I0721371

MARILYN TURK

Shadow of the Curse

A Suspicious Shores Novel, Book 2

by Marilyn Turk

THE SHADOW OF THE CURSE

to help those most in need plus characters who carry both physical and spiritual wounds of all kinds, and Marilyn Turk has penned yet another knock-out novel. Historical fiction fans will not be disappointed.

~ Julie Cantrell

New York Times and USA TODAY bestselling novelist of *Perennials*

Lexie Smithfield, a nurse at Bellevue Psychiatric Hospital in New York City in the 1940s, faces a curious melee of German spies, soldiers suffering from "shell shock," arrogant doctors, and danger. This World War II love story by award-winning author Marilyn Turk is filled with romance and intrigue. A treat for both history buffs and romance readers.

~ Suzanne Woods Fisher

Bestselling author of *Anna's Crossing*

Shadowed by a Spy is more than a love story. It explores the drive in each of us to be something more. I was profoundly affected by the plight of patients suffering from mental health issues, particularly those returning from war. This might be a historical novel set in World War II, but the issues Marilyn Turk raises within the world of her story are equally pressing today and deserve to be discussed honestly and openly as they are in this novel. The inclusion of a based-on-history spy story (that I bet you never knew about!) adds a layer of suspense to this important story.

~ Jodie Bailey

RT Reviewers Choice and Selah Award Winner
CBA Bestselling Author

Set against the backdrop of World War II and New York City, *Shadowed by a Spy* has it all—courageous soldiers, brave nurses, men and women entertaining the troops and spies who want to do damage to American soil. Marilyn Turk has written a page-turner based on real events that has surprises in every plot thread. With exquisite detail and a fast-paced telling, *Shadowed by a Spy* will give readers a new respect for the sacrifices many made during World War II and also take them back to a romantic, frightening time in American history.

~ Lenora Worth

Author of *Their Amish Reunion*

Dedication

To my daddy, who told me I was stubborn enough to do anything I wanted to do.

Chapter One

June 13, 1942, Long Island, NY

Conversation across the room sparked Lexie Smithfield's attention. She glanced over and noticed a group of four men entering the train station. The men glanced around before clustering on the side of the room to talk among themselves. Was it her imagination, or did they seem overly cautious? Her pulse quickened as she strained to hear their conversation; however, their low voices sounded like mumbling. Who were they?

Stop it, she chastised herself. Must she always suspect everyone around her? When would she get over that habit? She'd left her fears behind at Jekyll Island. But every day, the newspapers warned about Nazis patrolling the coast, so no wonder she was suspicious. She had enough on her mind without worrying about some strangers. Last night's conversation with her fiancé Russell, for one.

"So much for a chance to spend some time together," he'd said. "I sure wish you didn't have to go back so soon." He'd looked like a forlorn puppy when she'd said good night.

"I do too. I'm sorry. I hate to leave early, but the big

parade in the city made the hospital shorthanded."

"Well, at least we had the afternoon together and a nice dinner with Peg and Marian."

"And I got to see and hear you play at the USO dance."

"I could go back with you tomorrow." It was just like Russell to offer to cut his own free time short.

"No, you stay here and rest, and enjoy your day off."

Their goodnight kiss had been sweet and tender but brief. Someday, they'd be married, and everything would be different. But when was "someday"?

Ever since that kiss, something about him had been bothering her. Despite his actions, he seemed more remote. Was it her imagination, or had his attitude changed? Sure, Russell was as jovial as ever during the evening. He'd laughed and teased her like always. So why did he seem different? Or was she just worrying over nothing, feeling sorry for herself because she had to go back to work sooner than expected? It was her fault she had to leave, well, maybe not exactly, but since she was a student nurse, she had little to say about her schedule. Ever since they'd left Jekyll Island at the end of March, they'd had so little time together. Going to nursing school at Bellevue Hospital required her full attention. Plus, Russell's new job as assistant manager at the Martinique Hotel in Manhattan, as well as his moonlighting as a piano player for the USO, made his days long. But like most Americans, he wanted to do his part for the war effort, even though the schedule was exhausting. It was rare for him and Lexie to even grab lunch together most weeks.

The invitation from the elderly Maurice sisters to visit them at their summer cottage in East Hampton had been a welcome opportunity to spend time away from their busy routines. Convenient, too, since the cottage wasn't far from Montauk Manor where the USO show was held, so Russell could stay in the sisters' converted carriage house afterward.

Lexie stifled a yawn behind her gloved hand. A cup of hot tea would be nice right now. So many things felt wrong about today, and the chill of the foggy day was just one of them. Wasn't it supposed to be balmy and sunny in June? She rubbed her shoulders and stamped her feet to stay warm in the unheated room.

If only her plans hadn't changed. She'd asked for the two-day pass far enough in advance, but news about the huge patriotic parade in the city canceled any ideas she had to be with her fiancé. Nurses from every branch in the service—Red Cross, Army, and Navy—as well as Bellevue's student nurses, were required to march in the parade. She wasn't one of the nurses marching, but she had to return anyway so the hospital wouldn't be short-staffed.

Another man strolled into the station holding a copy of *The New York Times*. He sat down on a bench in the waiting room and opened the newspaper displaying a bold headline about today's parade. Chuckles from the group of men drew her attention. They nudged each another as they looked at the man with the paper. What were they laughing at? One of the men made eye contact with her before turning back to the group and rejoining their conversation.

A shudder trickled down her back. Why did they make her uncomfortable? She could imagine Russell telling her to quit suspecting everyone. Here on Long Island with such a large military presence, they didn't have to worry about the threat of Nazis, unlike the unprotected community on Jekyll Island. Lexie berated herself. *Quit worrying. You're safe here.*

The odor of cigarette smoke assailed her nostrils, prompting her to seek its source, and another glance at the group of men confirmed her suspicion. One man smoked while offering cigarettes from a pack to the others. Russell often teased her about her sensitive sense of smell. She'd always been able to detect odors before other people noticed. And since she was one of the few people who didn't smoke, it was easy for her to pick up the scent, especially since she disliked it so much.

Lexie shifted her gaze back to the train tracks outside. She was being rude staring at the men, much less trying to eavesdrop on their conversation. At times like these, she really missed Russell's company. A sudden thought jolted her. They were supposed to discuss their wedding this weekend, maybe even choose a place for it in East Hampton. But once again, they didn't have time.

She blew out a frustrated breath. Was Russell as concerned about their lack of wedding plans as she was? What if he was having second thoughts about marrying her? She shook her head. No, Russell loved her. She was sure of that. So what was causing that niggling feeling that something was wrong?

The mournful whistle of the approaching train summoned her outside to the platform. She pushed her gray felt hat down over her ears and pulled her coat together at the neck, wishing she'd added a scarf on this chilly morning. As the front of the train appeared through the fog, its screeching brakes slowed the rumbling engine to a halt. Lexie walked to the second railroad car. The men from the waiting room followed her outside as well, keeping their distance from other travelers.

Lexie waited for passengers to disembark, though she didn't expect any at that early hour on a Saturday. When she was certain no one was getting off the train, she grabbed the cold steel railing to pull herself up to the first step.

As she did, her foot slipped on the metal stair, and she stumbled. A man's arm reached out to steady her, and she glanced over her shoulder to see who it was. Her gaze locked with one of the men from the station, the one with the sandy-blond hair and wire-rimmed glasses.

"Oh, thank you," Lexie said. "The step must be wet from the fog."

The man nodded and said, "Be careful," before releasing his grip on her. Lexie's face warmed, embarrassed by her clumsiness. She climbed into the car and settled in a seat next to the window, even though all she could see outside were the ghostly shapes of trees and shrubs. She probably wouldn't even be able to glimpse the water when the train passed within view of the ocean.

Two of the men from the station moved past her seat and walked to the rear of the train car. She didn't notice where the other two went. Why did these men move so far away from her? It wasn't as if the car was crowded. Only a handful of passengers were on board. Was it her imagination, or were the men trying to get as far away from everyone else as possible? Maybe they didn't want anyone to hear what they were discussing. Why did she care what they talked about? She certainly didn't intend to converse with them or anyone else. The only person she wanted to talk to was Russell.

When she and Russell did have a chance to talk, she enjoyed telling him about her days at the hospital. He always appeared to be interested, but maybe he got tired of hearing about it and thought she spent too much time there. From the moment she made the decision to attend nursing school, he'd supported her choice, saying he was happy she was pursuing a goal that meant that much to her. After all, he had moved to New York for her. Could he be regretting that decision now?

Not everyone had approved of her becoming a nurse. She chuckled to herself, remembering the responses she'd gotten from acquaintances in the Hamptons. Some of them thought nursing wasn't a proper profession for people of their standing, people of Lexie's parents' standing at one time. The wealthy women of East Hampton helped the war effort in other ways—by contributing financially, rolling bandages, or collecting for the USO. Even the sisters had questioned Lexie's career choice, but they at least tried to understand and lend their support.

Peg and Marian Maurice, the two elderly sisters she'd met on Jekyll Island, were so special. They treated her like family and worried about her like parents. They fretted over her safety, and only the assurance that Russell worked near the hospital gave them any comfort. To them, a single girl in the city should have someone to look out for her, but Lexie knew their concern stemmed from a different era, a time when women didn't travel alone. The city was one place Lexie did feel safe and comfortable, a place where she didn't have to look over her shoulder all the time like she had in the past.

Besides, now that so many men were going off to war, more women were alone and finding it necessary to function without a man around to take care of them. Plenty of women her age were on their own without a husband or a boyfriend nearby. Of course, Lexie was seldom by herself anyway.

When she walked from the nurses' residence to the hospital, there were always other nurses to accompany her. The only time she didn't feel so safe was when she had to return to the residence after working a night shift at the hospital. She had to admit it was creepy outside the hospital at night, but thankfully, she didn't have far to go.

As the train rumbled toward the city, more people climbed aboard at each stop. The atmosphere inside the car lifted as the excited newcomers discussed the big parade they were on their way to watch. Lexie wanted to share their excitement, but her heart was back in East Hampton with Russell. She shot a quick glance toward the back of the car to see if the two men from the station were still there. This time, she noticed that one of the men was fidgety, constantly looking around. What was he worried about? Was there someone he didn't want to see? *Oh, bother, Lex. Stop imagining things.* If Abner, the old gardener from Jekyll Island, were here, he'd tell her she was "making a mountain out of a molehill."

She smiled at the memory of the old man who used to scare her. How was he doing now since the club had closed? He was one of the reasons she wanted to study the effects of shell shock on soldiers. The thought reminded her to look over some notes she took at the hospital last week. With still an hour before the train arrived at Penn Station, Lexie had time to review them. She pulled some folded sheets out of her handbag, opened the paper, and smoothed out the creases. A visiting doctor had been training the staff on a new procedure he'd used with mental patients in France. Maybe if this new form of treatment had been used on former soldiers like Abner, his life would have turned out better. At least someone was trying to help the returning soldiers. The scent of cigarette smoke wafted through the car. It had to be coming from the men in the back. Thank God, Russell had given up the habit when he learned she didn't like it. Last night at the dance, the ballroom had been full of smoke. She hated the way the odor permeated her clothes and her hair and hoped her quick bath this morning had removed the smell. It wouldn't do to have that odor on her nurse's uniform when she entered the hospital. She would barely have time to change into it when she returned to the dorm since uniforms weren't allowed to be worn outside the hospital grounds.

She glanced over her shoulder at the other passengers. A bespectacled older lady bent over her knitting, while a few other men in suits sat reading their newspapers. A cloud of smoke encircled the head of the jittery man from the depot, and she realized the other two men hadn't sat with them. *Wonder why all four men didn't sit together?* Perhaps they were getting off at different stops. Before she turned back around, the man who had helped her onto the steps caught her gaze and nodded, the slightest glimmer of a smile on his face.

She spun around, embarrassed to have been caught staring again. He was a nice-looking man, but she hoped he didn't get the wrong idea. Lexie had found the man she wanted to marry, someday. She hoped he still wanted to marry her too.

Chapter Two

*R*ussell yawned and spread his arms across the bed. As his eyes adjusted to the daylight, he surveyed his surroundings. Nice place.

Hard to believe this little house used to be where they kept horse carriages. The room showed the good taste of the Maurice sisters with its furnishings of plush fabric and intricate details—Lexie called it French Provincial. Although it only had one bedroom, a sitting room, kitchenette, and bath, the little cottage was big enough for him, and he'd be quite happy to stay there. Yeah, sure. If he didn't have to work for a living. His current home was in the hotel where he worked, in one of the plain rooms set aside for employees. Of course, his was slightly better than the rest of the staff since he was, after all, a manager, which meant he had his own private bathroom instead of sharing the hall bath.

Russell glanced at the clock on the bedside table. What a treat to sleep in for a change. Too bad Lexie couldn't have stayed another day too. The Maurice sisters put her up in one of the guest bedrooms in the main house, but maybe someday, when they finally tied the knot, he and Lexie could both stay here in this cozy little cottage. He surveyed the room again, wondering if she would be content to live in such a little place. What a comfy home it would be for just the two of them. He shook his head. *You must still be dreaming, pal.*

Already eight thirty. She might be at the hospital by now.

Russell swung his legs over the side of the comfortable bed and rubbed his eyes. He sure did miss spending time with Lexie. In fact, he was almost jealous of the patients who got to see her more often than he did. Nowadays, she was so busy they barely had a chance to get together anymore. Sure, he was busy, too, what with the hotel and the piano gigs. He thought back to last night and how cute she looked with her full skirt and white satin blouse, wearing her pearls as usual and a red ribbon tied around her blonde curls. She'd stood by the piano, her hand tapping the top to the rhythm as she scanned the crowd. When he motioned for her to sit next to him, she complied, keeping her foot moving to the tune. He knew she wanted to dance, but she politely refused the army guys who came over and asked, even when Russell motioned for her to go ahead. Poor fellas walked away looking so disappointed. Even when some begged her to dance, she shook her head more determinedly, smiling sweetly when she said, "No."

She was his gal, and she wanted those guys to know it. Thank God the two of them had been able to squeeze in a couple of dances together. Holding her close while they swayed to the music reminded him of the first time they danced back on Jekyll Island. Just the memory of her in his arms, the scent of her hair … wow, his pulse sped up just thinking about it. Back then, he'd never have believed she would be his fiancée. And now she really was, but somehow, they hadn't gotten around to setting a date for the wedding. Who had time? Someday they'd tie the knot. Maybe when she finished her nurse's training and he finished … what? Most everyone was focused on the war and what they could do to help.

Lots of folks had sacrificed something for the war effort. All he did was play at the USO. Big sacrifice—just giving up a few hours' sleep each week. He glanced at his deformed foot, the one that had been ruined by an errant bullet in a hunting accident and now made him unfit for military service. What else could he do for the war effort besides play the piano?

Russell stood and stretched. He needed coffee. First, he better get presentable before showing up at the main house. He stumbled to the bathroom and splashed water on his face, then staring at his scruffy reflection in the mirror, asked, "What does a girl like Lexie see in a guy like you?"

He shook his head, still not able to answer the question. After he shaved and finished with his toiletries, he put on some clean trousers and a casual, short-sleeved shirt before stepping outside.

A crisp wind blew off the ocean, forcing the morning mist to lift. The sun tried to assert itself into the scene, piercing through with daggers of light that bounced off the waves below, insisting that summer was indeed coming to Long Island. Pausing a moment, he listened to the ocean with its breakers keeping their rhythm, a sound he never tired of. They had their own music, God's music, he'd always thought. He was grateful the Maurice sisters kept their privet hedge trimmed, so the view was not covered up, unlike many of their neighbors. He always wondered why anyone would want a place on the water if they couldn't see it. But maybe other folks were content with an upstairs view, as protecting their privacy was even more important to them.

Russell turned and crossed the stone terrace between the carriage house and the main house. As he neared the sun parlor, he saw the sisters sitting inside, and they waved him over.

The smell of fresh coffee greeted him when he entered the French doors into the bright space, its rattan furniture with overstuffed floral cushions adding gaiety to the comfortable sitting room.

"Good morning, Russell," Peg and Marian, the gray-haired sisters, chorused.

"Good morning, ladies."

Peg relaxed on a chaise near the coffee table and motioned to the refreshments on it. A silver coffee pot and tea pitcher were surrounded by dainty cups and saucers. Nearby was a platter full of pastries.

"Help yourself to the coffee and rolls. Or if you'd prefer, Jane can make you a full breakfast. Would you like some eggs?"

"No, thank you. This looks delicious and quite enough for now." Russell poured himself a cup of black coffee and selected two of the pastries.

"Sit over here." Peg motioned to a spot on the settee beside the coffee table. "Did you sleep well?"

"I sure did. The bed was extremely comfortable, and I fell right to sleep."

"Good. You needed your rest after such a long day," said Peg. "I wish Lexie could've stayed longer and rested more too.

Seems like she'd get awfully tired of standing on her feet all the time."

"I'm sure she doesn't even think about being tired. She's so absorbed by her work," Russell said.

"She certainly is devoted to it," said Marian, pouring herself some tea from the small silver pitcher.

Peg nodded. "I admire her for that. Lexie says there's a shortage of nurses in our hospitals since so many have gone into the Army and Navy."

Marian took a sip from her cup. "It's too bad she couldn't visit with us longer. But I'm glad she didn't have to march in that huge patriotic parade. The paper said they expected over two million people in the city to watch it. I just can't imagine being in a crowd of people that huge."

Peg shook her head. "Nor I." She nibbled on a Danish before placing it on the saucer beside her cup, then lifted her teacup and said, "Have you two made any wedding plans yet?"

Russell sighed. "I'm afraid we haven't. Just never seem to get a chance to discuss them."

"Do you know where you'll have it? In East Hampton, perhaps?" Marian asked.

"Maybe so, if that's what Lexie wants." Russell studied his coffee before looking up. "Do you recommend a church around here?" No doubt they would.

"We like the Presbyterian Church here in town. It would make a lovely location for a wedding." Peg looked over at her sister who gave a nod in agreement. "The original church was established by the Puritans in the 1600s. Isn't that interesting? Of course, the present building is only a hundred years old."

"Only? Well, maybe I'll take a look at it this weekend."

Russell took a swig of coffee. "I know Lexie wants something simple, though. She doesn't want some big, fancy wedding."

Neither did he. Besides, who would pay for it?

"No one is having a big wedding these days. Extravagance is frowned upon during wartime. The government says if you have enough money for a big wedding, you can buy more war bonds," Marian said.

Peg pointed to the newspaper lying on the table. "Speaking of money, looks like we can expect a visit from the East Hampton USO fundraisers. They'll be going house to house looking for donations. The township has a quota of $6,000 to raise."

"They'll do more than that to get the money," Marian said, picking up the copy of *The East Hampton Star*. "The Devon Yacht Club is going to have a benefit dinner-dance too."

"May I see that?" Russell reached for the paper. "Wonder if they'll need a piano player?"

"I'll call Mr. Simons, the manager, and ask him," Marian said. "The club won't open for the season for two more weeks, but he's over there now, working to get it ready."

"Thanks. I'll make sure I can get the time off." He scanned the headlines, then laid the paper on the table.

Peg refilled her teacup, took the tongs, and dropped a couple of sugar cubes in the beverage. "I read there's going to be a softball game between a team from the Coast Guard and one from the Maidstone Club to raise money too. That should be fun to watch, don't you think, sister?"

Marian clasped her hands. "Oh yes, I do want to go see it. Russell, do you play softball?"

Glancing down at his bum foot, Russell said, "Not much anymore, I'm afraid. I'm not a very good runner."

Marian's face turned beet red. "Oh, I'm so sorry. I forgot about your foot."

Russell smiled and shook his head. "Please don't worry about embarrassing me. I used to be a pretty nice player before the accident. I wouldn't be very good at softball now, but I'm a decent golfer."

"Do you have time for a game of golf this weekend? Perhaps we can call George Champion and see if he can round up a foursome."

"Sister, I'm not sure the golf course is open now. The Maidstone hasn't had their official opening for the season yet either," Peg said.

"Well, pooh. I believe you're correct. Seems like everything will open the weekend of June 27th." Marian turned to Russell. "Perhaps another time this summer?"

"We'll see. Thanks for the offer, anyway." Russell drained his cup. "I'm pretty rusty right now, though." He stood and imitated a golf swing with his arms. "Need to practice my swing."

"Russell, did you and Lexie have an opportunity to dance any last night, or did you have to play all evening?" Peg asked.

"We got to dance a few songs when only the horns played, and the piano wasn't needed." He released a sigh. "She could've danced all night if she'd wanted to. Those Army guys kept asking, but she refused."

"Well, who wouldn't want to dance with such a pretty girl?" Marian said. "But I can see why she didn't want to give any of them the wrong idea. She's very loyal to you."

That was nice to hear. Not that he'd ever doubt Lexie's loyalty, but he was still amazed that it was him who she gave that loyalty to.

Peg spoke up. "I hear the military is adding more men at Camp Hero. Montauk Point will soon be full of soldiers."

"We can be assured we're safe from enemy invasion here." Marian nodded. "We're not vulnerable like we were on Jekyll."

"Quite right," said Russell. "We've gone from practically having no military there to having an abundance here on Long Island. The Nazis wouldn't dare come close to us."

Peg grew pensive. "I wonder how many of those boys at Camp Hero on the Point will be shipped overseas?"

The question had crossed Russell's mind too. "Probably most of them at some point, since that's where the fighting is."

"The *Star* lists all the local boys who have joined up. It's quite a list for this area," said Marian. "And so many are right out of high school." She tsked. "So young to be fighting a war."

Peg's head jerked up. "Russell, do you think Lexie might want to be an Army or Navy nurse? Oh, I do hope not."

"She hasn't mentioned it. Many of our wounded are sent back here from hospitals overseas. She can help them here just as well."

Anxiety quickened his pulse. Would she consider joining the military? He really wasn't sure. And if she did, what would he do? Keep his boring hotel job and play the piano in New York while everyone else was going across the ocean to serve the country?

He needed to find a better way to show his support, something he could be proud of. Something Lexie would be proud of as well.

Chapter Three

Lexie exited the train and climbed the steep steps to the main lobby of Penn Station. The cavernous waiting room was bustling with more people than usual for a Saturday. No doubt they'd come to watch the big parade and were eager to gain their spots along its route. Daylight filtered through the grand palladium windows and overhead skylights as Lexie hurried across the glass-tiled floor, her tapping heels echoing off the pink granite walls.

A glance at one of the station clocks that was suspended at each end of the room confirmed her timing. Not a second to spare to get back to the nurses' dormitory and change her clothes. As usual, people clustered below the clocks, popular meeting spots for travelers. Victory flags hung from the ceiling, encouragement for the men in tan uniforms and navy crackerjacks that were scattered throughout the room. Some of the soldiers chatted with women, probably girlfriends or wives, before their departing trains arrived. A bittersweet sensation touched her heart as she considered the fate of those couples. Would they see each other again? Would these men return wounded, even to the very hospital where she worked?

At least she knew Russell wouldn't be one of them, even though he sometimes made comments wishing he were. His damaged foot assured he wouldn't be drafted, but he was like most men, wanting to serve their country, especially single men. And Russell was still single, despite their plans to marry.

Lexie passed by the huge granite columns and joined the throngs of people who bumped and jostled their way through the arched east exit onto the sidewalk. The beep of car horns and rumble of busses greeted her outside where more men in uniform waited, some sitting on their suitcases while others stood by their canvas duffel bags. Many puffed on cigarettes, sending up smoke signals as they stared resolutely at the traffic that rolled past or stopped to pick up passengers.

As she approached, a bus pulled away from the stop spewing foul-smelling exhaust. Lexie covered her nose to keep from breathing it in, then turned to a man standing nearby.

"Do you know which bus that was?" He nodded. "Number 16 bus, miss."

"Thank you."

Her bus. Now what? Should she wait for the next bus or walk the twelve blocks to the hospital? In an effort to cut back on gasoline usage for the war effort, the city had reduced the number of bus routes. She checked her watch. No, she couldn't afford to waste time waiting for the next bus going her direction. She'd better walk, but fast. After such a long train ride, the exercise would do her good anyway and refresh her for the long day ahead. She crossed the street and headed down the sidewalk as the city woke up. Merchants raised their blinds and flipped the signs on their doors to "open" as she strode past.

Approaching the corner of 6th Avenue and 32nd Street, Lexie looked up at the nineteen-story Hotel Martinique where Russell worked. Although it would have been nice to have his company, she was glad for his sake that he'd stayed back in East Hampton. Lexie stepped off the curb to cross the street then recognized some men walking toward the hotel ahead of her. Two of the men were the ones who'd shared the train ride with her, the men from the Amagansett Station. But she didn't recognize the third man, a thin-haired, portly man. He must've joined them since their arrival at Penn Station.

She crossed the street, glancing over at the group again, still curious about the language they'd spoken. As she watched them, the blond man looked back and nodded. The other two turned her direction, then back to him, and said something. Her face heated. Why did he always catch her looking at him? Did he think she was interested in him, or even following him? How embarrassing when it was just a stupid coincidence. She wanted to explain, but that would be ridiculous. She gripped the handle of her overnight case, blew out a breath, and hurried on ahead until she'd passed the building. At least she wouldn't run into them again.

Karl Mueller's gaze followed the pretty blonde crossing the street. Who wouldn't? She was a very lovely young lady, especially with her curls bouncing as she walked. How amusing that they had traveled the entire distance together. A smile crossed his face seeing her blush and quicken her step when they made eye contact. *Wonder where she was going?*

"Karl!" Oscar barked, biting down on the cigar stuck in his mouth. "What are you doing? You have no time for women!"

Karl shrugged. "No harm in looking, is there?"

"As long as that is all you do. We have no time to get cozy with these people."

These people? Did he mean Americans? If so, he was one, too, even if he had moved back to the Fatherland. After all, he'd been born and raised in Indiana. Just because his family was from Germany didn't take away his citizenship. Not yet, anyway. In fact, that was one of the reasons he was chosen for this mission.

"Let's get you checked in." Oscar glanced around, then motioned to the door ahead. "We'll talk more when we get to your room."

Karl nodded as he and Henry followed Oscar inside. Why did Oscar have to be their contact here? He had never liked the obnoxious man who seemed to detest everyone but the Führer himself. Oscar didn't even know how to laugh, much less smile. Fortunately, Karl wouldn't be around him very long before he went on to his assignment. Besides that, Oscar still sounded like a German, which he supposed was acceptable for someone who worked undercover in a German bakery. The men got their room key—Karl and Henry would be sharing a suite—and walked to the elevator. Oscar pulled his hat low over his eyes and stared straight ahead, spitting out "Twenty-five" to the elevator attendant before taking his place in the back corner. Did the man have to be so rude? Karl and Henry followed him onto the elevator and asked the attendant politely for the same floor.

Two other passengers got on the elevator, each going to different floors.

"Yes, sir," the attendant replied to each passenger. "Going right up." Karl could sense the tension emanating from Oscar. Did everyone else? He was so committed to he mission, he didn't act human. More like one of those automatons Karl had seen in a carnival when he lived in the States. He never wanted to be like him, despite the fact they were on the same side.

Lexie dashed into the nurses' dorm passing other students, crisp in their blue-and-white-striped uniforms with starched white pinafores, on the way out.

"Hey, Lex! Better hurry! Don't keep the dragon lady waiting. She might spew fire if you're late." Lexie's amusing roommate Penny had a nickname for everyone, even their stern nursing instructor, Chief Nurse Harper.

"I'll be there in two shakes," Lexie called back as she scrambled up the stairs to her room.

Lexie set the record for getting dressed in the requisite white stockings and shoes, dress, and apron before attaching her stiff nurse's cap with the mandatory two bobby pins. A quick check in the mirror, then she ran down to the lobby and across the street to the hospital. She rushed into the back of the classroom in time to catch the last few words of Nurse Harper.

"We're glad you're here this morning instead of going to the parade because we have received some injured soldiers. They were wounded in the Philippines and sent to California for initial treatment." Nurse Harper scanned the room as Lexie hid behind another student who was standing too. "We will be processing each one into the hospital today, so we'll divide into groups."

The head nurse looked down at her clipboard and began assigning names to the different wards they'd visit. When she was finished, the girls stood and separated into their respective groups.

Penny slipped next to Lexie and whispered, "Sweetie, you cut it close. She didn't ask for you, so maybe she didn't notice you were missing."

"Nurse Smithfield, may I see you up front?" Lexie's heart dropped. Now what?

"On second thought, maybe she did." Penny hustled out the door to catch up with her group.

Lexie walked to where Nurse Harper had positioned herself.

"Nurse Smithfield. I didn't see you come in with the rest. You weren't late, were you?"

She took a deep breath before answering. "I'm sorry, Nurse Harper. I missed the bus at the train station and had to walk here. I was just a few minutes late."

"Nurse Smithfield, time is very important in the medical field. Someone could die if you were 'just a few minutes late.' Make sure it doesn't happen again. You must abide by the same principles here as everyone else, no matter *who* you are."

Lexie's face grew hot. Must the woman insinuate that Lexie

thought herself special?

"Yes, ma'am. I'm sorry." She had to concede defeat to this woman if she wanted to pass school.

"All right. Now let's get on with the patient processing."

A streak of fear raced down Lexie's back. "I'm afraid I didn't hear my name assigned to a ward."

"That's because you're going with me." Nurse Harper glanced at the other few students standing a few feet away. "We're going to the second floor of the psychiatric hospital."

The second floor? That was the ward for mildly disturbed male patients. Now she could see firsthand how wounded men were affected by the war and what she could do to help them. This is why she had come here.

Chapter Four

Nurse Harper unlocked the door to the mental ward, and the students followed her in, eyes nervously scanning the patient beds. Lexie mustered her courage among these patients with unusual behaviors, reminding herself they were just unfortunate people, not the freaks of rumors.

The large room had twenty beds, ten on each side, lining the walls. Men in this ward were the most normal-appearing patients in the eight-story psychiatric hospital. Here, the patients milled around, some sitting and others playing cards, so the room was fairly quiet save for an occasional snore from one of the sleeping patients. The students shuffled in with wary eyes, holding their notebooks against their chests and trying to stay quiet lest they alarm any of the patients. Nurse Harper motioned for them to come over to a bed in front of the barred windows.

In a low voice, she said, "This is John Doe. He was injured in the Philippines. Sustained a head injury and broken arm. Appears catatonic when awake. We will be considering him for one of the new brain treatments."

Lexie studied the young man with the bandaged head

and arm in a cast. His squared chin and broad shoulders showed strength the rest of his body lacked at the moment. While the others scribbled notes and moved on to another bed, Lexie couldn't take her eyes off John Doe. What had happened to him?

As she studied the motionless man, his eyes opened. She jumped back, startled. The eyes were blue but dark and unfocused. They looked straight ahead, failing to acknowledge her presence beside him. Did he see her or even know she was there? Did he know where he was?

Nurse Harper cleared her throat, garnering Lexie's attention. She glanced up and saw the head nurse's stern gaze from her position at the end of the row of beds. Lexie hurried over to join the others. Cutting her eyes at Lexie as a warning, Nurse Harper whispered, "Everyone needs to stay with the group."

While Nurse Harper reviewed the next patient's diagnosis, Lexie's mind wandered back to John Doe. How could she reach him? Was there a way? Maybe she'd get a chance to try.

A man cried out from the bed behind her, and the students gasped collectively as heads turned. The patient was sitting up, eyes wide as he grabbed his sheet and shrank back in terror.

"No, don't kill me! No! Stay away!" His screaming disturbed the other patients, and they began to respond as well. Some moaned, a few yelled, still others whimpered. The students huddled together in fear beside Nurse Harper like chicks around a mother hen.

"Shush. Now, now. Calm down." The nurse held up her hand to evoke silence. "We are just here to help you.

Settle down. We'll bring your medication in shortly."

The clamor quieted, but some mumbling continued. The patients watched with anxious eyes as if afraid the nurses meant to do them harm.

"Let's go out in the hallway," said Nurse Harper, motioning toward the door. The students hustled to the exit, casting glances behind them as they made their escape. Lexie watched John Doe's reaction to the disturbance, noting that there was none. If all that noise didn't affect him, what would? She couldn't wait to read up on the catatonic condition, and what she couldn't find in her textbook, she'd research in the hospital library as soon as she had a chance.

When the students were safely on the other side of the door, they whispered to each other as they followed Nurse Harper away from the ward, the door secured behind them.

"That man's scream wasn't human!"

"He sounded like a wounded wild animal!"

A girl near Lexie shuddered. "I hope I don't have to work in there. What if one of them grabs me?"

"I don't think they'll make us go in there alone," Lexie said to reassure the frightened girl. "Besides, this is the *mildly* disturbed ward."

"If I'm assigned here, I hope she'll let you work with me. You don't seem afraid," the wide-eyed girl said.

"I'm not. They're just people like us."

"Oh yeah? Like us? I don't think so," said a fiery redheaded student. "I hope none of us are that loony."

"You think they're loony, just imagine what they're like in the semi- disturbed and disturbed wards," said another student.

"No, thank you!" said several of the nurses at once.

Lexie's pulse quickened as her anger rose. Attitudes like theirs were to blame for the cruel treatment mental patients had endured for ages, even in this very hospital fifty years earlier. People had called her mother "loony" too. And they also said that about Abner at one time. Of course, Mother's illness was not the result of a war. She never got well, but Abner did. So maybe there was still hope for John Doe.

"Hey, Lex! You think I could wear my hair like this?"

"Hmm?" Lexie lifted her gaze from the book she was reading and turned to her roommate who lay prone on one of the twin beds, pointing to a picture in the *Look* magazine that was spread out before her. The photo showed a Hollywood starlet waving to a group of sailors on the deck of a ship.

Lexie studied the picture, then eyed Penny. "Sure, Penny. But it looks like it takes a lot of time to do, and who has time for that when we have to get dressed for duty?"

Penny flopped over on her back, holding the magazine aloft. "Yeah, you're right. Besides, what difference does it make when we have to pin that piece of cardboard in our hair?" She lowered the publication to look at Lexie. "But maybe next time I have a date—whenever that is."

"Maybe so." Lexie turned back to her book. *Catatonia is a state of neurogenic motor immobility and behavioral abnormality manifested by stupor.*

"Lexie, are you really going to spend all afternoon studying? Ya know, we're off duty now. Why don't we go window-shopping or something—get outta this room and get some fresh air? After all, it *is* Saturday. The parade's over so it won't be so crowded."

Lexie sighed and marked her place in the book. She obviously wasn't going to get much done with Penny around. Her roommate, the Jersey girl, was so different than Lexie was, always ready for fun. But maybe Penny was right about taking a break, even though Lexie wanted to spend more time researching.

"Sure, Penny. Where do you want to go?"

"Where else? Fifth Avenue!" She jumped up and opened the closet. "'Course I can't afford to buy anything, but I could at least look and dream." She selected a floral blouse and put it on over her slip, then took a navy-blue skirt off the hanger and stepped into it, buttoning it at the waist.

Lexie stood and stretched her arms over her head. "We're supposed to be saving our money for the war effort anyway." She pulled a light blue short-sleeve sweater out of a drawer and drew it over her head, then put on her gray men's-style trousers with the high waistband.

"You and those trousers. I don't understand why you want to wear those things instead of a skirt."

"I find them quite comfortable," said Lexie. She grabbed a blue ribbon hanging over the vanity mirror and tied it around her unruly curls.

"Well, they look good on you, but not on me. I'm a little too round in the bottom for them," Penny said, looking at her rear view in the mirror. "Besides, I don't think the dragon lady likes them."

Lexie shrugged. "I'm not wearing them on duty, so it shouldn't matter."

"Let's hope not." Penny opened the door. "Ready?"

Lexie nodded, and they went outside and headed down the sidewalk for Fifth Avenue. Trash from the morning's parade was still evident while street sweepers did their best to clean it up. Lexie and Penny spent the rest of the day strolling along in front of the stores, occasionally going in and out. The city was still filled with men in uniform, and Penny giggled every time one of them whistled as they walked by. Lexie tried not to notice, but Penny's head practically revolved to look at all the guys, giving them a big smile.

She squeezed Lexie's arm. "That one winked at me!" Lexie glanced over and saw several guys in sailor suits grinning at them.

"Oh, Penny. Calm down."

"How can I, with so many to choose from?"

"Penny! Come on. Those guys will be shipping out of here soon."

"Oh, I know. But isn't it fun just to flirt?"

Not for Lexie. She had Russell, thank God.

Lexie pointed to a store display to divert Penny's attention. In typical Penny fashion, she "oohed" and "aahed" over the latest fashions in the window. Many of them had military themes like navy-blue sailor dresses with white collars or khaki-colored jackets with epaulets.

Lexie looked on with little interest. Her mother had always loved to shop, spending quite a bit on her wardrobe and Lexie's too. She was intent on making Lexie look "pretty and fashionable," and no doubt to show off her taste to her friends in their elite social circle. The idea rankled Lexie. All her mother's "friends" had disappeared as she became more ill. What difference did nice clothes make when no one cared about the person in them?

"Lex, that would look great on you!" Penny pointed to a formal dress on display in a window. The creamy satin evening gown tied at the shoulders and draped at the neckline, cinched at the waist, and then flowed to the floor. "I bet that little number costs a fortune."

Lexie admired the dress, which was indeed beautiful. She envisioned herself dancing in a ballroom in Russell's arms. But when would that ever happen? Formal dances were a thing of the past during wartime. And even if there were such an event, would she and Russell have the time to go?

"It's nice."

"Nice? Are you kidding? It's fabulous!"

"You're right, it's quite lovely. But right now, I don't need anything like it, even if I did have the money."

Penny eyed her curiously. Lexie knew her roommate was aware of the Smithfield family's history of wealth, but Penny would never be convinced that Lexie was no longer in that income bracket.

"I'm getting hot, aren't you? And thirsty. Let's go get a shake." Penny headed to the street corner.

"Sounds good. Where do you want to go? The drugstore counter?" She nodded toward the drugstore on the opposite corner.

"Let's go to Mack's. It's on our way back to the dormitory. Besides, they have the best shakes in the city."

"Sure." Mack's Diner was one of the places Lexie and Russell met for lunch when their schedules allowed, since it was about halfway between the hospital and the hotel.

What was he doing right now out on the Island? She didn't expect him back tonight, since he had tomorrow off too. She enjoyed going to church with him on Sundays, but she'd have to go alone this time. Unless she could talk Penny or one of the other students into going with her.

Only a couple of men with their backs to the door were sitting   on the chrome stools with red vinyl seats at the counter when Lexie and Penny entered the diner. The noonday lunch crowd was long gone from the shiny, stainless-steel-accented room, although the smell of burgers and onion rings lingered. Two women who worked at Macy's cosmetic counter sipped milkshakes at a corner table, their perfume wafting across the room.

"Can we sit over there?" Lexie motioned to the opposite side of the restaurant.

"Sit where you like," said the waitress behind the counter as she grabbed menus and silverware.

She followed Lexie and Penny to a booth beside the diner's window, handing them the menus as they sat down.

"We just want milkshakes," said Penny. "What kind have you got?"

"Vanilla, chocolate, and strawberry—the usual."

"No cherry? Okay then, I'll take a strawberry, with extra whipped cream on top. And a cherry, too, if you have it." Penny patted her hands on the cold Formica table.

"I'll take chocolate," said Lexie, handing back the menu. "And a glass of ice water, please."

"Sure thing," said the waitress as she turned and walked away from the booth.

"I never heard of a cherry milkshake, Penny."

"I haven't either. I was just hoping." Penny glanced around the diner and back to Lexie. "So, when's your guy coming back?"

"I'm not sure when Russell is coming back—maybe tonight, maybe tomorrow."

"Aren't you miffed that you had to come back and he got to stay?" Penny admired her reflection in the window and twirled a piece of hair into place.

"No, not really." Lexie sighed and gazed out at the passersby on the sidewalk. "He deserves some time off."

"But what's he going to do out there in the Hamptons all by himself?"

"He's not by himself. He's staying with our friends Peg and Marian Maurice. "

Penny frowned at Lexie. "But aren't they a couple of old ladies? Why would he want to hang out with them?"

Lexie shrugged. "They're just nice people. Russell's known them longer than I have."

"Don't you ever get jealous? I mean, there's lots of single women out there, too, aren't there?"

Lexie shook her head. "No, I don't worry about Russell. I know he loves me and isn't interested in anyone else."

"So why don't you get married? What are you waiting for? There's married women in the school."

"True, but their husbands are in the military. You know, even if you're married, you have to live in the nursing residence until you graduate, so we'd still live apart. That doesn't matter when your husband is overseas."

The waitress brought their milkshakes and set them on the table. The women glanced up and smiled their appreciation. "Thank you," they chimed.

"Yeah, I guess you're right. So why don't you go ahead and plan your wedding for after your graduation? They really need nurses now, so I heard they're going to shorten the training."

"I heard that, too, just don't know when it will happen." Lexie ran her finger along the cool moisture on the outside of the glass.

Penny held her cherry above her head, then dropped it into her mouth. "I don't know. If it were me, I couldn't wait. You know, don't you want to snuggle, like a married couple?"

Lexie's face warmed at the suggestion. Of course, she wanted a real marriage relationship, and someday she'd have one with Russell. She stirred her shake with the straw and sipped, savoring the cool chocolaty flavor as it eased down her throat.

Penny slurped her milkshake, then quickly covered her mouth, "Oops! Got a little carried away. This is so good."

"I'm glad you had this idea." Lexie patted her mouth with her napkin. "It's very refreshing."

"Lexie, have you thought about joining the Army, being an Army nurse?"

Startled, Lexie raised an eyebrow. "No, I haven't. Have you?"

"Yeah, I have. Or maybe being a Navy nurse."

"I didn't realize you were considering either." Lexie couldn't imagine her frivolous roommate in the military.

Penny stirred her shake. "Well, I wasn't, until now. You know, they're begging for nurses in the military. Besides, what a good place to meet guys!"

Lexie smiled at her friend. "So that's the real reason?"

"Not altogether. But you have to admit it's a nice bonus."

Penny was honest, at least. Lexie didn't think she'd ever been as man-crazy as her roommate, though. Lexie hadn't even been looking for a boyfriend when she'd met Russell. Falling in love with him had been an unexpected surprise.

"Maybe you'll meet the right man when you're not looking. Like I did with Russell."

"Trust me, I'm always on the lookout." Penny eyed the counter. "Take those guys, for example. They're not bad looking, especially the blond guy with the glasses. He keeps looking over here. Do you know him?"

Lexie glanced toward the counter and flinched as the man sitting at the counter looked over his shoulder at her and nodded. It was the man from the train.

Chapter Five

"What are you looking at, Karl, those dames?"

"Henry, the name is Cal, remember?" Karl asked in a hushed tone, reminding Henry of his alias. "And yes, you might say I'm looking at the scenery."

"Don't get any ideas, Cal," Henry said, with emphasis on the name Cal. "Oscar warned you."

"I'm not worried about him. And he doesn't need to worry about me. I know what I'm here for."

Henry glanced over his shoulder at the girls in the booth. "Say, isn't that blonde the girl that was on the train with us?"

"The same. Seems like we keep running into each other."

Henry frowned, squirming on the stool. "You think she's following you?"

"Of course not. Relax, Henry, she's not spying on us."

"But how do you know she's not?" Henry lit another cigarette, forgetting he already had one burning in the ashtray in front of him. "Don't you think it's odd that she was on that train all the way from Long Island with us, and we're still running into her?"

"No, I don't. Pure coincidence." Karl lifted his coffee cup, then paused. "But maybe I should investigate, make sure."

Henry's head whipped around to face Karl. "You wouldn't. I mean, I don't think that's a good idea."

Karl patted his comrade on the arm. "Don't worry, friend. I'll be very careful." Then he turned on his stool, faced the women, and stood.

Russell sped along Further Lane on one of the bicycles the sisters kept for guests. The salt air was invigorating, the afternoon sun warming his face. He wasn't alone on the road since gas rationing and the government's encouragement had inspired more people to ride bikes instead of drive cars. In fact, there was barely any room for a car, with so many enjoying the summer day on their bicycles. Groups of carefree young women sporting shorts with blouses tied at their midriffs passed him along the way, waving and laughing, even flirting with him.

He waved back and smiled, missing Lexie even more and their bike rides on Jekyll Island. Following the road into Amagansett, he rode to Bluff Road, then continued on to Atlantic Avenue, where he turned down the path to the beach. The Coast Guard station sat on a sand dune by the water, and the place was swarming with activity. Men in uniform stood in groups on the porch, some holding binoculars, while others walked the beach, probing and searching the sand, apparently conducting a training exercise. Their presence affirmed the safety of the islanders. Thank God Lexie could quit worrying about danger.

Russell climbed off the bike, rolled up his shirt sleeves

and pants legs, then pulled off his shoes and socks to step on the sand, hoping he wouldn't get too many stares at his misshapen foot. The shooting accident had left its scars, but thankfully, he still had a foot to walk on. He sauntered to the water and let it wash over his toes. "Oh! That's cold," he said to no one in particular as he jumped back.

The sunny weather imitated summer, but the water still had some warming up to do. Russell turned and moved a few yards back to sit on the sand and watch the waves. The front page of today's *East Hampton Star* flashed through his mind. Boldly displayed on the front was the "Roll of Honor," a list of local people who served in the military, divided into Army, Navy, and Marines. At the bottom of the list were the names of two Army nurses. Would Lexie's name be there someday? If that's what she really wanted to do, then she'd have no problem joining up. But his name would never appear on that list.

He blew out a breath. *Quit feeling sorry for yourself, pal. Buck up.*

Fine. He was finished with all the sulking. After all, he had plenty to be thankful for. A great job, friends, his health, and the love of a beautiful woman. Why wasn't that enough? He closed his eyes and prayed. *Dear God, please show me what I can do to be part of the war effort and help me to be thankful for what I have.*

Standing, he brushed himself off, then went back to the bike, stopping to put his shoes and socks back on. He glanced back at the water, thankful for the chance to be near it. But there was something, no, someone, missing. She couldn't be with him today, but he could be with her tomorrow. Besides, he felt guilty knowing how busy the hotel must be with so many in town for the parade. He'd call Lexie when he got back to the cottage and let her know he would be coming back on the train tonight so they could spend Sunday together.

Penny and Lexie hurried down the sidewalk to the dorm.

"Why are you in such a hurry, Lexie? Nobody's chasing us!" Penny huffed as she tried to catch up with Lexie.

"I just want to get back, that's all."

"Was it the guy—Cal? Geez, all he did was introduce himself and his friend Henry to us." She stopped and grabbed Lexie's arm. "Hey, slow down, will ya?"

"All right. I'm sorry. I guess I was just embarrassed," said Lexie.

"So you've run into him before. What's to be embarrassed about? He seemed like a nice guy, nicer than that Henry, the 'nervous Nellie.' That guy kept looking around like a caged animal."

"You're right. I have no reason to be embarrassed. I just didn't want to encourage him or make him think I'm interested in him."

"Well, I think you made that pretty clear, the way you practically ran away."

"Did I? I didn't mean to be rude."

They reached the door of the nursing residence and went inside. "Are you Lexie Smithfield?" a girl said from across the room. "You had a phone call."

"Yes, that's me. Do you know who it was?"

The other nursing student handed her a piece of paper. "He left a message."

Pick you up for church tomorrow at ten. Love, Russell. Lexie's heart fluttered. Even though she'd just seen him the night before, she was excited to be with him again. Maybe she'd been worried about nothing. Besides, tomorrow would be different because he didn't have to go to work and neither did she. They could spend the whole day together before either of them had to report back.

"Good news? Must be, judging from that smile on your face," said Penny.

"Yes, it's Russell. He's coming back tonight."

"Hi, sunshine!"

Russell's dimpled grin lit his face as Lexie entered the living room of the nurses' quarters. Looking quite dapper in his double-breasted navy pinstriped suit, Lexie's fiancé struck a handsome pose as he waited for her, rocking on his heels and twirling his fedora in his hand. A new suntan made Russell's smile even brighter.

Lexie returned her own as her heart bubbled with excitement. They'd only been apart less than forty-eight hours, but he appeared more attractive than ever.

"Hello, Russell. Good to see you again," Penny said, walking beside Lexie. Whispering in Lexie's ear, she said, "That boyfriend of yours is a handsome devil. You better hold on to him, or I'll snatch him away!"

"You couldn't," said Lexie, whispering back. "He's only got eyes for me."

"Hello, Penny. What are you girls up to? You're not talking about me, are you?" Russell winked at them.

"Well, as a matter of fact, we are," said Penny, "but you don't need to worry about it."

Russell reached out to take Lexie's hand, lifting it to his lips and planting a kiss on it. "My lady, you doth look lovely today."

Lexie blushed as Penny rolled her eyes. "Okay, Lexie, you're right."

Russell lifted an eyebrow. "She is? Say, Penny, are you going to church with us?"

"Na, I don't think so. I might go to the chapel at the hospital." As she strolled away toward the door, she looked over her shoulder. "You kids behave yourself today. As if I have to tell you that. Tata!"

Russell returned his gaze to Lexie, pulled her close, and gave her a hug. "Boy, I missed you. I just couldn't stay away any longer."

Lexie gave him a little shove. "Sure, Russell. Did you get tired of all the young lovelies at the beach?"

"Actually, I did. They just weren't you, and when I thought about what I'd do today with my free time, I decided I'd rather spend it with you than Peg and Marian."

Lexie smiled. "I certainly hope so."

Russell placed his hand on the small of her back and pushed her gently toward the door. "So, are we going to Fifth Avenue Presbyterian today? After the service, how about we grab a bite to eat from the deli down the street from the church, take it over to Central Park, and have a picnic?"

"Sounds great." Lexie pulled on her white gloves, then adjusted her hat, using her reflection in the glass door as a mirror. "It's a beautiful day for a picnic."

After church, the park was full of people enjoying the warm June weather. Lexie and Russell strolled arm in arm along the sidewalk until they found an empty bench in the shade. Russell removed his suit coat and draped it over the back of the bench, rolled up his shirtsleeves, and loosened his tie. They sat down and unwrapped their sandwiches while pigeons gathered on the ground in front of them, waiting for a morsel. Russell pulled a bottle opener from his pants pocket and opened the two glass bottles of soda they'd bought at the deli, then handed her one.

"So what did you do yesterday on the I s l a n d ?" Lexie pinched off a crumb of her sandwich and tossed it to a pigeon that fought competition pursuing the morsel.

"I rode a bike for a while—down to the Maidstone Club and back over to Amagansett to the beach near the coast guard station. Boy, it was lively yesterday. Those guys were all over the beach."

"That's good to know." She took a sip of soda. "I didn't know the Maidstone was open yet."

"It's not. As a matter of fact, the paper said they're opening in two weeks. They're having a grand opening dance, and the sisters think they might be interested in having a certain piano player for the evening."

Lexie leaned back and eyed him. "That so? Would you like to do that? I mean, it's not the USO."

"I know, but I think it'd be a nice change. It's a fundraiser for the USO anyway. Besides, I might even get to meet somebody famous." He gave Lexie a wink.

"I suppose you might. You never know who's going to show up in the Hamptons."

"Think you'd like to join me?"

"Sure, if I can get the time off. But with the new patients that came in this week and more coming next week, I can't promise you I can make it."

"Of course." Russell glanced away, watching a couple stroll down the sidewalk, the man wearing an Army uniform, one of many soldiers enjoying the park today.

Lexie saw his jaw tighten. She laid her hand on his leg. "Russell, are you mad at me?"

He turned quickly and faced her, smiling. "No, dear, I'm not. I understand you might have other commitments." He placed his hand on top of hers. "So tell me, did you see any new patients yesterday?"

"Yes, I did." She nibbled the last bit of her sandwich, saving a piece of the crust for the waiting pigeons. "There was one young soldier in the mild psychiatric ward with a head injury. His arm was broken, too, but his head injury must've affected his brain or something because he's catatonic."

"And that means…"

"It's like he's in a trance. He stares but doesn't focus, like he's not aware he's in the world. He doesn't react to anything around him."

"So what is the hospital going to do for him? Can't they just snap their fingers and bring him out of it?"

Lexie shot him a glare. "Russell, it's not funny. Actually, there are a couple of treatments they could try. One of them would be electric shock therapy."

"You mean, you actually shock someone on purpose?"

"Yes, several times. It's been known to help, especially violent patients or schizophrenics."

"Sounds like torture—something you'd do to an enemy,

not a friend."

Lexie opened her mouth to defend the treatment, then changed her mind. She wasn't sure she approved of the procedure either. But she was just a trainee. Doctors much wiser about mental disorders knew more about their proper treatment than she did. Who was she to question such a practice? Especially if it had been successful with some patients.

She sighed. "I know. It does sound rather barbaric, but I'm just learning about the various treatments. And that one's not used on everyone. It's possible we can reach John Doe another way."

Russell lifted an eyebrow. "John Doe?"

Lexie sighed. "Yes, poor guy. He was found by a fisherman washed up on some remote island in the Philippines that the Japanese had not occupied yet. They think he might have been in a plane that crashed into the ocean. He had no identification papers, no Dog Tags, no nothing. He has been comatose ever since he was rescued. He's lucky to be alive. At this point, we don't know his real name, so we don't know how to contact his relatives either."

"That's too bad. Well, I'll pray you can help him come out of his trance and find out who he is. I'm sure God will use your compassion to minister to your patients—whatever their problem."

Lexie smiled at Russell, leaned over, and put her head on his shoulder. "I hope so."

Russell put his arms around her and gave her a squeeze. One of the things she admired most about Russell was his faith. Thanks to him, her own faith had grown.

What a perfect day. The church service had fulfilled her

spiritual thirst, and their time at the park was relaxing, renewing their relationship. Being close to him now was so comfortable, so natural. With his strong arms around her, she was safe, and nothing could harm her as long as she was with him. She didn't want to be apart from him, but she had to be, at least until she graduated from nurses' training. Then they could marry and live together as husband and wife. Maybe now they could talk about the wedding.

"Russell? Have you thought…"

A woman screamed, and people started running toward the sound. "My baby! Help!"

Lexie jumped up, and Russell followed as she hurried toward the woman's cry.

A small crowd had gathered beside the lake. Lexie pushed her way through the throng. "I'm a nurse," she said. When she saw the toddler lying at the base of a huge boulder by the water's edge, she rushed over to him, extending her hand to keep others back. "Don't move him!"

"I was sitting up there," the woman said, pointing to the top of the rock, "holding Toby for a picture, then he wiggled out of my arms and fell off!" The woman sobbed as Lexie knelt on the ground beside him and felt the child's pulse. The pulse was there, but the child was unconscious and must have hit his head when he fell, according to the gash and knot on his forehead.

"He'll be okay," said Lexie, hoping she was right. "Can someone get a policeman or find a payphone to call for an ambulance?"

"I just did," came a man's voice from the crowd.

Lexie looked into the mother's eyes. "I'll go to the hospital with him. Meet me at the emergency room."

The mother lifted a tear-stained face to Lexie. "Oh, thank you." She kissed the child on his cheek as the ambulance workers arrived carrying a stretcher.

"I'm a nurse at Bellevue," Lexie said to the men. "Can you take him there?"

The men nodded, and as Lexie began to follow the child to the ambulance, she turned to Russell. "I'm so sorry to have to leave you this way, Russell."

He nodded and smiled. "You go ahead. You're needed somewhere else. I'll talk to you tomorrow. Maybe lunch?"

She shrugged. "I don't know yet. I'll call you tomorrow."

As she climbed into the ambulance, she realized they hadn't discussed their wedding plans … again.

Chapter *S*ix

"*T*oby has a concussion," Lexie said to the boy's mother in the emergency room. "They're taking him up to Pediatrics on the fourth floor." Lexie patted the woman's arm. "We'll take good care of him."

"Thank you, Nurse…"

"Smithfield, I'm Nurse Smithfield." Lexie found it odd to hear the words come out of her own mouth.

"Nurse Smithfield. I'm so glad you were there. My husband, Toby's father, is in the Army, and I wanted a picture to mail to him. Oh, it's all my fault!" A sob erupted from the woman.

Lexie placed her hand on the woman's arm. "No, it's not. Accidents do happen, and God knows you did not intend for Toby to fall."

The woman nodded and sniffed.

"Go upstairs and check with the nurses' station to find out when you can see him."

"All right. I'll do that. Thank you again, Nurse Smithfield." She offered Lexie a grateful smile before turning around.

Lexie's heart was heavy with sympathy as she watched the woman walk away. How alone she must feel with her husband away in the service and now her child injured. Sometimes, life just didn't seem fair, no matter what she did to help.

Would she and Russell ever have a little boy like Toby? Or a girl? She sighed. Poor Russell. She'd left him again. She sure hoped he wasn't angry with her. But how could he not be? He came home early from the Island to spend time with her, and then she had to leave again. Her eyes filled with moisture. He'd say he understood, even if he didn't like it. She didn't like it either, but when it came to making choices about taking care of someone or spending the day with your fiancé, a nurse's choice would always be to put personal desires aside and the welfare of others first.

She glanced outside as daylight changed to dusk. No chance of going back out now. She should go to the nurses' residence and study for tomorrow. But while she was here at the hospital, maybe she could check on John Doe.

She walked over to the psychiatric hospital, the smell of disinfectant smacking her in the face when she entered the tiled hallway on the second floor. She stopped at the nurses' station to inquire about the patient.

"Can I help you, miss?" The floor nurse looked Lexie over.

"Yes, please, I'm one of the nurses in training, and I was here yesterday." The other woman crossed her arms, and, with a stern look, examined Lexie as she continued. "I just wanted to check on the condition of one of the patients—John Doe. Has it changed any?"

"Not that I can tell. If you were in uniform, I'd take you

in, but I can't when you're dressed in street clothes."

Lexie glanced down at her clothes, surprised to see how dirty she was after kneeling on the ground at the park, a run up one leg of her stockings. She had completely forgotten she wasn't in uniform. "Of course. I understand." Lexie was tempted to run back to the dorm and change but decided against it. The phone rang, and the nurse went to answer it, turning her back on Lexie.

Lexie started to walk away, then on impulse changed direction and went past the nurses' station over to the door of the psychiatric ward. She peered through the small window in the door, trying to see John Doe. When a face appeared on the other side, she gasped and jumped back. The patient who'd caused the ruckus when she had been in there with the other students was looking out. Seeing her, his eyes grew wide, and he began to yell and beat on the door. "Let me out! Let me out! They're trying to kill me!"

The door shook, and the knob rattled as the man tried to get it open. Lexie backed away, right into the floor nurse.

"What are you doing? You shouldn't be here! Leave at once."

Lexie hurried away from the angry nurse, embarrassed that her good intentions had not turned out well.

"Nurse Smithfield, do you mind telling me what you were doing yesterday in the psychiatric hospital improperly dressed?"

She had expected this. Lexie sat across the desk from the nursing supervisor and glanced down at her hands in her lap before answering. "I was at the hospital because I had helped someone whose child had fallen at Central Park yesterday. When I left the emergency room, I decided to go check on John Doe, but I forgot I was out of uniform."

"You forgot?" The volume of Nurse Addams' voice rose.

"I'm sorry. I really did." Lexie's face grew hot. "It wasn't until the floor nurse mentioned it that I remembered."

Nurse Addams shook her head in disbelief. "And then when she reminded you, you decided to go look in the door anyway?"

"Yes, ma'am."

"I've a good mind to put a reprimand in your file. However, I know you're smart, despite your unwise decision yesterday." The nurse tapped the desk with her pencil. "Nurse Smithfield, as you know, you entered the nursing school ahead of the other students because of your college degree at Vassar."

The head nurse stood and walked over to a bookcase in her office, picked up a picture from the shelf, and showed it to Lexie.

"This is my graduating class from nurses' training at Vassar in 1918."

Lexie's eyes widened as she scanned the old photo of nurses with their capes. "You went to Vassar too?"

Nurse Addams took the picture back, studied it, then replaced it on the bookshelf. "I did, but unfortunately, the nurses' program was discontinued after that, or you might have attended it too."

"I might have, although when I started college at Vassar, I didn't know what I wanted to study."

"But now you do. Apparently, you learned about mental

health care on your own."

Lexie nodded. "I've read a lot about the subject." Her heart weighed heavy with memory, and she looked down as she continued. "My mother had dementia, so I wanted to know more about it."

"I heard about that. You're not aware of this, but I've consulted Dr. Grainger from the sanatorium where your mother lived."

Surprised, Lexie lifted her gaze. "You did?"

"Yes, he tells me you assisted him on his rounds at times. That's unusual for someone who's not a nurse."

Lexie waited for the next reprimand concerning another time when she stepped outside the boundaries of proper procedure.

"He also told me he was confident you were as familiar with patient care as many nurses he knew. In fact, not only did he recommend you for our nursing school, he said you would make a fine doctor if that was your desire."

Astounded, Lexie couldn't believe what she'd heard. "A doctor?"

Nurse Addams nodded. "That's what he said. Apparently, you made quite an impression on him." She sat back down and clasped her hands on the desk, focusing on Lexie. "Since you've already passed the first-year nursing exam, you're presently a second-year student. Based on Dr. Grainger's recommendation, I will give you the second-year test next week. If you pass that, you'll be considered a senior, or third-year student. Would that be acceptable to you?"

Sitting up straight in her chair, Lexie said, "Yes, ma'am, it certainly would."

"Fine, then plan on taking it Monday a week. Now,

another thing, you have reached the point in your training where you can choose your preference of placement at the hospital. I assume that would be psychiatric nursing. Am I right?"

"Oh, yes, ma'am!"

"I know your mother had dementia, but I'm sure you know mental illness can have other forms."

"Yes, in fact, I encountered someone last year who suffered from shell shock after the Great War. He was put in a mental hospital when he returned from the service because his family didn't understand what was wrong. But when he got out, he was able to live a normal life." Lexie recalled Abner from Jekyll Island. "I'd like to learn how to help the soldiers who come back with shell shock."

"So you think our John Doe might be one of those?"

Lexie nodded. "Maybe."

"That's a distinct possibility. But we still have a lot to learn about mental illness and how to treat it. It's just not as simple as setting a broken arm or putting a Band-Aid on a scratch."

"Yes, ma'am, I know."

The nursing instructor leaned back and steepled her fingers as she studied Lexie. "As you know, we are desperate for more nurses, both here and in the military. There are plans in the works to implement an accelerated study program for nursing students instead of the three years that are now required. You are already on an accelerated schedule. Do you have any intentions of joining the military, Nurse Smithfield?"

"No, ma'am. I prefer to stay stateside." If Russell were in the military, maybe her answer would be different, but there was no chance he'd be leaving, so they could marry and stay here.

"Well, that's good for us, then. We could use you here." The head nurse scribbled something on a notepad. "As of today, I'm assigning you to the psychiatric hospital full time when you're not in class or needed elsewhere. You can alternate between the men's floors and the women's."

Lexie could not believe what she had heard. She exercised great restraint to keep from grinning, feeling as if she'd just won a small victory.

"One word of caution, though."

"Yes?"

"The psychiatric ward can be dangerous. You never know what will set one of the patients off. It's important that you remember to take precautions. Never turn your back to the patients, and keep the door locked at all times. Of course, some of the patients are just alcoholics that the police brought in, or even checked themselves in. They're not the most dangerous ones. Once they sober up, they're pretty harmless. It's the others, the ones with real mental illness, who can be dangerous."

"Yes, ma'am, I understand. I'll be careful."

"You may leave now. Go to class, then report to the quiet male ward this afternoon."

Lexie stood. "Thank you, Nurse Addams." Yesterday, the quiet male ward had been anything but quiet.

The instructor nodded. "You might not be thanking me in a few weeks, Nurse Smithfield, because the psychiatric ward can be depressing and usually the least favorite place for most nursing students. However, I pray you will find your work fulfilling."

Thrilled with her news, Lexie wanted to skip out of the instructor's office, but she wouldn't dare evoke Nurse Addams' ire right now. Lexie was assigned exactly where she wanted to be. She couldn't wait to   tell Russell. Now they were even closer to being man and wife, with graduation coming sooner than expected. But she didn't have time to tell him yet because she had to get to class. Her news would have to wait until lunch.

"Why can't we get a room? Your sign out there said 'Vacancy,'" the young man yelled across the front desk, his blushing wife standing behind him. The man leaned toward Russell, lowering his voice. "Hey, pal, we just got married, and I'm shipping out in two days. We need to be together, you know?"

Russell hated telling this couple they couldn't have a room. The "Vacancy" sign should have been removed. Truth was, the hotel was staying booked like every other hotel in the city these days. So many people were going and coming as men left for the military, their families and sweethearts visiting and saying "goodbye."

His brief respite in the Hamptons had quickly become a faded memory when he stepped back into his manager shoes Monday morning. He scarcely finished a sentence before someone asked him another question. His stomach grumbled, reminding him it was lunchtime. Yesterday, he had asked Lexie to join him for lunch today, but he wasn't even sure he could take the time to eat. Besides, he hadn't heard from her yet anyway. No doubt she was busy too.

Lord, help me help this young couple. Who knew when they would be together again?

One of his assistants came up beside him and whispered, "Room 420 just became vacant. You can put them in there."

Russell breathed a sigh of relief. He smiled at the couple as he offered the room. "If you can wait here in the lobby a little while, we'll get a room cleaned for you. We just had someone check out."

"We'll be right here," the young man announced. "Just don't give that room to anyone else, ya hear?"

"Wouldn't think of it," said Russell, taking the demand in stride.

A group of gentlemen passed the front desk, their hats shielding their faces, their heads down as they spoke to each other. Two of them glanced around the room as they followed the others to the elevator. They must be in town on business since they didn't have that eager, naive look of the young servicemen. Nor were they wearing officers' uniforms. The short, fat man in front reminded Russell of someone, yet he couldn't place him at the moment.

The phone near him rang. Seeing no one else at the desk, he lifted the receiver. "Hotel Martinique."

"Russell? Is that you?" Lexie's voice sounded surprised.

"Guilty. How's my pretty lady today?"

"Busy as usual. But I have something exciting to tell you!" Lexie dove into the episode at the hospital on Sunday and her meeting with Nurse Addams that morning. "And guess what?"

"You're being promoted?"

"Not yet, but I get to take the second-year test next week, and if I pass it, I'll be a senior! But guess what else? I'm being assigned to the psychiatric hospital! Now I get to spend more time with John Doe." The excitement in her voice reverberated through the phone.

"That's great, Lex. Just what you wanted." Should he even ask about lunch? "So I guess you'll be too busy for lunch."

"Lunch? Oh, I completely forgot that you asked me to lunch." She paused before continuing. "I'm so sorry, no, not today. Maybe later?"

"Don't worry, sweetie. I don't really have time to sit down today anyway." Even though he didn't, he regretted not seeing her just the same. "Say, thanks for telling me your good news. I'm sure you'll be an asset to the psychiatric department. And I'm glad you'll be able to keep a close eye on John Doe."

"Thanks for understanding, Russell. Gotta run now. Love you!"

"Love you, too, Lex." Russell hung up the phone, embarrassed about the twinge of jealousy he had for John Doe.

Chapter Seven

Karl studied the four newcomers who had arrived from Florida. He remembered them from the Abwehr school in Germany, all former U.S. residents, all trained to sabotage the American war effort. They had been prepared to blend in with the population after landing their rafts—his group on Long Island and the others on the coast of Florida.

Each of them had been pretty confident when they were selected to the elite spy mission, but Karl wondered if they were so sure of themselves now that they were back on American soil. Except for his group's brief encounter with the lone guardsman on Long Island, it had been relatively easy to get on shore from the lifeboats the submarines had launched. The new guys joked and told how they had caught busses to New York, proud of how simple the "invasion" had been.

Now, here they all were in the same hotel room without creating any unwanted attention. Nobody would notice them among the throngs of men in the busy city. To avoid suspicion, they weren't staying in the same place. Karl's group had split in two and was rooming at separate hotels. The other group had also divided and would be headed out of town to their assignments soon. By the time they got back together in Cincinnati on July 4th, their missions would be completed, and the United States would be reeling from their handiwork.

Oscar, with his typical cigar stuck in his mouth, unrolled a map and spread it across the bed. "George, here's Niagara Falls," he said, pointing to the chart. "You and Peter will place your explosives in these places." His finger poked several points on the paper.

George tapped his temple with his finger. "I've got them all memorized."

Peter nodded. "We'll retrieve the boxes we buried on the beach tomorrow night, then head north."

"So you don't think the guardsman told? What if he did? Will we be able to get our supplies?" Karl asked. What would they do if they went back to get them and they weren't there? Or worse, if there was a trap set for them?

"We should've killed him when we had the chance," said Peter.

"We have backup," said George. "Oscar's been stockpiling what we need, just in case."

Karl glanced at Oscar, who nodded, then continued. "Karl and Henry, here's your targets. Karl, the aluminum company here in New York, and the cryolite plant in Philadelphia." Oscar chewed on the cigar clenched between his teeth. "Henry, this is where the locks on the rivers are, the ones you'll destroy."

The men muttered their acknowledgment as Oscar unrolled another chart. They were not seeing this information for the first time. It had been drilled into them before they left Germany. How could they forget?

Edward, the leader of the Florida group, stepped up to scrutinize the new diagram. "Here are the railroads and bridges we will take care of." He glanced up at the other three members of his group. "Herbert, Bernard, and Max, these are yours." Each of the men pointed to their targets, nodding.

A knock sounded on the door, and the men shot nervous looks at each other. "I'll get it," said Karl, walking toward the door. "I ordered some coffee for us."

He reached into his pocket for some change as he opened the door, then handed some coins to the room service maid and took the tray. "Thank you."

The maid thanked him in return, smiled, and left. Karl came in with the tray, pushing the door closed with his shoulder.

Oscar glared at him. "Why are you being so careless? Do you want to compromise our mission?"

"Relax, Oscar." Karl set the tray down on a small table. "The maid couldn't see anything. Besides, I think you're acting too suspicious. You should act normal. We're just some men conducting business." Karl lifted a cup and the coffee pot, looking at the others. "Coffee, anyone?"

Peter frowned at Karl as he poured himself a cup of coffee. "Oscar's right. You should exercise more caution."

Karl restrained himself from commenting. The stocky German was the last person to preach caution, with his reputation for being a hothead. If there was anyone to worry about, Karl thought it would be Peter overreacting to some imagined offense.

The men spent the next hour in the smoke-filled room discussing their assignments before the conversation turned to events back in Germany. Karl opened a window for some fresh air while considering how different they all were. Their work experience varied—he was an electrician like Peter, two of the men were car mechanics, one was a cook, and one a butler. Some of them had belonged to the Nazi party. Others didn't. Five had left families behind, families who thought they were serving in the army. Two of them were divorced, devoted only to the Führer. Karl was single and the only one who still had family on this side of the Atlantic. His mother and sister had moved to Canada to live with his uncle when he went back to Germany, shortly after his father died.

What the men did have in common was their mission and the fact that only they and their superiors knew what that was. But Karl wondered if they also differed in their reasons for accepting the mission. Patriotism? Revenge? Or maybe just fear. Fear of what would happen to their families if they didn't accept, or maybe fear of failure if they did. Karl's gut wrenched at the thought. Perhaps there was a reason he had never married, why he'd avoided commitment. It was one thing to be responsible for himself. He'd hate for someone he cared about to suffer the consequences of his behavior.

Lexie followed the psychiatric head nurse into the men's ward after the door was unlocked. The patients were calm, some sleeping, some flipping through old issues of magazines. Lexie noted that the man who had caused such a ruckus on earlier occasions was strapped down to the bed, asleep. He had been sedated, according to the nurse.

Nurse Martin carried a clipboard with notes about each patient's condition. She pointed out the man's information to

Lexie, and in a low voice said, "He's scheduled for shock therapy tomorrow." She checked the patient's pulse, then noted it on the chart.

Lexie studied the man's relaxed features, so different from the panic and terror he'd displayed before. Would shock therapy help him? Would he be able to live a normal life afterward?

They moved to the next bed where a patient mumbled incoherently, his arms crossed tightly in front of his chest.

"Good morning," said Nurse Martin. "What is your name?"

The man blinked several times before uttering, "Sam." Lexie glanced at the chart and noticed his name was Sam Hall.

"What is today's date, Sam?" The nurse continued the mental status assessment required for each patient every day.

"Sunday?" The man offered a guess, his eyes darting back and forth between the nurses.

"It's June 15, 1942. And it's Monday."

Nurse Martin reached for the man's arm and tried to dislodge it from his chest.

"Do you know who the president of the United States is?"

"Roosevelt."

"That's right!"

Mr. Hall's arms remained crossed.

"May I take your pulse, Mr. Hall?"

The man looked up at the nurse with childlike wonder. "Please?"

Nurse Martin repeated, gently tugging on the man's

wrist.

Sam Hall slowly extended an arm, which Nurse Martin took, holding it as she counted his pulse. Releasing his arm, she said, "Thank you. Would you like some water?" He nodded and returned his arm to its former position. "Good, we'll bring you some in a few minutes." The nurse turned to Lexie. "When we get finished in here, you can refill their water pitchers outside and bring them back. Make sure you get some paper cups."

Lexie nodded, noting the man's vital signs on the chart. They continued checking each patient who was awake, asking the same questions and taking each pulse. She glanced down the row at John Doe every so often, hoping to see some change, but he still stared straight ahead.

When they got to his bed, Nurse Martin spoke to him as well, but there was no response. She checked the bandage on his head. "His head wound is healing nicely. We might be able to take off the bandage this week." Nurse Martin waved her hand in front of his face, and he blinked. "Involuntary movement," she said, explaining to Lexie.

"Wonder if he's thirsty too?" Lexie ventured.

"You can try, but you'll probably have to open his mouth and pour it in. I'm sure he could use something to wet his throat. He's dehydrated." She motioned to the bottle of saline solution hanging on the IV pole next to the bed connected to the tube taped to the man's arm.

Why this one man intrigued her so much, she didn't know. Maybe it was because he was so young. A young soldier who shouldn't end up like Abner Jones had after the last world war—forgotten by society and left to cope with his dilemma alone. Lexie was determined to get a response from

John Doe, even if it was to help him drink some water. Seeing his uncovered toes, she grabbed the thin blanket and pulled it over them.

They finished making the rounds of the ward, then left the room. Once out in the hall, Nurse Martin faced Lexie. "The stainless-steel water pitchers and paper cups are in the utility closet. You'll find a tray and cart there too. Just fill the cups and roll the cart in. Unlike most wards, we don't keep pitchers in this ward—a safety precaution." She handed Lexie a key. "Make sure you keep the door locked."

Lexie took the key and put it in her apron pocket. "Am I to go in by myself? I thought someone was supposed to accompany me."

"Everything's calm in there today, so you shouldn't have any problems." She studied Lexie's face. "Are you afraid to go in alone?"

Lexie shook her head. "No, ma'am." She hoped she sounded believable enough to convince two people—the nurse and herself.

"Good. You'll manage just fine." Another nurse approached, asking for Nurse Martin's assistance at the nurses' station, and they walked away.

I will be fine. Lord, please take away my fear. Lexie found the supplies she needed in the utility closet where the sink was. She filled three water pitchers and assembled them with the cups on a tray. After she located the cart, she put everything on it and rolled it to the ward door. The nurse's warning to be careful reverberated through her mind as she went through the motions of unlocking the door, pushing the cart through, then relocking the door behind her. She made her way to the end of the row of beds and began offering water to those who were awake and receptive. As she moved through the room, she hummed a hymn she'd heard in church the day before.

Watchful faces followed her through the room, some with wary glances while others smiled. She wasn't sure if it was permissible for her to hum, but she didn't see a reason not to. Some of the patients appeared to enjoy her effort to add a form of music to the quiet room. She reached John Doe's bed and walked to the side. "John, would you like some water?" Protocol was to address the man as Mr. Doe, but she wanted to be less formal.

He didn't say yes, but he didn't say no either. So she took the cup, and placing her hand gently behind his neck, lifted his head. She poured a tiny bit of water into the partially opened mouth, watching as his Adam's apple bobbed when he swallowed with a little dribbling down the side of his face. She dabbed his wet face with a cloth, then poured a little more water into his mouth. A sense of triumph made her smile. "There, now. That must feel better," she said. She offered some more, which he also swallowed, and Lexie wanted to shout with excitement. The next time she put the cup to his lips, they were closed shut. Did that mean he'd had enough? Was he telling her that? Only God knew what the man was thinking, if he was indeed thinking.

"All right. That's enough for now," she said, letting him know she got the message if he was sending her one.

After she passed out all the water to the rest of the patients, one of them said, "I know that song."

She looked back at the man, an older gentleman with a sad face, who was sitting up. "You do?"

He nodded. "Heard it a long time ago. I think my

momma sang it. Or my grandma. I forget."

"It's 'Amazing Grace,' one of my favorite hymns. We sang it in church yesterday, and I can't get it out of my mind." Lexie immediately regretted her words, knowing some of the patients had problems with recurring thoughts.

The man nodded his head. "'Amazing Grace.' Maybe it will be in my head now."

Lexie smiled. "It's not a bad thing to have in your head. The song is about God's grace for us."

The man lay back against a propped pillow. "Please keep humming. It makes the voices shut up."

So her humming was better than sedation? Maybe, somehow, God's message would get through to him too. She hoped so. Did John Doe also hear her humming? Did he know the song? Perhaps one day she could ask him, and he'd answer.

Chapter Eight

Russell sat in the hotel dining room staring at the morning newspaper. *US Flyers Attack Italian Fleet in the Mediterranean Battle* and *Flyers Bomb Jap Ships Off Alaska—Jap Carrier Sunk.* He turned the page and found *Nazis Kill Hundreds of Polish.*

He slapped the paper shut and put it down on the table. The world had gone crazy. Hard to imagine such devastation. Why? How could men like Hitler be so evil? The man was a monster, according to all he had read. *Lord, God, please help us stop this evil from spreading.* If only he could do something about it besides pray. Every day he watched young men leave for the military, ready to give their lives for their country. Russell gritted his teeth—he might as well be an old man who was too old to fight since he couldn't sign up either.

"More coffee, sir?" The hotel waitress stood beside him with a coffee pot in her hand. "I can't read the paper anymore," she said. "I just get so worked up about what's going on, I can't sleep at night. And I worry about our men."

Russell lifted his cup for her to refill. "I suppose you know someone who's in the service?"

"Yes, sir, my brothers—both of them, one Army, one Navy."

"Well, I'll pray for their safety." He peered at her name badge. "Lois, that's one thing we can do for them."

"Yes, sir, I know. And the preacher on Sunday said that's one of the most important things we can do too. It just doesn't feel like I'm doing anything."

"I know what you mean, Lois." He sipped his coffee. "Good thing God doesn't depend on our feelings, now, isn't it?"

She propped one hand on her hip, holding the coffee pot with the other and appeared to consider his comment. "You're right. Faith and feelings aren't the same." She glanced at another table where a patron was signaling her. "I'd better go take care of that customer. Have a nice day, Mr. Thompson."

"You do the same, Lois."

Russell watched her walk to the other table and recognized two of the men he'd seen in the group the previous day. One of them appeared relaxed, while the other was fidgety and a chain-smoker. Watching the man smoke made him glad he had quit for Lexie's sake. He had to admit he felt better since he'd quit five months before.

He glanced up to see his assistant manager coming toward him. "Phone call for you, sir."

Russell nodded and pushed his chair back. He reached into his pocket and pulled out some change to leave on the table, then tucked the newspaper under his arm, grabbed his coffee cup, and followed the man out to the lobby. He picked up the black receiver and heard a conversation going on.

"Have a good one, Lex," Penny's voice was heard in the background. "Okay, see you later, Penny," Lexie said.

Russell cleared his throat. "Good morning, Lexie."

"Oh, you're there. Hello, Russell, are you busy?" She sounded especially cheerful today.

"No more than normal. Why?" Maybe she could spread some of her cheer his way.

"Well, I'm working the second shift in the ward today, so I don't have to report until 2:30. Of course, I still have some classes this morning, but I'm free for lunch if you are."

"Now how can I pass up an invitation like that?" Russell smiled as he pictured Lexie's face. "I promise I'll make time to have lunch with my special lady. The diner or here?"

"Let's meet at the diner. That way, you won't be interrupted by hotel business."

"Good point. See you at noon?"

"Sure. I can't wait to tell you what happened in the ward yesterday."

"John Doe talked to you."

"No, not yet. But he will. At least I hope he will."

"Lexie, sweetheart, who wouldn't want to talk to you?"

"Oh, Russell."

She paused, and he imagined her expression. "I'll see you at noon. Bye."

He hung up the phone in a better mood than he'd answered it. If anyone could brighten his day, it was Lexie.

The diner was packed when Russell entered, pushing his way through the crowd standing inside the door as they waited for a seat. Every stool at the counter was taken with lunch customers, and every booth appeared full as well. He scanned the room, about to give up hope of finding an empty space, when Lexie's blonde curls came into view as her head popped up from one of the high-backed booths. She flashed a bright smile and waved him over.

He strode to the booth, leaned down, and gave her a kiss. "How's my girl? Pretty as a picture, like always."

He loved the way she smiled with her eyes, a smile so inviting, it melted his insides. He placed his hat on the pole at the end of the booth and slid onto the red vinyl cushion across from her.

"I got here just in time to grab this booth for us." She looked around. "They're really busy. Glad you got here before I had to share the table with a stranger."

"Perish the thought!" He glanced toward the grill where above it, a row of menu signs was mounted side by side running the entire length of the counter. "I'm hungry for a patty melt, how about you?"

The waitress came over with her pad in hand, pulling the pencil from behind her ear. "What can I get for you kids?" She kept a steady rhythm with her gum as she waited for their answer.

Russell looked at Lexie. "What will you have, Lexie?"

Lexie glanced up at the waitress. "Grilled cheese and a Coke, please."

The waitress faced Russell. "And you, sir?" *Crack!* She popped her gum.

"Patty melt, pickle on the side. I'll have a root beer, please."

"Oh, I'd like a pickle too," Lexie added.

"Sure thing. Be right up." The waitress finished writing, then flipped the page over as she approached the next booth.

Russell clasped his hands on the white tabletop between them. "Well, sweetie, what exciting things happened at the hospital yesterday?"

Lexie described the scene when she gave water to the patients. "When I was humming 'Amazing Grace,' one of the patients recognized the tune. Said he remembered it from his mother or grandmother. Isn't that great?"

"Yes, Lex. Did John Doe like it too?"

Lexie shrugged, rearranging the utensils on the table before her. "I don't know. I don't know if he listened." She paused, then glanced up. "But he did drink some water!" Lexie proceeded to tell Russell how she'd poured water down the man's mouth.

"So, I suppose this is progress?"

"Yes, I think so. He also closed his mouth, so maybe he was telling me he'd had enough."

Russell rubbed his chin. "Could be, I guess. Of course, I don't know anything about such things." He wished he could share her excitement.

"Well, I don't know much, but I'm learning. I remember when I gave Mother water when she was in the sanatorium and she behaved the same way, although she normally looked at me."

The waitress brought their sodas and handed them straws. Lexie took a sip of hers.

"And he will too. I'm sure of it." He searched her bright blue eyes and clasped her hands in his. "You know, Lexie, I think God is using you to minister to these men's spiritual health as well. Just keep humming hymns, and maybe it'll connect their minds to God."

"I hope so, Russell."

"What time is your shift tonight?"

"It starts at 3:00 and normally goes until 11:00. I've never worked at night before, so I'll get to see what goes on when the nurses change shifts."

"Well, I hope things stay calm for you. What happened to the man that was causing all the ruckus the other day?"

"When I saw him last, he was strapped to his bed and asleep—sedated, the nurse said."

Their food arrived, and Russell took her hand and said grace. Lexie nibbled pensively on her sandwich. "You know, Russell, the nurse said they were going to give that man electric shock therapy today. I've never seen that given before—only people after they'd had it. "

"Will you get to see them give it to him?" He took a bite of his sandwich, then sipped some soda.

"Nurse Addams told me they'd wait until I came on duty so I could watch how it's done."

"So the doctors do this in the operating room?"

"No, I think the nurses administer it themselves."

Russell leaned back in his seat, eyes widened. "The nurses can do that? It seems like a procedure only a doctor would do."

"I know, but I guess the doctors are too busy with other things, and nurses are trained to administer it."

"Wouldn't it be dangerous if you gave the patient too big a shock?"

"I suppose so, but I'm sure the nurses know what they're doing. I've never heard of anyone overdoing it."

"Don't you think it's odd that something we use to execute

criminals can also be used as therapy?"

"Russell, there's no chance we'd give someone *that* much voltage!"

"I sure hope not." Russell finished his sandwich and pushed his plate away. "Lexie, thanks for calling me today. It's good to get out of the hotel, especially to see you."

"Russell, I felt so bad about leaving you at the park Sunday. I didn't want the day to end that way. We were having such a nice day."

He touched her hand. "We *did* have a nice day, Lexie, even if it was cut a little short. We'll do it again soon."

Lexie nodded and smiled. "Russell, thank you for being so understanding."

Russell leaned forward and peered into her eyes. "I love you, Lexie, and I know what you do is important to you. So it's important to me too. Okay?"

Lexie's eyes sparkled her response.

Russell glanced at his watch. "Guess I better get back to work."

"Me too," said Lexie. "I have to change my clothes before I report to the ward."

They slid out of the booth, and she put on her gloves as he grabbed his hat. Two more customers came in as they approached the door, and Russell recognized them from the hotel dining room that morning. Lexie froze in her step and glanced uncomfortably at the two men. The blond one tipped his hat and smiled before Lexie hurried out the door Russell held for her.

"Do you know that man, Lexie?" She appeared frightened by the men.

"Not really." She walked quickly away from the diner. "He

and that other man and a couple others rode the train into town with me from Long Island. Penny and I ran into them Saturday afternoon when we came in for a shake. He introduced himself before we left."

"Hmmm. I think they're staying at the hotel. Guess he didn't notice your engagement ring."

Lexie rubbed the ring concealed by her glove. "Maybe not if I was wearing gloves."

"Well, I can't blame him for wanting to meet such a lovely lady." Russell smiled at the blush on Lexie's face. "Too bad you're already taken."

Lexie eyed him warily. "Too bad?"

Russell pulled her to him. "Terrible!" He winked at her, then said, "For him. Poor sap." He kissed her on the forehead. "Call me tomorrow and tell me how your evening goes. Okay?"

Lexie tossed her head and gave him a big smile. "Sure thing, Russell." As she turned and sauntered away, she lifted her hand and gave him a little wave over her shoulder. "Toodles!"

Chapter Nine

"You're just in time," Nurse Addams said as Lexie approached.

"In time for what?"

"We're going to administer the electric shock treatment to Claude this afternoon."

"Claude?"

"You remember Claude Graham. He's the patient that's been having outbursts."

"Who's going to administer it?"

"We are. You and I."

"I am?"

"Yes. You can do it. Just watch and do what I say. You need to learn how to administer the treatments yourself. Don't worry, you'll never do it alone." She pushed the ECT cart toward Lexie. "Come on. You can follow me with the cart."

Lexie eyed the machine, a tingle running up her spine at the prospect of participating in such a procedure. Maybe she wasn't ready for this yet. She did as ordered, though, and pulled the cart carrying the machine into the hallway, then followed Nurse Addams down the hall.

"Wait here, and I'll get the other supplies." The nurse went into a storeroom, then came out with a tray containing syringes, saline solution, an anesthetic, and a gum shield. Handing her keys to Lexie, she said, "You open the door and push the cart in. I'll follow with the tray. You can lock up behind me."

When they entered the ward, the room fell silent, all eyes focused on the nurses. Lexie and the head nurse took the machine and procedure supplies to the bed where Claude Graham lay, his eyes growing wider as the women approached. Nurse Addams went to the opposite side of the bed, glanced at Lexie, and said, "Pull the curtain, please."

The patient began squirming in the bed, pulling against the restraints that held him down.

"Mr. Graham, don't worry. We're here to help you," Nurse Addams said in a quiet, soothing tone.

"No! No! You're going to kill me!" The man continued to fight against the bed restraints.

"Calm down. You'll feel much better soon."

Nurse Addams prepared the syringe with the anesthesia, then administered it by injecting it into the man's arm. Afterward, she patted his arm, and said, "There, that will help."

Within seconds, the man had relaxed. "Go ahead and prepare him," Nurse Addams said, addressing Lexie.

Lexie nodded, trying to remember the way they'd been taught on the dummy in class. The smell of alcohol permeated the air as she wiped his temples to cleanse them. Next, she applied the gel. Then she took the end of each cord connected to the machine and placed an electrode firmly on each gelled position.

Nurse Addams took the rubber mouth shield in her hand. "Now, open wide." She looked over at Lexie as if asking for help.

What could she do to get him to cooperate and relax? She could tell him a story. Lexie looked Claude in the eyes and said, "You know, Mr. Graham, when I was a little girl, my mother wouldn't let me ride horses. You know why? Because she was thrown by a horse when she was a girl and was afraid the same thing would happen to me. But she didn't need to fear all horses. You see, the horse she was on had not been broken. It wasn't ready to be ridden. It was still too wild and afraid of the saddle. But when I went away to college, I rode horses that were stabled there, gentle, calm horses that were not wild. They were safe. They weren't afraid of me, so I wasn't afraid of them either."

Nurse Addams lifted an eyebrow as she listened to Lexie's story and placed the mouthpiece in the patient's mouth without a problem while he watched Lexie. Soon, his eyelids began to droop.

"Mr. Graham, this treatment is to help you get rid of your fears and anxiety. It has helped many other people, and I'm sure it will help you too," said Nurse Addams. "You'll experience a little shock, but it will be over in just a few seconds. Afterward, we'll bring you something to eat because I'm sure the fasting has made you hungry." She patted his arm. "Are you ready?"

The man nodded slightly, then closed his eyes.

Nurse Addams turned to the machine, dialed the gauge, then flipped the switch on. A buzzing noise ensued, and Lexie held her breath for the second the electricity was applied. Mr. Graham jerked and went into a seizure as Nurse Addams turned the electricity off, then counted the seconds from her watch as the seizure continued for a full minute, the patient's muscles alternately twitching and relaxing. When he stopped, Lexie eased out a breath.

"Good," Nurse Addams said, removing the mouthpiece from the man's mouth. "We'll monitor him this evening, and he should be awake and ready for a snack in a couple of hours. You can remove the electrodes now."

Lexie followed the nurse's directions, thankful to release the man from the machine. Her nursing manual said nurses should be sympathetic to their patients. She had no problem with that rule, especially after seeing the shock treatment applied. If she hadn't read about the treatment's effectiveness, she wouldn't be able to watch.

"We'll do this again in two days," said Nurse Addams as she pushed the cart away from the bed.

"So soon?" How much could a person take?

"That's right. It must be administered twice a week for at least six weeks to be effective."

The nurse eyed Lexie. "You must understand this is for the patient's good, despite your feelings." She nodded toward the curtain. "You can push that back now."

Lexie did so, aware that the patient in the next bed watched her. She offered her best reassuring smile.

The patient glanced nervously at the machine as Nurse Addams pushed it by. "Are you going to do that to me too?"

"Only if you need it," answered Nurse Addams over her shoulder.

The man looked back to Lexie, his eyes pleading. *I don't need it.*

"Okay? I'll be real good."

Lexie nodded. "Don't worry." What else could she say? She hoped he wouldn't need it. She really didn't enjoy participating in the treatment. As they passed John Doe's bed, Lexie glanced to see his response, thinking she'd sensed him watching her. But she must've imagined it. He still stared straight ahead, oblivious to his surroundings.

"Nurse Addams, should I check his bandage?"

"Go ahead. We might take that off today."

Lexie approached the bed. "Let's see how you're doing."

She lifted the bandage gently and checked the wound on his forehead. The gash had closed thanks to the stitches.

"What do you think?" asked Nurse Addams, who had come up beside her.

"It looks well enough to me. When will the stitches come out?"

"Let's unwrap the bandage and give the wound some air. The doctor will make his rounds tomorrow, and he'll probably take the stitches out then."

Lexie took the end of the bandage and began to unwrap it from John Doe's head. As she removed the bandage, the patient's chestnut-brown hair fell across his face. She picked up the loose locks and finger-combed them into the rest of his hair. "I bet he'd like to have his hair washed."

Nurse Addams raised an eyebrow. "You think so?"

Lexie blushed, realizing the man's condition and that he was likely not aware of his hair's condition, much less anything else. "Well, I'll wash it anyway, if you don't mind. I know I'd want my hair washed if it had been wrapped in a bandage for weeks."

"That sounds like a good idea. Perhaps it would provide him more comfort. You'll have plenty of time after the patients have their supper tonight."

If she could make him more comfortable, she would be happy to wash his hair. In fact, she was tempted to give him a shave too, whether he knew he needed one or not. The fuzzy whiskers didn't look natural, and she sensed they hadn't been there when he was serving in the Army. She had a great urge to see more of his face, as if it would provide any clues to his identity.

Nurse Addams whispered to Lexie, "He might be the next patient for treatment."

For a second, Lexie didn't know what treatment the head nurse referred to. Then she looked from the ECT machine to the patient and realized. She cringed at the thought. For some reason, it didn't seem fair to apply the treatment to someone who had no understanding of what was being done to him, much less give his consent for the therapy. Of course, she wanted to help him any way she could, but was that the only way? Surely, there was another. An idea struck her. She'd tell him about it when she came back later to wash his hair. He might not understand, but at least she'd give him the opportunity to know about it. Perhaps somewhere in his subconscious, he'd hear what she said.

Lexie carried a basin of water, a towel and washcloth over her arm, and a bottle of shampoo tucked in her pocket. Most of the patients were sleeping when she made her way over to

John Doe's bed and placed the basin on the bedside table. She felt the water temperature—nice and warm. Speaking softly, she said, "Mr. Doe, my name is Nurse Smithfield. I hope you don't mind me washing your hair. It's been a while since it was washed, and I think you'll feel better when it's clean." Taking the washcloth, she dabbed it in the water, then began to wet the man's hair. She placed the rolled towel behind his neck, gently lifting his head. While she washed his hair, she hummed softly, trying not to disturb the other patients.

She used a little water to rinse the hair, then patted it dry with the towel. A sense of tenderness touched her as she cared for the man, and the sensation surprised her. As she took a comb from her pocket and began combing the man's hair, she wondered if the feeling was like a mother caring for a child, doing something for them they couldn't do for themselves. Was this why she wanted to be a nurse? She finished combing and exchanged the pillowcase for a dry one, studying the man's face as she did.

John Doe had high cheekbones and a squared jaw—a face that would display strength under normal conditions. She wiped his face with the washcloth, wishing she could see him without the whiskers. He couldn't be much older than she was. Maybe not as old as Russell. What if this were Russell? But no, he wouldn't end up like this because he wouldn't be fighting in the war. Was she wrong to be glad about that?

And what about John Doe? Did he have a girlfriend or fiancée somewhere? Or maybe a wife, a family? The Army thought everyone in his unit had been killed, but without his dog tags, how would they know who the survivor was? Surely, they'd figure it out eventually, but in the meantime, who needed to know he was alive? If only he could talk to her. For now, though, she could talk to him, and maybe he'd hear.

"Mr. Doe? We want to help you. I want you to understand that. There are some medical treatments that might relieve your condition, and they are being considered so we can determine the best one for you. I want you to be aware of them so you won't be surprised. One of them is called ECT, and another patient received it today. We expect favorable results from his treatment." All the while she spoke, she tried to convince herself as well as the unresponsive man in front of her. "I'll try to let you know at least a day beforehand when we'll administer the treatment to you."

There, she'd told him. Her effort to communicate might not mean anything to him, but her conscience was relieved. She patted his arm. "Good night, Mr. Doe."

After gathering up the hair washing supplies and damp linens, she tiptoed away from the bed, then glanced around the room to make sure the other patients were still asleep. Confident they were, she left the ward, locking the door behind her, and properly stored the supplies before going to the nurses' station to document her patient reports for the evening. She only wished she had some progress to report on John Doe's condition besides clean hair.

Although her shift ended at 11:00, it was almost midnight before she finished her paperwork, barely able to keep her eyes open. She craved a cup of hot tea, but she needed to go to bed.

Crossing the street to the residence at night made her uneasy, but streetlights helped show the way, even though they'd been dimmed according to the war mandate. Often other medical personnel from the hospital went back and forth during the night as well, so she shouldn't be afraid. She steeled herself as she stepped outside and hurried along the walk and through the wrought iron gates separating the hospital from the outside world. The muted lights crafted fuzzy shadows on the ground, creating images like the haunted forest that frightened a character in a cartoon she'd watched as a child. The scene had always haunted her, and even now the memory tingled her spine. But she wouldn't act like that character and run screaming through the night. *Fear not, for the Lord is with you.* She quoted this scriptural promise over and over as she traveled the distance to the residence building, reaching the entrance just before her late pass expired.

When would she quit being afraid? She knew now there really were no family curses. And she knew she was far away from Nazis landing near her home. Times like these were when she wanted Russell's arms around her, his comforting voice reassuring her that she was safe. But she needed to be able to cross the street without being afraid, without depending on Russell to always protect her. The Lord was with her, and that was enough.

Chapter Ten

"Gee, some gals have all the luck!" Penny leaned against the door frame watching Lexie pin her cap on.

"Whatever do you mean?" Lexie faced her roommate.

"I dunno. I know you work hard, but you come from a rich family. You have a college degree and a handsome fiancé. Where was I when they were dishing out the good life?"

"Penny, you *do* have a good life. You have a big family back home. I don't have any family … anymore."

"Oh, I'm sorry. You're right. Guess it just seems like things are easier for you, you know, grades and stuff. You're already ahead of me, and now you're going to be a senior too!"

"Only if I pass the exam. I'll have to study hard for it. They don't just hand out promotions."

"Yeah, I don't envy you that. I'm having enough trouble with 'Theory and Practice.'"

"It's only because I studied it in college that I was able to pass the test." Lexie grabbed her books. "Besides, you know I'm a lot older than you, so I have more experience." She winked at her roommate.

"Oh, I forgot how *old* you are! All of two years older than me, right?"

"Almost three. I'll be twenty-three this year." Lexie hooked her arm onto Penny's. "Come on, let's go before we're late for breakfast."

"So I guess you're going to study all day long? Are you going to see Russell today?"

"Maybe. I haven't talked to him yet."

"Well, don't ignore him. If you do, somebody else will grab him!"

"Not a chance." Lexie laughed.

"I just wish I had a boyfriend. You know, somebody to see on the weekends when I can get a pass. I like to go home, but it sure would be nice to have a man waiting for me. But, gee, all the guys are leaving for the war."

"Hey, I have an idea." Lexie stopped and faced Penny. "Next time Russell plays at a local USO dance, we can go together. That would be fun, wouldn't it?"

Penny's face brightened. "Yeah, sure! Hopefully, I'll be able to get away from here. You get more passes than I do."

Lexie put her hands on her hips. "You know why too. If you go to church, you get two passes a week instead of one."

"All right. All right. You might talk me into going to church with you after all."

"It wouldn't kill you. I'll call Russell later and see when the next dance is."

After breakfast, Lexie returned to the residence to use the phone and called Russell at the hotel.

"Hi, babe." He always sounded like he was smiling.

"Hi, Russell. You have time for me today?"

"I think I can work you in. Something exciting happen last night?"

"You might not think so, but I'd still like to see you."

"Music to my ears. Would you like to come to the hotel for lunch?"

"Sure. Noon? I'm working again tonight."

"Perfect. See you then."

Lexie hung up the residence phone, then returned to the hospital and made her way to the library. She opened her books and began studying for her tests, getting so engrossed she forgot the time. When her stomach growled, she remembered lunch and checked the time. It was already a quarter past noon! She'd have to hurry, but she had to change clothes first. What a frustrating rule that she couldn't wear her uniform off the hospital grounds. She raced upstairs to her room, grateful it was on the second floor so she didn't have to wait for the elevator.

She thought about calling Russell to tell him she was running late but decided not to take the time and practically ran the blocks to the hotel, dashing into the lobby out of breath. She peered into the dining room and scanned the tables searching for Russell but didn't see him anywhere.

A waiter approached her. "Can I help you find a seat, miss?"

"I'm looking for the hotel manager, Russell Thompson. Has he been in here?"

The waiter nodded. "Yes, he was sitting over there about fifteen minutes ago, but someone came and got him. You might check at the front desk and see if they know where he is."

Lexie went back to the lobby and waited for the desk clerk

to finish with a customer before he came over to her. "May I help you?"

"Have you seen Russell Thompson? I was supposed to meet him for lunch."

"Ah, yes, ma'am. He left a note for you." The clerk reached beneath the desk, withdrew a piece of paper, then gave it to her.

"Lexie, sorry I had to leave. The hotel owner called an unexpected meeting with all the managers, and I have to attend. Will make it up to you later."

What would she do now? She might as well return to the residence and get ready for her shift. She left the hotel and headed back. But as she neared the diner, the craving for a club sandwich propelled her inside. Since she was alone, she opted for one of the two seats that were empty at the counter. The waitress came over, took her order, then returned with a glass of Coke. As she sipped her soda, a gentleman sat down beside her. She glanced over and almost choked on her drink.

The same man, the one who'd introduced himself as Cal, was sitting next to her. Why did she keep running into him? She thought about leaving, but she had already ordered her sandwich. Besides, she was hungry.

He took off his hat, placed it on the counter, then turned to her with a surprised look.

"So we meet again."

Lexie offered a smile, hoping he didn't notice the blush that her warm cheeks confirmed.

"How are you today … did you say your name was Cal?"

"You have a good memory. And I believe your friend said your name was Alexandra. Is that correct?"

"That is my given name, yes, but most people call me Lexie."

The waitress brought Lexie's sandwich and turned to Cal. "What'll you have, hon?"

"Coffee and…" He looked at Lexie's sandwich, "I'll have one of those."

"Club sandwich? Coming right up!"

Lexie bowed a second to bless her food, then took a bite.

"Didn't your friend, Penny, I think, say you were both nursing students?"

Lexie swallowed and took a sip of her drink before answering. "That's correct. We're students at Bellevue."

"So if I may ask, why did you decide to be a nurse? Is that something you've always wanted to be?" Cal's sandwich arrived, and Lexie welcomed the chance to formulate her answer.

"Maybe it's because my mother was ill." She paused, not wanting to divulge the nature of her mother's illness.

"It's a tough profession." He drank some coffee. "I saw a movie about nurses a long time ago."

"You did? Which one?"

"Let's see. Oh, it was called *The White Parade.* My little sister wanted to see it, so I took her."

Surprised, Lexie faced him. "I saw that too. I forgot about it because it was so long ago."

"So maybe it influenced you, huh?"

Lexie pondered the idea. "Maybe it did, but I didn't realize it. Did your sister become a nurse?"

"As a matter of fact, she did."

"Does she live here?"

Cal paused, his gaze drifting off. "No, she lives in

Canada."

"You're Canadian, then?"

He ran his finger around the inside of his collar as if it were too tight. "No, but my family moved there a few years ago. My uncle is there."

The man seemed uncomfortable, and Lexie was afraid she'd overstepped herself. "I'm sorry, I didn't mean to pry."

His broad smile returned. "Oh no, you didn't. I was just thinking it's been a while since I've spoken to them."

"You live on Long Island?" Seeing his puzzled look, she said, "You know, I saw you on the train from Long Island."

"Oh, that. No, I was visiting friends there."

"Actually, I was, too, in East Hampton." Lexie bit her tongue. Maybe she was giving this stranger too much personal information. She didn't want him to get the wrong idea. "My fiancé and I were there visiting friends."

Cal lifted an eyebrow. "Your fiancé? I suppose that is the man I saw you here with yesterday."

"Yes, that's him. He's the manager at the Martinique Hotel."

"I thought he looked familiar. That's where I've been staying."

"Oh. So you don't live here?" There she went again being nosy. Why else would he be staying at the hotel?

"No, I'm just in town a few days wrapping up some business. Then I'll be going to work at the Aluminum Company in Massena."

"I thought maybe you were in town to sign up for the Army or Navy." The expression on Cal's face was curious, like she'd suggested something very unusual. She looked down at her watch, then jumped up. "I'm sorry. I need to get back to the hospital." She reached into her purse for money to pay for her lunch, and Cal put his hand over hers.

"I'll get this."

"That's really not necessary," she said, pulling her hand away to get her money out and put it on the counter. "But thank you anyway."

"All right." He put on his hat and stood. "It was very nice talking with you, Alexandra, or Lexie."

"You too," she said and dashed out of the building. As she hurried down the sidewalk, she mulled over the conversation she had with Cal.

So his sister was a nurse? How interesting. Why hadn't he seen his family for a while? She wondered who he had been visiting in the Hamptons. Maybe it was someone she knew. If not, the sisters probably did. Maybe some of the men he was with were the people he'd visited. He sure did act strangely when she suggested he was joining the military. Well, what he did was not her concern, even though he was a nice man. Too bad Penny hadn't been there to talk to him since *she* was the one who wanted to meet men.

Scenes from *The White Parade* flitted through her mind as she remembered the movie. She recalled the nurses struggling with their duties and relationships. Was the movie realistic? In some ways, she remembered the situations as similar to those they faced at the hospital.

But the movie had seemed so dramatic when she saw it. One part that stood out in her mind was when the main character, played by Loretta Young, had to make a choice between love and her job. Lexie would never allow that dilemma in her own life. Even though the instructors at

Bellevue were unmarried, and a few former instructors had resigned to get married, that choice was no longer necessary. In today's world, a woman could have both, even if managing each was difficult.

Like studying too late and missing lunch with your fiancé. Lexie could kick herself for that. Good thing Russell was such a nice guy. Some guys might get peeved, but not him. Too bad Penny couldn't find some nice man like Russell. She smiled remembering Penny's warning to keep tabs on Russell so some other woman wouldn't snatch him away. Russell wasn't like other men, and he certainly wouldn't be attracted to someone like Penny. Thank God, Lexie could trust Russell. He was a loyal, God-fearing, moral man, and he had his priorities straight. She worried that working at the Martinique wasn't as fulfilling for him as being manager of the Jekyll Island Club had been. Hopefully, he would come to like his new job as much as his last.

Chapter Eleven

*Ru*ssell strolled up to the front desk, exhausted from the meeting he'd been in.

"Anything I need to handle?"

"No, sir, not at the moment." The desk clerk finished tallying a bill. "Oh, yes, that young lady came by looking for you."

"Beautiful blue eyes, blonde curls, about this tall?" Russell held his hand shoulder high.

"Yes, sir, that would be the one. She blew in here pretty fast and canvassed the dining room before she came to the desk."

"Yep. Sounds like Lexie. Late again. Guess she was sore I wasn't here waiting for her."

"Disappointed, I'd say. She left the hotel when I told her you had to leave for a meeting."

Russell blew out a breath. That's the way things were going with he and Lexie these days—never enough time for each other. He leaned over the desk and turned the registration book around. "How are we doing on vacancies?"

"A few checked out, but just as many checked in. We're

still full."

Russell rubbed his chin. His business wasn't slowing down any, that's for sure. And now that he'd found out the company was losing a couple of its managers to the military, he'd have even more work. He wouldn't mind the work if he enjoyed it. But New York City was so different from Jekyll Island. The city was not a resort, and the Martinique was not a club. He hated the hectic pace of the city, so unlike the relaxed pace of Jekyll.

He lifted his gaze when a man entered the lobby and passed by on his way to the elevators. It was the same guy that Lexie said she saw on the train from Long Island. Russell nodded in his direction. "Say, you know who that man is?"

"No, sir. I don't think the room he's in is registered in his name."

"Wonder how long he's staying?"

The desk clerk shrugged. "I saw him with some other men this morning, but they left."

Russell scanned the book again, trying to figure out which rooms had changed in the last twenty-four hours. But there were too many rooms and too many people for him to know. Which was another thing he didn't like about the hotel. At Jekyll, he knew everyone who came to the hotel, as well as the island. And they knew him too. He was important there. Even if he wasn't one of the club members, he was their "go-to" man. He had everyone's respect because they knew he handled his responsibilities with skill and professionalism. Anything they needed, he could provide, or would at least try to, and the members appreciated him for that.

Here at the Martinique, only his employees and the owner knew who he was. Yes, there were a few customers who came in more than once—just some regular business travelers who he'd become familiar with. But others, like the stars who stayed when they performed on Broadway, didn't even give him a nod. *Russell, your pride is showing,* he admonished himself. He should be content just having a job after the Jekyll Club Hotel closed. He should be thankful to be near Lexie so they could see each other occasionally. Well, that's one thing he was thankful for. Seeing Lexie, even if it wasn't as much as he wanted, added joy to his life and made his job more bearable. Still, he just didn't feel like he was making a difference, doing something that made the world a better place.

Two servicemen walked into the lobby and up to the front desk. He straightened and spoke to them. "Good afternoon, gentlemen. Do you have reservations?"

The two young men seemed barely old enough to be out of high school, if indeed they were. They looked at each other and shrugged. "Do we have to have reservations?"

Russell smiled, thinking how innocent they were, how unprepared for the world they were about to defend. "It would be a good idea. Most New York City hotels are staying booked these days."

He turned to the desk clerk. "Glenn, see if we have anything available."

The clerk looked at him with raised eyebrows but perused the reservation book anyway.

"I'm afraid we don't, sir. Not at this time."

The young men were crestfallen. "Oh, okay. Do you know someplace else we can go?'

Russell had an idea and turned to the clerk. "Say, Glenn, why don't you call the McAlpin and see if they have any vacancies?" The McAlpin Hotel, at twenty-five stories was larger than the Martinique's nineteen and was owned by the same company. Russell knew from the meeting he'd come from that the hotel had vacancies.

"Yes, sir." The clerk phoned the other hotel and determined there were indeed rooms available. "They're holding two rooms for you," he said to the men when he hung up the phone.

"Gee, thanks," one of them said. "Where is it? We're new in town."

Russell picked up a pad of paper and drew a map for them. "It's only a couple of blocks south of here. You won't have any trouble finding it." He tore off the paper and handed it to them.

When the men left, Glenn turned to Russell. "That was real nice of you. You go the extra mile to help people."

"Shouldn't we all? The Golden Rule, you know."

"What's that?"

"Treat others the way you'd like to be treated yourself." Hadn't everyone heard of the Golden Rule?

The clerk's forehead creased in thought. "Ah, yes, that's a good thing to remember."

"Sure is, Glenn. So let's try to treat all our patrons that way." Russell slapped the desk with his hand for emphasis. "Our hotel should have a reputation for the good service we give, don't you agree?"

"Yes, sir."

The phone rang, and Glenn picked it up. "Hotel Martinique. How may I help you?" He winked at Russell, who smiled his approval. Then he handed the phone to Russell. "For you."

Russell leaned against the desk, propping his elbow on the top. "Russell Thompson, at your service."

The USO was on the other end. He chatted with them a while before they asked if he could play piano for their dance Friday night. Russell accepted the offer, happy to know the dance would be at the Martinique. Maybe Lexie could come, too, since it was so close to her.

Karl entered the hotel room to find Henry pacing the floor. "Where have you been?" The fellow conspirator puffed out his words with ever-present cigarette smoke.

"I went out for lunch. And some cards." Karl held up the deck of playing cards, frowning at the overflowing ashtray on the nightstand, and strode to the window to make sure it was open as far as possible. "Don't you get tired of this room?"

"Sure I do, but I don't want to take any unnecessary chances." Henry glanced anxiously at the window.

"Like I do, you mean?" Karl crossed his arms and leaned against the wall nearest the fresh air.

"Yes, like you do." Henry pointed at Karl. "Oscar told us to stay low while we wait for our supplies."

"Oscar is not my commanding officer." Karl frowned at the notion.

Hands on hips, Henry walked over to face him. "But he is our leader for the operation here."

Karl shrugged but stood his ground. "He's our contact person, nothing else. He does not decide what I do with my time."

"Don't underestimate him, Karl. Oscar can be a dangerous man to cross."

"Yeah? What's he going to do to me? Kill me? How will that affect the operation? Wouldn't that create more attention than we want?" Karl's anger threatened to take over the good mood he'd had when he arrived at the room.

Henry backed down, but Karl had a suspicion the man struggled with the situation.

"Henry, let's go downstairs for some coffee. You need to get out of here before you go crazy."

Henry flashed an apprehensive look. "I don't know. I…"

Karl strode to the door and grabbed the knob. "Come on. I'm buying." He offered a slight smile to his edgy roommate.

Scanning the room as if searching for an answer, Henry finally nodded. "Well, all right." He grabbed his hat off the table. "But just downstairs, nowhere else."

Karl grinned as he opened the door wide. "So I guess a walk in the park would be out of the question?"

Henry took a step back, surprise in his eyes.

Motioning with his hand to come on, Karl said, "It's a joke, Henry."

They took the elevator down to the lobby and passed the front desk on the way to one of the hotel's restaurants. When Karl saw the hotel manager near the desk talking on the phone, he remembered that the man was Alexandra's fiancé. Not a bad-looking fellow, dressed well and seemed pleasant enough. He caught some of the phone conversation as they walked past.

"Yes, the beach at Amagansett was hopping when I was there Saturday. Never saw so many coast guard personnel around there before." He paused while he listened, then continued. "Yes, I know there's a station there, but this is the first time I've ever seen so much action around it. I figured they were conducting some type of training exercise. I saw them digging in the sand, like hunting for buried treasure."

An alarm went off in Karl's head. Buried treasure? Did they find anything? He followed Henry to the farthest table in the restaurant, choosing a seat that faced the lobby. He wanted to keep an eye on this fellow.

When the man hung up the phone and walked away, Karl noticed a slight limp. What was wrong with his foot or leg? Had he been a soldier? The girl didn't say anything about it. And with all the rampant patriotism going on in the country, she might have bragged about his service or his injury.

What had the man been talking about? The place they hid the munitions boxes was near the coast guard station he mentioned. Had the guardsmen found them? Of course, Karl and the others knew the possibility existed, which was why Oscar had stockpiled some backup. Even so, he shouldn't worry. They couldn't trace his team. It had been foggy and dark, and the only man the coast guard had seen clearly was Peter when he shone the flashlight in his face. Apparently, the bribe didn't work. And what were the chances the guy would run into Peter again? He tried to push away his increasing doubts about the mission. The waitress brought coffee, then left. Karl looked at Henry, his head low over his coffee cup as if he were trying to hide inside the beverage. How could he get the guy to act more relaxed? "Henry, tell me about your family."

Henry's head jerked up. "Why?"

"Just curious." He took a sip and set his cup down. "You have two children, right?"

Henry's face brightened. "Yes, Hilda and Hans. They are six and eight years old." He reached for his wallet, then stopped. "I used to carry pictures … back there."

Karl nodded. "And your wife … her name is Hazel, I believe?"

"Yes, she is a very wonderful wife." A look of worry clouded his features. "I hope they are safe."

Karl lowered his voice. "They're in Berlin?"

"No! I sent them to the country to stay with my parents."

"They should be safe then. What are you worried about?"

Henry lit another cigarette, pulled a drag on it, then put it down in the ashtray. "I miss them. And I can't contact them."

"I suppose that's one advantage I have—no family wondering where I am."

"No family? Not even parents or brothers, sisters?"

"My father died after I went back. He loved the Fatherland and wanted to go back too, but my mother and sister wanted to stay here. But after he died, they went to live with my uncle in Canada."

"And they don't know you're here, I guess."

"No," Karl said. "It's better that way." But it had crossed his mind to try calling them, just to talk. But then, how would he explain where he was? He knew Mother and Gretchen would not approve of his mission. Knowing they were no longer in the States had made it easier to accept the assignment, but their strong Christian values would oppose such destruction. A wave of guilt washed over him. They probably prayed for him too. That notion was somewhat comforting if it protected him. Then again, when he decided to participate in the mission, he knew the risks.

Henry mumbled, "I guess I'll never see my family again."

He wiped away moisture from his eyes with the back of his hand and sniffed. "I should've thought about that before I agreed to do this."

"Yeah, well, you never know what might happen." Karl mulled over various scenarios of their future, none of them appealing.

Henry raised an eyebrow. "What do you mean?"

"Oh, I don't know, just dreaming, I guess."

Hunching over his cup toward Karl, Henry said, "Do you think there's a chance we…"

Karl glanced up to see Oscar coming toward them, his face contorted in anger. "Shhh! Oscar's here."

Henry twisted around as Oscar stormed up. The man pulled out a chair and plopped down in it, red-faced and perspiring as he slammed his cigar butt into the ashtray. He glanced back and forth at the two of them, then focused on Karl, hissing through clenched teeth.

"I saw you with that woman!"

Karl leaned back and raised an eyebrow, feigning confusion. "A woman?"

"Yes! That woman you know from the train. I told you to stay away from women!"

Karl bit his tongue as his temper rose. "I was not *with* any woman. She just happened to be in the same place at the same time when I went for lunch."

"You were talking to her!" Oscar growled.

The idea that the man was spying on him enraged Karl, but he would not let the fellow dictate his activity. He took a deep breath, then exhaled slowly.

"So, Oscar, are you following me? Because if you are, you're a greater threat to our mission than my talking to a young woman who happens to be sitting next to me at a lunch counter.”

“I am not following you!” Oscar’s eyes darted around the room. “I was making a delivery for the bakery and saw you go in there. And when I passed by later, you were still there, sitting next to her and making conversation.” He lowered his voice even more. “Who is she, Karl? What does she know?”

“Oscar, calm down. She’s a nobody, just some girl I’ve run into a few times. We’ve made polite conversation.” He shrugged. “That’s all.”

“But you keep running into her? Don’t you think that’s strange, Karl? What if she’s on to us?”

Karl leaned forward and put his face as close to Oscar’s cigar breath as he could bear. “Calm down, Oscar. Listen. Trust me, the girl just lives in this area. She has no idea who I am or what I’m doing here. She. Is. Not. A. Threat.” Karl clenched his fists below the table. Wouldn’t he love to punch the guy in his flabby face?

“Trust you? Ha! I trust no one.” Oscar leaned back in his chair and blew out a breath, then signaled the waitress over. “Bring me a drink—uh, Coke.” The waitress’s expression changed from pleasant to disgusted as she nodded and walked away.

“Speaking of … I overheard something that you need to know.” Karl glanced around the dining room where only two other tables had patrons, and those were some distance away. He spoke in a low voice. “I think the guy we ran into at the beach talked.”

Oscar frowned, leaned over, and huffed. “Why? What did you hear?”

Karl nodded toward the lobby. “Heard a man on the

phone talking about lots of coast guard personnel on the beach Saturday, probing and digging in the sand. Chances are they found our boxes."

Oscar looked out to the lobby. "Who said that? How do you know he was talking about the same beach?"

"The manager of the hotel. He's the one out there on this side of the desk talking to the clerk on the other side. He mentioned the name of the coast guard station that was near where we landed, so I know it's the same beach."

Oscar glanced over his shoulder at the lobby. "Peter was right. You should have killed the guy."

"But we didn't, Oscar, so we're going to need what you can get us."

"All right. It'll take some time to round it up." He drained the Coke the waitress handed him in practically one noisy gulp, slurping the ice when the liquid ran out. "I'll have to tell Peter and George too." He pushed back his chair, stood, then leaned over, planting his palms on the table, his eyes shifting from Henry to Karl. "You two stay put." He pointed his finger at Karl. "And you, stay away from that woman!"

Karl held back his response. The last thing he wanted was to give Oscar a reason to stay in his company any longer. As Oscar stormed out, Karl clasped his hands in front of him and twirled his thumbs, fighting for control of his temper.

Henry peered up from his cup like he'd been hiding in it while Oscar ranted. "Told you he'd be angry."

Karl shrugged. "So he's angry. Let him be angry. I have no intention of staying here twenty-four hours a day until everything's in place. This is my first trip to New York City, so I might as well enjoy it while I can."

Henry's shocked expression was almost amusing.

Apparently, Oscar had the guy scared to move. "But what if you run into that woman again?"

Karl shrugged. "What if? So, I'll speak to her, say hello. Don't you think it'd be strange if I ignored her now that we've exchanged pleasantries?"

Henry shook his head. "I don't understand you. You act like we're here on holiday."

"We're not? Well, maybe not, but we can act like we are, can't we?"

"No, no, I don't think we can. At least I can't. This is not fun, Karl, and I'm not enjoying it one little bit. Have you forgotten why we're here?"

Karl became serious. "No, Henry, I haven't forgotten. We don't know what will happen to us, whether we succeed or fail. But until then, I plan to enjoy my life while I still can—Oscar or no Oscar."

Chapter Twelve

"Guess what, Penny?" Lexie asked with a smug grin. The girls had run into each other in the ladies' lounge at the hospital after lunch before heading on to their afternoon assignments.

"You've just been made the head nurse on the psychiatric floor." Lexie gave her a playful shove. "No, silly. Guess again?"

Penny put her finger under her chin and gazed up at the ceiling. "Ummm—you're pregnant! No, I'm sure that can't be true."

Lexie planted her hands on her hips. "Really, Penny! That's not even funny, much less possible."

"Okay, okay. I give up. What?"

"There's a USO dance at the Martinique Friday night, and Russell is playing in the band." She grabbed Penny by the shoulders. "Do you want to go with me?"

Penny's grin spread across her face. "Do I? You bet your bottom dollar, I do!" She clapped her hands together.

Lexie put her finger to her lips. "Shhh! Not so loud."

Penny's face clouded over. "I hope I can get a pass."

"Oh, surely you can, Penny. You've been a good girl this week—no problems. You've kept your uniform clean and ironed, been on time for class and work, done everything right."

"I'll keep my fingers crossed. But what about you? But what about your new schedule? Will that interfere?"

Lexie chewed on her cuticle. "I hadn't thought about that. I really hope not. Let's go ahead and put in our requests."

"Okay, sure thing. Say, are you going to see John Doe again today?"

"No, at least I'm not assigned to the men's ward today." She looked in the mirror and straightened her collar. "I have to work in the women's semi-disturbed ward instead."

"Well, you can't have all the men all the time!" Penny teased, laughing.

"Penny, you're impossible!"

They parted ways, and Lexie went over to the psychiatric hospital and entered the women's wing.

"Good afternoon, Nurse Smithfield." A nurse with silver-white hair pulled into a tight bun met Lexie at the nurses' station. Nurse Pritchard was a robust woman, and she meant business. "I'll take you in and introduce you to our patients. We've got a mixed bag of cases."

Mixed bag? Whatever that meant, Lexie would soon find out as she followed the nurse into the ward where twenty women made their temporary home. At one end, an elderly lady in a rocking chair held a doll and cooed at it. Beside her, another woman with frightened eyes mumbled, watching as they passed by. Still another whimpered and huddled in a fetal position. Some were dressed in street clothes while a couple wore hospital gowns. A few were asleep, and others were awake and acted fairly normal. Until they attempted to answer Nurse Pritchard's questions. The answers they gave made no sense at all. Lexie pitied these women, wishing she could counsel them and help them. But she was not skilled in psychiatric counseling. All she could do was smile, be friendly, and try to make them comfortable.

One woman was practically bald from pulling out her hair. Her arms were restrained in a straitjacket to prevent her from further damaging herself. The nurse led Lexie from patient to patient, explaining their condition, and tried to talk to them. At the bedside of a rather large woman strapped to her bed with her eyes closed, Nurse Pritchard said, "This is Big Bertha. She's sedated because she can get pretty wild." Lexie eyed the woman, hoping she stayed asleep during her shift.

The patient named Happy Kathy smiled and giggled as Nurse Pritchard introduced Lexie. "Hi! Will you be my friend? Will you play with me?" Lexie guessed the woman who sat cross-legged on the bed, bouncing as she spoke, was in her forties.

Lexie smiled and said, "Of course I'll be your friend. Maybe we can play later."

Happy Kathy clapped her hands rapidly. "Oh goody, goody, gumdrop!"

When they left the ward and locked the door behind them, Lexie released a breath. Nurse Pritchard glanced her way. "This is a different kind of nursing, isn't it?"

Lexie nodded. "It's so hard to know how to help."

"Mental illness is a different kind of sickness. There's so little we can do for these patients, but we keep trying."

"Big Bertha, has she had electric shock therapy yet?"

"Yes, she's had two treatments so far, but it's going to take more than that."

Lexie wondered what she meant by that statement as they walked to the nurse's station, and the elder nurse handed Lexie the keys to the ward. "Well, my shift is over, so you're taking charge. Most of the patients will go to sleep for the night. Be careful when you go in, and remember, do not turn your back on any of them."

How could she accomplish that feat with beds on both sides? Lexie spent the next two hours reviewing each patient's chart since these were kept in the nurses' station. She checked to see what medication or treatment was needed and when, then went to the medical closet to gather what she needed. The hospital was quiet, and she let her mind wander. She was sorry she'd missed Russell for lunch but was hopeful she'd be able to go to the USO dance on Friday and spend some social time with him again.

As she went through the motions to prepare for her evening rounds, her conversation with Cal Miller replayed in her mind. She'd enjoyed talking with him but hoped he didn't think she was too forward and that he understood her relationship with Russell was solid. Cal was a gentleman and well-spoken, maybe even too much so, if that were possible.

Lexie pushed the cart to the ward door, unlocked it, and slipped into the room, trying to be discreet as she shoved the cart inside and locked the door behind her. She studied her medicine cards and began at one end of the long room, going from patient to patient administering their medication. The windows emitted no light from the nighttime sky outside, and the lack of bright lights in the city added to the darkness.

Lexie checked all around her in case one of the patients decided to get up and go somewhere or bother someone else.

When she got to the other end of the row of beds, she came to Happy Kathy. The juvenile woman looked expectantly at Lexie.

"Did you come to play with me?" The voice was that of a little girl, but the body belonged to an older woman. Had she quit maturing at some point or regressed back to childhood for some reason?

"Shhh. Let's not wake anyone. It's bedtime."

"But you said you would play!"

Lexie sensed a tantrum coming on. "How about I tell you a story?" Maybe that tactic would work.

"A story? Really?" Happy Kathy clapped her hands again.

Lexie reached into her repertoire of stories but couldn't think of any that wouldn't be frightening to a young girl. She thought about the Disney movie, *Snow White and the Seven Dwarfs*, but there was a wicked witch in the story that might scare her. If only she had a children's book with her, but she didn't. Guess she'd have to make up a story.

"Once upon a time, there was a little girl named Alexandra. Alexandra had an older brother named Robert." Lexie paused as the image of her brother Robert came to mind. Her eyes misted over, but she wouldn't cry and upset the patient. "They lived in a big house with their mother and father and grandmother and grandfather. Robert always took care of Lexie. But their mother was sick. They didn't know it at first, but when she got sicker, they knew something was wrong."

Kathy's eyelids grew heavy as Lexie continued her story. Then suddenly the girl's eyes opened wide with fear, and she pointed behind Lexie. Lexie jerked around in time to see Big Bertha holding a rocking chair over her head, about to crash it down on Lexie's head. Lexie reached up to shove the chair away as it came down, and in the process pushed Bertha off balance, making her fall to the floor. Lexie grabbed the call button and pushed it a couple of times before running past Bertha before she got back up. Lexie made it to the door and, with shaking hands, unlocked it and ran out, slamming the door behind her and locking it with fumbling fingers.

She jogged to the nurses' station, called the emergency room, and asked for help. Hearing a crash, she assumed the medicine cart had been rammed against the door. It seemed like forever, but in reality, it was only a few minutes before the elevator opened and four attendants got off. She pointed to the ward door and handed one of the men the key. The ER doctor came running from the stairs. "Prepare a shot of phenobarbital!" Lexie ran to the medicine chest, prepared the medication, then hurried back to the doctor with the syringe.

"Get ready." Lexie followed the doctor inside the ward and found the four attendants struggling to hold Bertha down on her bed. The doctor managed to get the needle injected into Bertha's arm, and soon her thrashing abated. The attendants applied restraints to the bed after replacing the one she had ripped off earlier. Looking at Lexie, the doctor asked, "Are you going to be all right?"

"Yes. Thank you for coming so quickly."

"You're just lucky we weren't busy downstairs tonight."

He smiled at Lexie, then he and two of the attendants left, but he asked the other two to wait until Lexie finished in the room. She went to each patient and spoke in soothing tones to settle them back down after the disturbance in their sleep. Fortunately, the sedatives she'd administered earlier were taking effect. While she dealt with the patients, the two men picked up the mess Bertha had made. When Lexie got back to Happy Kathy's bed, the woman sat up and asked, "Is the story over?"

"For tonight it is." Lexie patted the woman on the hand. "I'll tell you some more of the story next time. Okay?"

"Okay." Happy Kathy let her head drop against the pillow. "Good night."

"Good night, Kathy."

She and the attendants moved to the door, and she scanned the dimly lit ward one more time. Assured all was calm, they left the room, remembering to secure the door again. She thanked the men, then took the cart with the supplies down to the utility room to wash them since procedure called for each stainless-steel needle and glass syringe be cleaned and sterilized before it could be used again. When she finished washing them, she wrapped them in clean cloth and sent them down a chute to Central Supply where they'd be sterilized in the autoclave the next day.

Lexie was exhausted when she finally sat down to write her report of the night. Her watch told her it was almost midnight again, and she still had an hour of paperwork to do. Today had been one of the longest days in her life, but she was thankful she'd made it through. When she considered the timing of all that had happened that night, she realized there were several "coincidences."

First, that Happy Kathy's reaction to Bertha had alerted Lexie just in time to keep the chair from hitting her. Then, she'd had enough time to get out of the room before Bertha got back up. And the emergency room wasn't busy tonight, so she got help right away. No, she knew it was more than coincidences. Thank God, He was looking out for her, proving she had no reason to fear, just like He said.

Chapter Thirteen

"*I*'ve got my pass!" Penny waved the slip of paper in the air. "Now what am I going to wear?"

"Anything but this uniform," said Lexie, as she hung hers up.

"I'm so excited!" Penny danced around the room in her slip. "Maybe I'll meet Prince Charming tonight."

"Maybe you will." Lexie stood in front of the closet. "Eenie, meenie, minee, moe. Will it be blouse number one or blouse number two?"

"You mean, the white one or the white one?"

"One of them is cream colored, not white," said Lexie.

"Big difference. But seriously, you look great in either one." "Okay. I'll wear the cream one tonight. With the gray skirt."

Penny held two dresses up by the hangers, one to either side of her. "Now you tell me—the dress with the flowers or the solid navy one?"

"Hmmm. The flowers are more fun."

"Then flowers it is! I have no intention of being serious tonight."

Lexie sniffed the air. "Do you smell smoke?"

Penny's eyes widened with fear. "You smell a fire?" She started sniffing the room and moved to their room door, which was kept open as required by the house rules. She stepped out into the hall and looked back and forth.

"No, it smells like cigarette smoke," said Lexie. "It's easy to smell here since nobody is allowed to smoke."

"Well, you've got the nose. If someone around here has smoked recently, they'll be in big trouble because it's against house rules, you know."

"I know. Wonder who it is?"

The two started guessing names of the possible culprits but didn't believe anyone would jeopardize their standing in nurses training by breaking the rule. Ten minutes later, the housemother marched down the hall. "Who's smoking?" When she stopped in front of Lexie and Penny's room, they shrugged.

"We smelled it too," Lexie said.

"Well, somebody better confess, or the whole floor will lose their privileges tonight."

Lexie and Penny exchanged shocked expressions. They *had* to go to the dance. But thirty minutes later, no one had owned up to the offense, and the housemother restricted all the nurses from their floor to the residence for the evening.

Lexie was furious, but Penny was vindictive. "If I get my hands on the girl who did this to us, she'll wish she hadn't!"

"It really isn't fair. We've worked hard all week for our privileges."

"Are you going to call Russell and tell him we can't make it?" Penny plopped down on the bed.

"I guess I better." Lexie walked over to the door but put

her hand on the door frame and stopped. Turning to Penny, she said, "Maybe I don't have to."

"What do you mean? He'll be looking for us."

Lexie put her finger in front of her lips and lowered her voice to a whisper. "I have an idea."

When the housemother called, "Lights out," Lexie and Penny complied. They climbed into their beds fully clothed and pulled the covers up to their chins. They waited until the matron passed their door, her flashlight sweeping the room as she did a bed check. When the girls heard her go back downstairs to the first floor, they stuffed the pillows under the covers so the beds looked occupied, then tiptoed down the hall to the back stairs. Lexie held her breath as they pushed open the side door, praying it wouldn't creak. They quickly slipped out, hurried away from the building, and around the corner. Once a safe distance away, they trotted the blocks to Russell's hotel and rushed through the lobby to the ballroom where throngs of servicemen had gathered for the USO dance.

Lexie spotted Russell at the piano beside the orchestra and hurried over. Penny stopped to chat with one of the servicemen.

"Hi, sweetheart." Russell gave her a broad grin when he saw her. "I thought you'd be here earlier. Was afraid you'd been given a last- minute assignment." He patted the piano bench, signaling her to sit beside him.

Relieved to catch her breath after the hasty walk to the hotel, Lexie eased onto the seat. While he played, she relaxed and let the rhythm of the song take control of her heartbeat. Watching Russell's fingers fly over the keys always impressed her, and she marveled at his skill. She gazed at his face, admiring his strong cheekbones and square chin, and inhaled the scent of Old Spice aftershave on his smooth skin. He must have known she was staring at him because he glanced over at her with sparkling eyes and winked, his dimpled smile melting her heart as always. As her gaze traveled to his lips, she craved his kiss. A whole week had passed since they'd really kissed, and that was too long. She tucked her hand inside his elbow and squeezed, giving him a mini-hug. He hit a wrong note and laughed, then gave her another look, this time more intense.

He got the message because as soon as the song ended, he turned to her and engulfed her in his arms, leaning his face toward her and covering her mouth with his warm lips. She surrendered to his embrace, allowing herself to be immersed in the moment. She had no idea how long the kiss lasted, but the sound of a drum roll caught her attention, and she remembered where she was. She pulled away from Russell as the cymbals crashed. They both looked over at the band, who laughed and applauded. Lexie's face flamed with embarrassment.

"Hey, can't a guy kiss his girl?" Russell lifted his palms up. "And this isn't just any girl. She's my fiancée!"

"Looks like you two better go ahead and tie the knot," said Artie Davis, the band leader.

Russell looked back at Lexie. "He's right, you know. We should be able to kiss like that any time we want to—without an audience."

If a minister had been in the room, Lexie would have gotten married right then. She was tired of waiting too. "I'd like that," she said.

"So I guess we better set a date," said Russell. "Have you any idea when that could be?"

Lexie shook her head. "No, not yet. But maybe it'll be sooner than we thought if I can get my training accelerated even more." Unless they got caught sneaking back into the residence. The band leader began counting and signaled with his baton for the musicians to start the next song. Russell shot her a regretful look, then joined the song as the band began playing. Lexie glanced around the room, searching for Penny before spotting her on the dance floor, where she appeared to be having the time of her life. What if they did get caught going back? What would that do to Penny's chances for graduation? Lexie began to worry. If they got into trouble, it would be her fault because it was her idea. What had she done? And what would happen to her? She'd already had one reprimand. It hadn't hurt so far, but two reprimands would have greater consequences.

They couldn't stay out too late, that's for sure. But she hoped they'd stay long enough for her to get a chance to talk to Russell some more. She wanted a chance to tell him what happened in the women's psychiatric ward. But first, she needed to let Penny know what time they'd be leaving.

Lexie turned to Russell. "I've got to tell Penny something."

"Sure, sweetie. Don't go far. After this number, we're taking a break, and maybe you and I will have a chance to talk … privately."

"I'd like that." She smiled and gave him a peck on the cheek before leaving the piano bench.

When they finished the set, Russell stood and stretched,

then scanned the room for Lexie. He spied her at the refreshment table and headed toward it. Boy, was he thirsty. He reached her side and eyed the cup of punch in her hand. She held it up to him, and he took a drink.

"Ahh. Just what I needed. Thank you."

"Here, you take this one, and I'll get another." She reached for another one of the cups filled with red liquid. "Would you like some cookies? They're pretty good." She extended her arm toward trays of sweets.

"No, thanks. I'm just thirsty." He looked around, then back at her. "Let's get out of here a minute. It's stuffy, and I need some fresh air. How about you?"

"Sounds good to me."

Once outside, they walked a few steps around to the side of the hotel, away from the front entrance. Lexie leaned against Russell's chest, and he put his arms around her. They stood in silence for a few minutes while Russell just enjoyed having his girl close to him. She sighed, and he put his finger under her chin and lifted her face toward him.

"Is something wrong, or are you just tired?"

"A little of both, I'm afraid."

"Tell me."

"Well, we … I mean I did something rather foolish tonight."

Russell held her out at arm's length and studied her face. "You? Do something foolish? I don't believe it."

"It's true. Somebody smoked on our floor of the nurses' residence today, and since no one owned up to it, the housemother canceled all the passes for those of us on the second floor."

"So how did you get out?"

"We snuck out. I convinced Penny to pretend we were asleep for room check, then we went out the side door."

"You didn't!" Russell chuckled, and an old memory surfaced. "So the little girl who climbed out her window at the family cottage on Jekyll Island is still alive and well!" He couldn't help himself from laughing out loud.

Lexie gave him a playful punch. "Well, it wasn't fair. We weren't the ones that were smoking. Besides, we'd earned our passes, and I wanted Penny to have a night out."

"Now, now. Don't get riled at me. I didn't restrict you. Forget Penny—tell me you were just dying to see me and your lips were itching to kiss me."

She pursed her lips, then a teasing smile eased across her face. "You think so?"

His pulse raced, and he fought to control himself. Aiming a steady look at her, he whispered, "I hope so."

She lifted her face to his, and he accepted the invitation to kiss her. He pulled her close, one hand on the small of her back and the other grasping her head, his fingers delving into her soft tresses. He pressed his lips against hers, conveying his love and passion in the kiss. But the ramifications of what she'd told him came to mind, bringing him back to reality, and he reluctantly pushed her gently away. "You need to get back before it's too late." Lexie nodded, and he took her hand. "I have to get back inside, but I want to walk you home. How much longer can you stay?" Russell glanced at his watch.

"When does the dance end?" Lexie fidgeted with her pearl necklace, looking worried and conflicted.

"Ten o'clock. Most of these guys are shipping out tomorrow, so they can't stay out too late." He guided her inside the door. "We have one more set. I can walk you and Penny back after that, if you can wait." Although it wasn't unusual for women to be out unescorted in Manhattan, he wasn't used to the idea, especially late at night, and particularly when it came to Lexie. Although she acted brave, he knew she still struggled with fear like she had before, even if not as much.

"All right. I'll find Penny and tell her we're leaving promptly at ten, just in case she has any idea of tarrying with some guy."

Lexie waved at Penny across the room, but her roommate was so involved in conversation with a sailor that she didn't see Lexie. The band started up again, and soon the dance floor was full of USO hostesses and GIs working off their last bit of energy. Lexie waited until the first song ended, then managed to get to Penny through the crowded floor.

She grabbed Penny's arm to get her attention. "Penny, be ready to leave as soon as the band quits. We have to hurry back."

Penny frowned and appeared annoyed at the interruption. She glanced at her dance partner who stood nearby, grinning from ear to ear. "So soon?" Then realization crossed her face.

"Russell's going to escort us back to the residence."

The sailor spoke up. "Hey, if you girls want an escort, I'm the man. Me and my buddy Frank'll be glad to go with you."

"Sorry, pal, you know the rules," Lexie said, winking at Penny who looked confused. "You know we hostesses aren't allowed to fraternize with you guys outside the dance." Although they weren't officially USO hostesses, it was convenient to use their rules as an excuse.

"Oh all right. Guess you gotta go by the book," the disappointed sailor said.

"You still have time for a couple more dances, though, so enjoy yourself while you can." Lexie said as the next dance started.

She headed toward Russell. But halfway across the room, her hand was grabbed by a young GI, who started jitterbugging with her. She started to walk away, then thought, "Why not?" and gave in to the urge to dance. During part of the song, she saw Russell watching her and smiling. Good thing he wasn't the jealous type. Much as she loved to dance, she still felt a twinge of guilt dancing with someone else.

When the song ended, she hurried over to Russell.

"You have fun out there?" He grinned and winked, easing her conscience somewhat.

"Sorry, Russell. The guy grabbed me, and I believe he thought I was one of the hostesses, even though I'm not wearing the armband. Anyway, I went ahead and danced with him. You know USO hostesses aren't supposed to refuse."

"Lexie, you know I don't mind. I want you to enjoy yourself instead of hanging around waiting for me. You looked great out there."

She blushed, and he laughed. "How many more songs do you have to play?"

"The next one will be the last, then I'll be free to leave."

"Good. I told Penny to be ready."

He nodded toward Penny. "Looks like she's having a

good time."

"She is, and I'm glad. I hope our little act of rebellion will be worth it."

"I hope so too."

The band leader led off with his clarinet, then the rest of the musicians joined in to play "Stardust." The romantic song was one of her favorites, and Lexie wished she and Russell could be dancing to it. Maybe someday they would, but not tonight.

When the song was over, the band leader thanked everyone for coming, and the crowd began to disperse. As the band members were putting away their instruments, Artie Davis came over to Russell and extended his hand.

"Say, Russell, thanks for helping us out tonight. You know, our regular piano player has joined the army, so we have an opening if you're interested."

Russell shook his hand and smiled. "Thanks, Artie, but I have another job, you know."

Artie shrugged. "Suit yourself, but we're going to start auditioning for a new piano man, and you have first dibs."

"I'll keep that in mind." Russell grabbed Lexie's elbow to lead her out but called over his shoulder. "Keep me in mind for a fill-in, in the meantime."

"Will do."

Penny joined them as they crossed the lobby to the front door. Cal Miller walked in when the door opened. He smiled and nodded at the group.

"Say, isn't that the guy that was in the diner?" Penny asked Lexie.

"Yes." Lexie hadn't shared the fact that she and Cal had a conversation at lunch earlier in the week and didn't want to discuss it now. She quickly changed the subject. "Did you have a good time, Penny?"

"I had a swell time! Thanks for the evening, Lexie … and Russell."

"I hope you'll thank me tomorrow," said Lexie. "If we get in trouble, I'll take responsibility. It was my idea."

"They won't buy that, Lexie, but it's nice of you to offer. I came with you because I wanted to. I'm a big girl and can make up my own mind. I could've said 'no.'"

Russell chimed in. "It was nice seeing you girls enjoy some time off. You work really hard and deserve to have a little fun."

"Lexie deserves it more than I do," Penny said. "I don't risk my life when I work in a ward like she does."

Russell raised his eyebrows. "You don't say. Lexie, did something happen I don't know about?"

"Go ahead and tell him about Big Bertha, Lexie."

Lexie described Big Bertha's attack on her and how she managed to escape unharmed. "The orderlies and doctor arrived pretty quickly."

"Why were you in there alone? Weren't there any other nurses on duty?"

Russell was alarmed like she'd expected him to be, always worried about her protection. "Russell, there just aren't enough nurses to go around."

"I didn't know it was that bad." Russell shook his head. "I don't feel very comfortable about you being in that situation."

"One of the things we nurses have to learn is to be able to cope with unusual conditions. And the nurse warned me about turning my back on the patients. I just need to be more careful."

"You won't see me volunteering for night duty on one of the psych wards!" Penny shook her head. "That's not my cup of tea."

"Strange as it seems, I prefer working in the men's psychiatric ward. They don't seem to be as dangerous." Both Russell and Penny gave her perplexed looks. "Maybe I just haven't seen anyone so violent there." *Yet*, she didn't say but assumed her companions were thinking the same thing.

"Suit yourself," said Penny.

They walked a few moments in silence before Lexie recalled the band leader's offer to Russell.

"Russell, would you consider joining a band like Artie's?"

"No, those musicians live in a whole different world than I do." "What do you mean?"

"They work every night, sleep half the day. Most of them don't have families because the lifestyle isn't good for a home life. Besides, they travel all the time."

"Sounds exciting to me," said Penny. "You'd get to go to a lot of places."

"Maybe so, but I want to stay in one place, settle down with my girl here." He gave Lexie's shoulder a squeeze.

"Yeah? So have you two set a date?" Penny glanced from Russell to Lexie.

Russell looked at Lexie with a questioning expression. "Not yet."

"Penny, we're waiting to find out when I graduate from nursing school. It would be difficult to be married before that."

"Maybe so, but I've heard it's possible."

"But most of the married girls have husbands that are in

the military, and they've shipped out," Lexie said, reminding her roommate and herself why she and Russell still waited.

"Well, you two don't have to worry about that, do you? I mean, you're not joining the Army or Navy, and neither is Russell, so you'll both be able to stay stateside."

Lexie sensed Russell's uneasiness whenever the topic of joining the military came up, knowing he couldn't. Why did Penny have to mention it?

"That's right, Penny. We can support our country right here. Somebody has to stay home." Lexie had to help bolster Russell's ego.

They were within half a block of the nursing residence. Lexie stopped and turned to Russell. "Thank you for being our escort, Russell, but I think you shouldn't come any farther."

"All right. I'll watch from here and see if you get inside okay."

"Of course, you won't find out what happens until Lexie calls you tomorrow," Penny said. "We might be confined to quarters."

"I hope not. Lexie, call me tomorrow as soon as you can and let me know if you get in trouble." He wrapped his arms around her, leaned down, and gave her a kiss. It wasn't as long a kiss as he'd like, but with Penny standing there, it would be awkward to prolong the goodbye. "Good night, Lexie. Good night, Penny. Take care."

The girls told him good night and walked the rest of the way in silence. They reached the side door and turned the knob, thankful it was still unlocked. Breathing sighs of relief, they slipped inside, removed their shoes, and tiptoed up the stairs to the second floor and into the hall. The floor was quiet, except for a snore that came from one of the rooms.

As they undressed and climbed into their beds, Lexie's thoughts returned to Russell. She was glad he could escort them home. So Artie Davis had offered him a position with his band. That was quite an honor for a musician. Was he refusing to join because of her? Maybe he really wanted to but felt obligated to her. He'd moved to New York because she did. Was he staying here for the same reason?

If he did leave, she would miss him terribly. The warmth of his lips was still on hers, and it was hard enough to be away from him for even a few days. What would happen to them if he really did leave? Would their relationship survive? But was it fair that she was pursuing her dream when he wasn't?

Chapter Fourteen

"Hi, Russell. It's Lexie. Everything's fine. Except that I have to work today—back on one of the men's psychiatric floors." Lexie didn't divulge any details about slipping into the residence the night before, in case the wrong person overheard her conversation.

"Thanks for calling, sweetheart. I'm glad to hear you didn't run into any problems. Will you be free for church tomorrow?"

"Sure. I need to make amends for my misdeeds."

Russell's laughter was welcome. "Good. I've heard a lot about the minister at Marble Collegiate Church, Dr. Norman Vincent Peale. I'd like to go there tomorrow if it's okay with you."

"Sounds swell. I've wanted to hear him preach too. Do you mind if I invite Penny?"

"Not at all. I'll come for you at a quarter past ten. See you tomorrow, darlin'."

Lexie hung up the phone. She didn't want to work on a Saturday, but it had been a few days since she'd seen John Doe, and she was anxious to see him again and find out if there had been any improvement in his condition. She checked her reflection to make sure her uniform was correct, then crossed the street to the psychiatric hospital and went to his ward. The floor nurse smiled at her from her seat in the nurses' station. "Welcome back, Nurse Smithfield. I heard you had some excitement the other night on the women's floor."

So everyone knew about Big Bertha's attack on her now. "Oh yes, it was exciting, to say the least."

"From what I heard, you handled yourself well. Glad to hear you weren't hurt."

"Thank God, I turned around in time." Lexie appreciated the compliment but realized that without God's intervention, things could have turned out much worse.

"Well, congratulations on your quick thinking. That patient is scheduled for a lobotomy. Nothing else has worked on her."

The nurse's words shocked Lexie. She'd heard about lobotomies being performed in last-resort situations, but the procedure frightened her. Cutting and manipulating a person's brain was a dangerous surgery. And hopeless. From what she'd read, the procedure might remove the symptoms of mental illness, but the side effects were alarming. People who'd had lobotomies were completely changed in personality, and some had even died from the operation. As frightened as she'd been of Big Bertha, she actually felt sorry for the woman now.

"The men's ward seems pretty calm, compared to my experience in the women's, but then I've only worked on the mildly disturbed ward."

"Oh, we've had our share of excitement here too.

Fortunately for you, we haven't had any while you've been on duty." The nurse peered up over her glasses at Lexie. "But that can change any minute, as you know."

Lexie nodded and thought of Claude, the wildest person she'd seen in the ward. "How is Claude Graham doing? Have the electric shock treatments helped?"

"Yes, I think they have. He's much calmer now. If he has another episode, he'll be moved to the 'semi-disturbed' ward." She pushed her chair away from the desk and stood. "Let's go see our patients. Wonder if they'll remember you?"

She hoped they would, especially one patient in particular. Nurse Addams opened the door, and as they entered, a few heads turned toward them. Four men played cards at a table. One of them pointed at Lexie. "It's the humming nurse! Will you hum for us again?"

Lexie's face flushed, and Nurse Addams faced her with raised eyebrows. "The humming nurse?"

Lexie lowered her gaze and muttered, "Yes, ma'am. It was so quiet in here. I wanted to add some music. That's not against the rules, is it?"

"Not that I know of. As long as it doesn't upset the patients, I suppose it's okay. What did you hum? Show tunes?"

"Oh no, I hummed a hymn. The tune had been fixed in my mind ever since I attended church last Sunday." She nodded toward the man who recognized her. "He said he used to hear the same hymn from his mother and grandmother."

"Hopefully, he had good memories of them," Nurse Addams whispered.

Lexie hadn't considered anything to the contrary and was surprised at the comment. They moved around the room, checking with the patients and assessing their mental condition as usual, asking about the date, the year, the president, etcetera. The men were having a good day, and most answered correctly, proud of themselves when they did, as if they'd passed a test.

Claude sat quietly by himself. "Claude, how are you today?" Nurse Addams asked.

His eyes darted from Lexie to the head nurse before answering. "I'm better, I think."

"That's very good, Claude." Nurse Addams offered the man a smile.

"Do I have to have another one of those treatments today? I don't think I need any more."

"Not today. We'll see if the doctor thinks you need more treatments."

"Okay. Maybe then he'll let me go home."

Lexie wanted to know what his home was like. Did he live with a wife or parents or anyone? Wherever it was, she hoped it was better than staying here.

They stopped at John Doe's bed, and Lexie noticed the wound on his head was practically gone. He was still hooked to the IV, a sign that he wasn't eating yet. Nurse Addams moved her hand in front of his eyes, and the man blinked but didn't focus on the women. "The doctor wants to wait until his injuries are healed before we give him shock treatments so he won't reinjure himself in the process."

Lexie hoped he'd come out of his trance before his injuries healed. Maybe he wouldn't even need the shock treatments once he regained consciousness.

They finished the tour of the ward, then went back to the nurses' station. "You know what to do now, so I'll leave our men in your capable hands. I don't think you'll have any problems today unless they bring someone new in."

Lexie nodded, and the head nurse left. She gathered the water pitchers, refilled them, placed them on the cart with some paper cups, and reentered the ward.

"Are you going to hum today? Please?" the older gentleman named Bob asked.

"If you'd like me to, Bob. Would you like me to hum 'Amazing Grace' again?"

"That would be real nice. And anything else you want to hum. Just don't stop."

She smiled and began going from patient to patient, offering water and trying to be friendly. Lexie hummed as she went through the room and the work developed a pleasant rhythm, lifting the atmosphere. Not all the patients welcomed her gesture, but most of them looked pleased, and the music seemed to have a calming effect on them.

When she arrived at John Doe's bed, she spoke to him. "Hello, John. Would you like a drink of water?" There was no response, but she offered the cup to his lips anyway as she had before, pouring a scant amount of liquid between his open lips. When he swallowed, she offered more with the same result. When his lips closed, she put the cup down on the bedside table. "Had enough?" She leaned over and gently removed his pillow, fluffed it up, and replaced it under his head. "There, that should be more comfortable." She also adjusted his sheet and blanket to make sure he was well covered.

She continued to talk to the unresponsive man. "Your head looks much better." She touched the healing scar lightly with her fingertip. Then she stroked the arm in a sling. "I wonder how long before your arm heals?"

The man in the bed next to John Doe leaned on his elbow and faced her. "He can't talk."

"Maybe he can, but he just doesn't want to," she said in John Doe's defense.

"What if he can't hear you? Why do you keep talkin' to him when he don't say nothin'?"

"Because I think he might be able to hear me. He had a head injury in the war, but even though he's not talking doesn't mean he can't hear." She offered the man a smile, then moved over to his bed. "Would you like some water too?"

The man sat on the edge of his bed, a magazine in his hands. "Is that all you got? Why don't you bring some scotch with you next time? I'd like to have a scotch and water."

"I don't think that would be a good idea."

Mo was his name, and he'd been brought in two nights ago when the police found him acting bizarre in the park, according to his chart. Since he'd reeked of alcohol when he was brought in, he was most likely an alcoholic.

"Well, I'm not stickin' around here much longer if I don't get a good drink."

Unfortunately, he was probably telling the truth. He'd dry up in the hospital, get released, then go back to drinking and end up back in one of the wards, hopefully the alcoholic ward, if there was room. At least he seemed to be mentally stable when he was sober, not like the others. What irony that the drunks had enough control to leave the hospital, but they didn't have enough control to stay out.

As she stepped away from him, she sensed being watched. She spun around, the alarm bell going off in her head, wondering if she'd gotten herself into another vulnerable position like she had with Big Bertha. But no one was threatening her this time. In fact, none of the other patients even looked her way. Was she becoming paranoid because of the experience? She blew out a breath. *Steady, girl. No one's out to harm you now.*

She moved on to the next patient, who nervously tapped his foot on the floor. "Good afternoon, Tom."

"You know me?" He squinted at her. "Do I know you?"

"I'm Nurse Smithfield. Perhaps you were asleep when I was here before."

Tom sat forward, searching her face. "Nope. Don't know you." He looked away from her.

She offered him water, which he accepted after some hesitation. He studied her face again and said with excitement. "You're the humming nurse!" Then he frowned. "Aren't you? Why aren't you humming?"

Lexie chuckled. "I was, but I guess I stopped. Would you like me to continue humming?"

"Yes, yes I would. They should give us radios in here."

Some wards were allowed radios, but there wasn't one in this room, the thought being a news story might upset a patient.

"I'll ask around and see if I can get one for you." There was no harm in trying anyway. The sensation returned. Someone was watching her—the skin on her back tingled with awareness. She turned slowly, glancing at each patient. But once again, she didn't find anyone looking at her. Was her mind playing tricks? Or was someone else playing a trick on her?

She finished handing out water. It was time to get the medications ready for those who needed them. She wheeled the cart down the aisle, checking to see if any of the patients were unusually interested in her. Still, no clues for her suspicions. Before she left the room, Bob shouted from the card table at the other end.

"Do you know the words to that song?"

She put her finger in front of her lips and went toward him. "I know a few of them. Why?"

"Just wondered if you can sing too. Or if you hum because you can't sing."

Lexie laughed and said, "I guess I can sing well enough. Maybe next time I come in, I'll sing. I need to brush up on the words, though."

"You do that, okay? You'll do that for me?"

She nodded. Bob must have been the one watching her, and she didn't realize it. That was the obvious reason for her feeling. So much for her suspicions.

Lexie went back to the nurses' station to make notes in the patient charts. At the same time, she made a list of meds and their dosages to give the patients that night. She also wrote up a requisition for a radio, hoping the request wouldn't meet any opposition. When dinner time arrived, she rolled in the dining trays and handed them out. To her surprise, Bob and Tom came forward and helped pass out the meals.

"Thank you, gentlemen. You're a big help." Bob beamed with pride, and Tom just nodded and continued helping. Only one patient wasn't able to eat regular food. John Doe. Lexie eyed him with concern.

His neighbor Mo spoke up, "I'll take his. He don't need it."

"We don't have an extra, Mo. He's still on a drip." She

pointed to the bottle suspended from the hook on the IV pole.

Mo shrugged. "Some kind of life."

Bob spoke up. "Hey, Mo! That man's a hero. He was hurt in the war. Give him some respect."

"Yeah, sure. Poor sap."

Lexie seethed beneath the surface. She wanted to say something to put Mo in his place, but she wasn't allowed. If only John Doe could defend himself against the man's remarks.

She busied herself while they ate dinner by straightening up the tables and chairs in the activity area and walked around the room closing the window blinds. When they were finished, she, Bob, and Tom collected the trays and stacked them on the cart.

"All right. Time to get ready for bed. Change clothes and wash up. I'll be back in a little while to give you your meds."

"You're going to tuck us in?" Tom asked.

"Of course. Be a good boy and be in bed when I get back."

Lexie rolled the cart stacked with dirty dishes out of the room, locked the door, and pushed the cart down the hall to the utility room to be washed, one of the night nurse's duties. Someone from the kitchen would pick them up in the morning.

Now, to prepare the meds. She checked the time and hurried to get the supplies before the men drifted off to sleep. When she returned to the ward, most of the men were in their beds. Those that weren't went to their beds when they saw her. Not all the men required medication, but some did only for sleep, and they passively submitted to the injection she gave them. Thank goodness Mo was already snoring. He was not one of her favorite patients, and she was glad she wouldn't have to deal with him when she went to John Doe's bedside.

She checked John's IV drip first, but, wanting to do more for him, used the damp washcloth beside him to wipe his face. As she moved about his area, the sensation of being watched returned. But once again, a scan around the room confirmed that the other patients were asleep or had their eyes closed. Then she saw John Doe's eyes follow her. She swallowed the gasp that was her first reaction, observing the rule that nurses should not show shock around the mental patients. But her face probably registered surprise.

In a soft voice, she said, "John, are you looking at me? Can you see me?"

He didn't make a sound, but he blinked. Did that mean something, or was it an involuntary reflex?

She moved her finger in front of his eyes. "Can you follow my finger?" His eyes obeyed, and he blinked again. Excitement bubbled inside her, and she wanted to run down the hall to tell someone. But no one else was on the floor.

"My name is Nurse Smithfield. You're in Bellevue Hospital in New York City. You were injured in the Pacific, taken to California, then brought here. Your dog tags were missing when you were found, so we don't know your name. Maybe you can tell us sometime."

He continued to watch her every move. She touched the healing wound on his head. "Does this hurt?"

He didn't blink, but his gaze remained fixed on her. She stroked his broken arm in the sling. "Your arm is broken, but it is healing quickly. Perhaps you can get the cast off soon."

What else could she talk about? She was running out of things to tell him. Without a response, conversation was difficult. "Is there anything I can get you? Some water, maybe? I'm sure you're looking forward to eating real food."

Still no response.

Lexie straightened his covers, then said, "We usually give back rubs to our bed patients, but I'm afraid to move you without doctor's permission. This will have to do for now." She put her hands on his shoulders and gently massaged them. His eyes followed her everywhere, making her self-conscious. She smiled at him, hoping to draw a smile from him in return. Perhaps she wanted too much too soon. However, she was certainly thankful for the progress, no matter how small. Sleeping noises filled the air, and John Doe needed to go to sleep as well.

"I better go now and let you rest. Good night, John, or whatever your real name is."

Even in the dim light, she could still feel his eyes on her as she left.

Chapter Fifteen

Sunday morning when Lexie walked into the residence living room, Russell was waiting with his welcome smile, standing with his hands behind his back.

"Good morning, sunshine!"

Lexie bounced over to him and stood on tiptoes to plant a friendly kiss on his lips.

"Why, that's a nice surprise! Did you miss me?"

"You know it."

When he didn't embrace her, she got curious. "Hey, what's behind your back?" She leaned around to see what he was hiding.

He angled his body so she couldn't see. "Something's behind my back?"

She placed her hands on her hips. "Russell…"

When he revealed his hands, he extended a bouquet of yellow roses toward her. "You mean these?" He laughed. "Pretty roses for a pretty lady."

Lexie gaped at the gorgeous bouquet. "Russell! They're lovely! But what's the occasion?"

Penny happened by and, seeing the flowers, said, "Watch

out, Lexie. He's been up to no good."

Russell shook his head. "Nope, not me. I've been as good as gold. I just wanted to surprise my sweetheart."

"Well, you sure did. Thank you." Lexie grabbed his neck with her free hand and pulled his face to hers. She gave him a kiss meant to show her appreciation.

"Wow. I think I need to give you flowers more often."

"It can't hurt," Lexie said. "Hold on a minute and let me find something to put them in." She disappeared for a few moments and returned with the flowers resting in a crystal vase. "The housemother had one." She set the bouquet down on the coffee table. "I think I'll leave them here for everyone else to enjoy until I get back."

"Good idea. It'll help my reputation with the ladies." Russell winked at her.

Lexie gave him a playful punch, then grabbed him by the crook of his arm. "I'm the only lady you need to impress, and don't forget it!"

Russell laughed out loud then escorted her through the door. "Couldn't convince Penny to go today?"

"No, she said she had to study."

"That's too bad. Just keep asking, and maybe she'll change her mind."

They rounded the corner and turned up the street. "I think the main reason she refuses is because she doesn't want to be a third wheel. You know, she feels a little out of place with us."

"Maybe so." Russell snapped his fingers. "Say, I know a fella at the hotel that might like to go, and then Penny will come with us too. Why didn't I think of that before?"

"You know she can't date right now."

"Perhaps not. But there's no rule against going to church." Walking arm in arm down the sidewalk with Russell was one of Lexie's favorite things. And the fact that they were going to church together made it even more special because it reminded her of a time when she was a little girl going to church with her family. So long ago, before everything changed. Now they were all gone, and times had changed, but thanks to Russell, this Sunday tradition had returned to her life.

"Are we going to the church you suggested, the Marble Collegiate Church?"

"Yes, if that's all right with you."

"Sure, I'd like to see what it's like. I've heard good things about the pastor."

They arrived at the old church at the corner of Fifth and West Twenty-Ninth Street noted for its marble exterior and for being one of the oldest Protestant congregations in the country. Lexie pointed to the wrought-iron fence surrounding the building. "Someone told me they put up the fence in the 1800's to keep cows from rubbing up against the marble. Can you imagine cows grazing on Fifth Avenue?"

"Pretty hard to believe, with all these buildings and concrete here now." Russell placed his hand on Lexie's back and ushered her inside the building where throngs of worshippers were gathered to hear the popular minister.

Lexie opened a hymnal to "Amazing Grace" and tried to memorize the words so she could sing them to the patients next time she was in the ward.

Russell glanced down at her with raised eyebrows before turning his attention to the front of the church.

Dr. Peale's sermon was motivational, encouraging, and

inspirational, and Lexie noticed many of the congregants smiling and nodding as he spoke. Even the young men in uniform looked hopeful. Worshippers eagerly shook Dr. Peale's hand when they exited the front doors of the sanctuary, thanking him for his positive message.

As they walked away, Russell said, "I liked what he said about our attitude—'Change your thoughts and you change your world.'"

"I like that, too, and I wish it was that simple."

"You disagree?"

"What about the war? Can we just change our thoughts about it and it'll go away?"

"Think of it this way. Hitler has changed Germany by changing the thoughts of the people. Of course, that kind of change is bad. But couldn't we do the opposite? For instance, at the hotel, if we act like we're happy to be there, then others will be happy to be there too. I'm going to try it and see."

Something about what Russell said touched a nerve. "Russell, are you saying you're not really happy? You have to pretend?"

The hint of a shadow passed over his face before his smile returned. "Sure I am. I've got the perfect girl!" He gave her an arm hug.

"Russell, you don't have to pretend with me. Aren't you happy with your job at the hotel?"

His expression became more serious. "I wouldn't say I'm 'happy,' but the job is good and steady, and I'm thankful to have it." His perpetual smile returned. "But I'm happy to be so near you."

"Russell, seriously. Do you have any regrets about coming to New York?"

"No, I don't. I'm sorry we had to leave Jekyll, but that couldn't be helped." He shrugged and lifted his hands. "I just have to get used to the change, that's all. Make the best of it. These days, everyone is having to make adjustments."

They continued down the sidewalk passing other couples dressed in their Sunday best. "Where shall we go?" Russell said. "Would you like to go to Madison Square Park? It's just down the street from here."

"I'd love to," said Lexie, "but can we get something to eat first?"

"Did you hear my stomach rumbling in church?" Russell laughed and rubbed his midsection. "There's a little cafe around the corner. Let's go there."

At lunch, Lexie continued reflecting on Dr. Peale's message. "Russell, I wonder how being positive can work in my job. Do you really think I can make people well by being happy?"

"I don't know that you can make them well, but perhaps you can help them feel better. You know, emotionally. Don't you feel good when you're happy? Maybe if you're cheerful, it will improve your patients' attitudes too."

"I do try to be helpful … and positive. It actually says in our manual that we should portray a cheerful attitude to the patients. I'll try to do a better job of that. Sometimes it's hard to be cheerful, though, when you see sad situations."

"I'm sure it is. But you can do it. After all, you changed my world for the better."

Lexie's heart swelled. "You always know what to say."

After lunch, they strolled in the park, looking at the various statues and fountains before stopping to sit down on one of the park benches. Russell sat beside Lexie, spreading his arms out along the back of the bench and tipping his hat back to look up. From their vantage point, they had a good view of the Flatiron Building, the once-tallest building in New York, rising high above the park's trees. A cool early-summer breeze blew the foliage gently, and Lexie's attention was attracted to movement on the red lantanas blooming nearby. She pointed and whispered, "Look at that gorgeous butterfly."

Russell followed her gaze and nodded, smiling. "He's attracted to those colorful flowers."

"I wish I could bring some back with me to the ward."

"The city fathers might not appreciate your gesture if you remove the park's flowers." Russell winked at her.

Lexie elbowed him. "I don't mean take these flowers! But I wish the patients had more color in their lives. The hospital is so drab, with white floors and dull white walls."

"If the market's still open, maybe you could pick up some flowers to take to the hospital. We could stop on the way back and get some."

"I'll have to see if it's allowed first. Nobody brings flowers to the men in the psych ward, and they need something cheerful as much as any other patients. But hardly anything is allowed in their wards in case it would present a danger."

Russell arched an eyebrow. "How dangerous could flowers be?"

"You'd be surprised. For one thing, the vase might be used as a weapon. Plus, I've even heard of patients eating flowers. On second thought, I doubt flowers would be allowed."

Russell shook his head. "I'd never considered those possibilities. That's too bad."

The tune of a hymn they'd sung in church that day ran through Lexie's mind. "Russell, do you miss playing piano for a church like you did at the chapel on Jekyll Island?"

He studied the ground for a few minutes, then lifted his gaze. "Yes, I do. Sometimes I slip away to the piano in the ballroom and play a little, just for my own enjoyment, but those times are few and far between." He faced her. "Why do you ask?"

"I was just thinking about how much I missed the tranquil atmosphere of Jekyll, especially listening to you play in the chapel. Life is so different here."

"It certainly is." He gave her a wink. "The bands I play with don't play hymns. They're not exactly dance music."

"No, I guess not." Lexie studied Russell's face as he gazed at the scenery. "You seem like a different person when you're playing with the band."

He turned toward her. "Different? Maybe not as spiritual?"

"Maybe not. Guess it's just the different atmosphere."

Russell slapped his thigh and put both feet on the ground. "I'm tired of sitting. Ready for a stroll down Fifth Avenue?" He stood and extended his hand to her.

"Sure." She accepted his hand and stood. He didn't let go, and they walked along the sidewalk swinging hands. Sunday was the day to promenade down the city's main streets, a decades-old custom. Women dressed in their Sunday-best clothes, complete with matching hats and gloves, strolled alongside well-dressed men in their suits and ties, their fedoras perched on their heads, and their handkerchiefs folded just right to peek out of their suit pockets.

Lexie enjoyed people-watching more than window-shopping, especially on a day that wasn't so crowded and hurried like the weekdays. A group of sailors in their white Cracker Jack uniforms walked by, and Lexie paused, seeing her brother Robert in each of them.

Russell watched her, his brows knitted with concern. "Is something wrong?"

She shook her head. "No, I was just thinking about Robert when he first joined the Navy."

Russell squeezed her hand. "He loved being in the Navy."

Lexie nodded, her eyes moist with tears. "He was so proud to wear that uniform."

Putting his arms around her, Russell gave her a hug. "He was doing what he wanted to do and serving his country."

Lexie wiped her eyes and pushed away. "What happened at Pearl Harbor was just so wrong, so unfair."

"You're right, and that's why those guys joined up." He nodded toward the guys who had walked by. "They're going to make sure that doesn't happen again."

"I hope they'll be successful."

"They will be. We won't be caught off guard again."

They stopped to look in some store windows, all decked out in red, white, and blue. Everywhere they looked, there was a symbol of patriotism. Posters advertising war bonds were plastered on windows, as well as signs promoting service to the country by rationing. Every storefront proudly displayed a Victory sign.

"Say, I've got an idea," Russell said. "How about going to the top of the Empire State Building?"

Lexie looked ahead at the highest building in the world and shuddered. Shaking her head, she said, "No, I can't do that."

"Lexie Smithfield, where's my brave girl?" he teased.

"I don't like heights." She could barely stand to look up at the tall building. Seeing people on the outside gallery sent shivers down her back.

"They didn't seem to bother you when you were in my office tower at Jekyll, not to mention when you climbed a tree from the second-floor window of your house."

"Russell, that building is a whole lot taller than the tower at Jekyll and the tree I climbed! There's no comparison."

"Are you sure? I'll hold your hand if you want to go up." Russell gave her a wink. "Don't you want to see the view from up there?"

"Maybe someday, but not today." Or never. "I'm content to admire it from here."

Russell laughed, displaying his endearing dimple. "Okay. You let me know when you change your mind."

They walked past more stores before Lexie stopped to admire a navy-blue dress with white polka dots. While she peered through the store window, she caught the reflection of someone who looked familiar. She spun around and saw the backs of two men walking away. She wasn't certain, but the blond man looked like Cal Miller, and based on the smoke ring around his head and the nervous way he looked around, the other man was the man she'd seen with Cal. Funny how she kept running into these two men from the train in a city so full of people.

"Who are you looking at?" Russell asked.

"Those two men over there. They looked like the men on the train." Was she imagining they were the same men?

"I can't tell from their backs, but they also look like some men staying at the Martinique."

"Then those are the same guys." Somehow, Russell's affirmation didn't make her feel better.

"What about them?"

"I don't know. It just seems strange that I keep seeing them." How could she explain the feeling of uneasiness the two men gave her?

"Guess you travel in the same circles."

"Well, it's a good thing I'm not suspicious anymore, or I'd think they were following me." Why did she even admit the thought that entered her mind? Of course they weren't following her. Why would they? Her old paranoia was trying to creep back in, but she pushed the thought away and wouldn't let it.

They spent the rest of the afternoon strolling around the city, even spending a little time at the library. Lexie enjoyed the relaxing time with Russell, and, for a while, it felt like the time they spent together back on Jekyll—peaceful and unhurried.

As they exited the stately library, Russell paused to admire one of the stone lions guarding the entrance beside the steps.

Lexie crossed her arms and studied the statue. "Looks pretty powerful, doesn't it? Wonder which lion it is— Fortitude or Patience?"

"Whatever he wants to be," said Russell with a wink. He glanced down at his watch. "Say, don't you have a test tomorrow?"

Lexie's eyes widened. "Oh my gosh! I do! I completely forgot about it. Guess I better get back and do some studying."

As they scurried down the rest of the steps to the

sidewalk, Lexie saw the men again. She halted, and Russell stopped beside her. He followed her gaze and nodded when he spotted them.

"So we cross paths again," he said.

"And you don't find that odd?" The uneasiness crept back in.

"Lexie, it's just coincidence."

Hands on her hips, she said, "Of course it is. But I hope they hurry up and leave. I'm tired of running into them."

Russell looked at her with raised eyebrows. "Why? Did they make a pass at you?"

Lexie sighed. "No. I just have a strange feeling about them, that's all." Russell raised an eyebrow. Lexie knew he must be thinking she was being overly suspicious. She faked a laugh. "Oh, don't worry, Russell. It's nothing, I'm sure."

He took her by the arm. "Let's get you back to the nurses' residence so you can study. I'm going to hang on to you tightly so some guy can't steal you from me."

"Oh, Russell. *Steal* me? Don't be silly." She peered up at him.

"Well, just in case…" He tucked her arm into the crook of his elbow.

Lexie's head told her the men were not a threat. Why did they make her uneasy anyway? Cal had seemed like a polite man, and she hadn't talked to the other guy. It didn't matter. She didn't have to worry about them as long as she had Russell by her side.

Chapter Sixteen

*R*ussell kissed Lexie goodbye before leaving her and walking back to the hotel, a spring in his step. Being with Lexie always had that effect on him and reminded him why he had followed her to New York in the first place. He shook his head. Why was Lexie so worried about those strangers? Sometimes she was too suspicious, but other times she was too trusting. No doubt the men were harmless, but he needed to stay close to Lexie if only to send them a message that she was taken.

He looked up at the Martinique as he approached. The 1910 French Renaissance façade with its stonework balconies was a piece of art amid the more modern buildings that had been built since. The hotel's style was one of the things he liked about it because he appreciated its history, as he had the Jekyll Island Club and the old homes on the island.

When he walked into the lobby, he scanned the room for activity. Because it was a Sunday, most of the guests were out enjoying the day in the less-busy city. He crossed the room to the front desk, admiring the inlaid mosaic tile floor with its intricate, multicolor patterns, a unique floor no other hotel could boast.

"Any messages for me?"

"Yes, sir." The desk clerk retrieved a note, glancing at the piece of paper in his hand before giving it to Russell. "This call came in at four o'clock."

"Thanks. I'll be in my office if you need me." Russell descended the stairs to his private office, entered, and sat at his desk. Artie Davis' name was by the number. He must've called to ask Russell to fill in again this week. Russell picked up the phone and asked the operator to give him an outside line before dialing the number. After a couple of rings, Artie answered.

"Artie Davis, best band leader in the biz, at your service."

Russell laughed out loud. "Hey, Artie. This is Russell Thompson. You called?"

"Hey, Russ! Man, I need to talk to you. I've got a proposition for you." Artie's enthusiastic voice brought a smile to Russell's face.

Russell sat back and put his feet on the desk. "That so? No, thank you, but I'm not joining your band."

"Hold on! You haven't heard the proposition yet."

"All right. I'm listening."

"You like playing for the USO, right?" Artie asked. "Yes, I enjoy it. Got to do my service for the country."

"Right. Well, how would you like to do even more for your country?" Artie's eager voice was intriguing.

Russell put his feet down and sat up, his elbows on the desk. "You have my attention."

"This is the deal. My band has been asked to go on a USO tour. And you know we need a piano player. If you want to do something really big for the country, come with us. We'll perform for soldiers who are away from home and won't be back for a while. Will you consider it? I'll match your pay at the hotel. Maybe you can take a leave of absence or something so in case it doesn't work out, you'll still have your day job to come back to. What do you think?"

Rubbing his chin, Russell tried to take in all Artie was saying. Travel with the USO? He'd never considered that as an option. But Artie's argument made sense. He could help to raise soldier morale much more when they'd been far away from home. Maybe this was the chance he'd been waiting for. But what would Lexie think? Could he leave her here alone? If he were going into the military, he would leave her behind like all the other guys did who served. He needed to talk to her first before deciding.

"I don't know, Artie. That's a big decision, and I can't make it without giving it a lot of thought."

"I get that. Tell you what. We're playing at the Stage Door Canteen tomorrow night. I'd like you to play with us there, then we can talk about the other gig. Will that work?" Artie was persistent if nothing else.

"Yes, I can do that. See you tomorrow night." Russell hung up the phone, his head swimming. He could actually be overseas where the Army and Navy were. He could do something that really mattered, more than he could do here at home, where he basically helped send soldiers off before they knew what it was like to be out of their own country among strangers and enemies. He'd prayed to do something significant for the war effort since he couldn't serve in the military himself. Was this the answer to his prayer? Part of him wanted to jump at the opportunity, but part of him said to take it easy and not react too fast. He closed his eyes. *Lord, is this what you want me to do?*

He needed to talk to Lexie before giving Artie his answer. If he decided to go overseas with the USO, how would that affect their wedding plans? He'd been waiting for her to have time, to finish her studies, but now, she might have to wait for him instead. Not that he needed her permission, but she'd want to know about it before he made his decision. He checked his watch. He should call her before it got any later, not knowing when he'd have a chance to discuss it in person. Maybe she could come to the Stage Door Canteen tomorrow night, and he could talk to her then.

Russell picked up the phone and called the nurses' residence. When the housemother answered, he asked for Lexie. Drumming his fingers on his desk, he tried to picture himself with Artie's band overseas.

"Hello?" Lexie sounded out of breath. "Hi, Lexie. It's Russell."

"Russell? Is anything wrong? You just left."

"No, no. Um, I'm playing at the Stage Door Canteen tomorrow night and wondered if you could come."

"On a Monday night? I couldn't come, even if I didn't have to work, which I do. I'm on the night shift tomorrow again after I take my test in the morning."

"Oh, of course." He had forgotten about her big test, not to mention the fact that she couldn't get away on a weeknight.

"Russell, isn't the Stage Door Canteen where the movie stars hang out with the servicemen?"

"Yes, that's the place. I haven't played there before, but Artie just called and…"

"Russell, you might get to meet somebody famous—like Bette Davis or Bob Hope or something!"

"Maybe so, but I wanted to talk to you about something."

He heard excited voices in the background. It sounded like the other girls were talking to Lexie about the names she'd mentioned.

"Sorry, Russell, did you say something? There's a bunch of nosy girls around here." Lexie laughed, and so did the girls standing near her.

Nosy and noisy too. "Lexie, can you hear me? Lexie, I need to talk to you." He frowned at the interruption. He had hoped to talk to her alone, but chances of that happening in the main living room at the nurses' quarters were slim to none. Frustrated, he stood and paced in front of his desk with the phone in his hand, waiting for Lexie's attention. He could hear her voice talking to the other nurses.

"Would you girls be quiet? No, I didn't say Bob Hope was on the phone. No, I didn't see Bette Davis today." She giggled. "Quit going bonkers on me. Go away."

Russell waited, his patience growing thin. He raised his voice. "Lexie!"

"Russell? Are you yelling at me? What on earth for?"

"You said you couldn't hear me." He seethed through clenched teeth.

"Sorry. I can hear now. The other girls left the room. What did you want to tell me?"

"I … I really wanted to discuss this with you in person, but I don't know when we'll get a chance."

"Discuss what?" Her voice had a worried tone. "Artie asked me to join his band, you know."

"Yes, you told me. And you told him you weren't interested." She paused. "Did you change your mind? Are you going to accept? Is that why you're playing at the Stage Door tomorrow night?"

"Whoa. Wait a minute." He took a deep breath. "Yes and no. He did ask me to join the band, and I told him 'no.' He called today to ask me to play tomorrow night, and I said 'yes.' But … he asked me about something else that I want to talk to you about before I give him an answer."

"Something else? What, Russell? Tell me," she insisted.

"His band is going on an overseas USO tour, and he wants me to join them. Lexie, I'm tempted to accept."

"Gee, Russell. That's quite an honor. But what about your job here at the hotel? Will you quit?"

"I'm not sure. I don't know when the band is leaving or how long it'll be gone, so I don't know what to tell the hotel. Artie suggested I ask for a leave of absence so they'll hold my job for me when I come back, but I don't know if they would."

"What are you going to tell him?"

"I don't know, Lexie. You know I've wanted to do something more for the country, and maybe this is it. But if I leave, I don't know when I'll be back."

"Russell, you already do plenty, but I know you don't think so. Have you prayed about it?"

"Some. But I had to speak to you about it too. I wouldn't make that big a decision without you."

"I'm glad you wanted to talk to me first, but I'm not going to tell you what to do. I think we both need to pray about it."

"Lexie, what about our wedding? It might be delayed even longer if I go." Russell waited during her silence. Was she upset about that?

"You know, Russell, our wedding has been postponed by my nurses' training, and you've supported me with my decision to go to school. I want to support you, too, if you choose to accept the offer."

Russell's heart swelled with the love he had for her. She cared about what he cared about, whatever the consequences. "You know, we can get married by a justice of the peace real quick before I leave town, just like all the soldiers and sailors are doing."

"We could, but why? So we'll be married while you're gone? No, I want the real deal, and I want to be married in a church. Plus, I want my husband to be here with me afterward."

"You know, kiddo, you're something. You *are* the real deal, and I love you for it."

"I love you, too, Russell, and I'll love you wherever you go."

"All right. I'll pray about it. And I'll see how things work out tomorrow night at the Canteen, see if I want to be with those guys more than a night."

Lexie laughed. "You have a good time, and I'll be praying about your decision too."

"I'll let you know as soon as I decide. Meanwhile, go study. I want you to score flying colors on your test."

"Yes, sir. I'll get right to it, as soon as we hang up. Good night, Russell."

"Good night, sweetheart."

The tables along the wall were filled with platters of cookies and cake when Russell entered the basement of the 44th Street Theater, the home of the Stage Door Canteen. Servicemen were already lining up outside for the opening shift of the night, which began at 6:00 p.m. Although the canteen could hold 500 at a time, more than 2,000 came each night, according to Artie, so the servicemen were divided into shifts, with tickets for four shifts issued every night. Decked out in patriotic red, white, and blue aprons, the women who were hostesses chatted with each other while they waited for the men to come in.

Russell waved at Artie and hurried over to the stage. "Looks like everything's ready."

"Yeah, the folks have been working here a couple of hours already." He pointed to the piano. "Have a seat, and let's run through a couple of songs before they open the door."

Soon the place teemed with servicemen being served food and drinks by some of the stars from Broadway shows. Russell glanced over and saw Tallulah Bankhead serving coffee and Ray Bolger serving sandwiches. The band took a short break while a vaudeville comedian performed on stage to entertain the crowd. Afterward, the band started playing again, and the dance floor was packed with sailors and soldiers dancing with the hostesses.

The band took another break when the shift changed, and new servicemen entered the room. They, too, were treated to sandwiches, dessert, fruit, and drinks. Russell couldn't believe how much food they would go through each night. He was thankful to learn that no liquor was served to these men who might be shipping out in a few hours. They didn't need to start out their service on the wrong foot. Russell felt a sense of patriotism as part of such a morale-boosting event for these guys. Too bad Lexie wasn't able to come tonight and share the experience with him.

When the last song ended at midnight, Russell was beat.

What a long day, working at the hotel eight hours, then coming to the canteen and playing almost six. He closed the piano lid and stayed seated on the bench, taking a few minutes to regroup as he watched the other band members pack up their instruments. True, he was tired physically, but somehow he was also energized mentally, knowing he'd contributed to a good cause.

Artie came over and pulled up a chair beside him. "What d'ya think? Are you ready to take this show overseas?"

Russell nodded and faced him. "Artie, I want to do it. I've talked to my girl and my Big Boss, but I haven't talked to the hotel yet."

Artie's eyebrows met. "I don't get it. I thought the hotel was the Big Boss. If they're not, who is?"

Russell smiled and pointed skyward. "The man upstairs. Had to talk it over with Him first." He chuckled at Artie's reaction. "Do you know when you're going to leave?"

"Well, here's the thing. I just got word that they want us to fly out in two days."

Russell's mouth dropped open. "Two days? That's a lot sooner than I expected."

"Yeah, me too. But some folks in another band got sick, so they need us right away."

"That doesn't give me much time to give notice to the hotel. I feel kind of bad about that."

"I know, but people are a lot more understanding about things like that these days, especially if you're serving your country. And that's what you'll be doing."

He was. And he would be. Finally.

Chapter Seventeen

"*H*ey, Lexie. Any chance you can meet me for lunch today?" Russell's voice was especially animated Tuesday morning.

"Sure, I guess so." Lexie ran over all she had to do that day, wondering how she could fit a lunch date with Russell into the schedule, but she heard the urgency in Russell's tone.

"Great. I'll meet you at the diner at noon. Okay?"

"See you then." Lexie hung up the receiver and stared at the phone a few seconds. Had Russell made a decision about going on a USO tour? He must have, or he wouldn't be so anxious to see her today. She'd had a hard enough time focusing on studying for her test after he'd called Sunday night. Hopefully, she'd passed, even though Russell was in the back of her mind. But whatever he decided, she needed to act as supportive of his decision as he was of hers. Yet, deep inside, she hoped he had turned down the offer.

"Lexie! Time for inspection!" Penny tagged her as she passed.

Snapped back into her immediate duties, Lexie lined up with the rest of the girls. She restrained herself from tapping her foot as she endured the scrutiny of the nursing supervisor once again. Everyone's uniform had to be clean, starched, and ironed. Every shoe had to be scuffless, polished lily-white, the seams in their white hose straight, and the hats pinned on in the proper place on their heads. Lexie thought she could put on her uniform blindfolded now that she'd done it so many times. This ordeal was one she looked forward to leaving behind when she graduated from nursing school.

As soon as the girls were released, they reported to their classes. This afternoon after lunch, she'd report back to the psychiatric hospital for duty. Did Nurse Harper have her test results yet? When would she tell Lexie how she did?

The pharmacology class ended just minutes before noon, giving Lexie little time to change to meet Russell. Lexie practically ran to the diner, hoping Russell had arrived early enough to claim a seat.

She squeezed in the door through waiting customers and spotted him at the counter where he waved her over.

Russell smiled and kissed her on the cheek as she climbed up on the stool. "Sorry I couldn't grab a table," he said, nodding toward the tables. "They were already taken."

"That's okay. I don't mind sitting here." She didn't mention the last time she sat there it was next to Cal Miller.

The waitress stopped in front of them with her pad and pencil ready.

Russell glanced at Lexie. "Do you know what you want yet?"

The smell of bacon frying tantalized Lexie's taste buds. "Yes, I'll have a club sandwich and a Coke."

"Make that two."

The waitress scribbled on her pad, then walked away. Lexie faced Russell. "You made a decision, didn't you?"

Russell's smile dimmed as he got serious. "I did. But I wanted to tell you in person."

"You've decided to go." She forced herself to swallow the lump in her throat.

"Yes." He took her hand. "You know I don't want to leave you, but I have to do this. I have to do more for the war. I have to do my part."

Lexie nodded, wishing the moisture in her eyes would go away. She sniffed, then said, "I know you feel that way, Russell."

Russell reached with his thumb and wiped away the tear that escaped from her eye and ran down her cheek. "I know you don't really understand, but thanks for trying."

She searched his face. "Do you know when you'll be leaving?

He cleared his throat. "That's one reason I needed to see you today." He squeezed her hand. "We leave tomorrow." Noticing her shock, he said, "I know it's kind of sudden, but another band had to cancel, and Artie's was asked to fill in."

She blew out a breath. "Tomorrow." She tried to let that fact sink in. "Do you know where you're going?"

"Yes, first we'll go to a base in England, then we'll fly over to Northern Ireland to some bases there."

Their food arrived, and they began eating in silence. Lexie struggled to swallow, fighting the urge to cry and argue. He didn't have to go. He wasn't military. But he was going anyway. And she needed to support him and keep her own misgivings to herself.

"Thank God the Germans aren't bombing England anymore."

"Yes, thank God. I'm sure the people of England are

happy about that too. Hitler's changed his focus to other countries now."

"Are you flying over or going out on a ship?"

"Flying. Special Services has arranged for us to leave with a convoy of military planes. Don't worry. We won't be in any danger."

Who was he kidding? There was always danger, especially from the Germans, but she'd keep that thought to herself.

"I'll pray for your safety."

"Thanks, Lexie. And I'll pray for yours too."

She leaned back and twisted to face him. "*My* safety? I'm staying here, safe in the good old USA." Much as she liked having him close by, she wouldn't let him know she had any fears about him leaving.

Russell gave her his wonderful dimpled smile and winked. "Since I won't be here to be your knight in shining armor, I have to pray for your protection while I'm gone."

"Prayers are always welcome. But you might want to pray for me to get through school while you're at it."

His eyes widened. "Sorry, Lexie, I forgot to ask you. Did you get your test scores back yet?"

"Not yet, but maybe tomorrow." She looked down at her Coke and stroked the sweating glass. "Do you know how long you'll be gone?"

"No, I don't. Artie didn't know for sure. Anywhere from a week to a month, he said."

"So you won't be here for the Fourth of July."

"Probably not. Are you thinking about staying here instead of going out to East Hampton with the sisters?"

"No, I'd still like to spend it with them, especially if you're not here."

"Sounds good. Be sure to give them hugs and kisses from me."

"I will. What did your boss at the hotel say? Are they sore because you're leaving?"

"They don't like it, but they left an open door for me to come back if I want to. I just wish I had been able to give them more notice."

Lexie glanced at the big round clock on the wall. "Russell, I need to get back to the hospital."

He followed her gaze. "Yes, you do."

Russell left money on the counter for their meals, then they went outside. On the sidewalk, Russell put his arms around her and drew her close. "I know it's broad daylight, but I can't leave you without a proper kiss."

"If that's the case, don't make it too proper," Lexie said, tilting her face to his.

Russell threw back his head and laughed, then leaned down and kissed her with as much passion as he could in a public place. When he let her go, she was dizzy from euphoria.

"Lexie, you take care, and remember I love you with my whole heart."

"I will. I love you too. And I'll be praying for your safety."

He let go of her, and they parted company and headed in opposite directions. Lexie looked back at him once more when she got to the next corner, and he turned, too, and, smiling, gave her a wave. She waved back, giving her best effort to smile back at him.

Her feet were like blocks of stone as she walked back to the hospital. She caught a whiff of cigar smoke as the German baker charged by, cutting a glance at her when he passed. She had no idea why the man didn't like her, but the feeling was mutual, even though she had a ping of guilt for being judgmental. However, she wasn't going to waste any thoughts on that rude man. She had more important things on her mind.

Like Russell leaving. Tomorrow. It was so hard to believe. So sudden. She knew he'd been unhappy he couldn't join the military, but she never thought he'd leave the country, never thought he'd have the opportunity. Was she being selfish to think he should stay with her while so many other women were saying goodbye to their men who were going off to fight? She didn't dare think it wasn't fair. War wasn't fair.

She trudged back to her room, changed clothes, then noticed her reflection in the mirror and the sad face looking back at her. Somehow she had to change that face into a cheerful one. Speaking of not fair, life hadn't been fair for her patients either. She wasn't about to add to their misery by showing up with such a pitiful expression. *Smile, Lexie*, she commanded. As she worked the edges of her lips up into a smile, a thought struck her, slapping the smile away. What if this wasn't his only trip with the USO? What if he liked it so much, he'd travel all over the world performing for soldiers like Bob Hope was doing? Even if she graduated early, if Russell wasn't around, what difference would it make? When would they ever get married?

There was no doubt in her mind that Russell loved her. That's the last thing he said. The last? She trembled at the implications. *Stop it, Lexie.* She couldn't allow her mind to take that negative route. She remembered Dr. Peale's words to change her thoughts and thereby change her world. She needed to focus on positive thoughts. Her fiancé was a wonderful man. He would be safe. He would be happy finding his place in the war. He would be doing a good thing. Meanwhile, so would she. She plastered a smile back on her face and left for the hospital.

"The humming nurse is back!" Bob exclaimed across the room when he saw her enter the ward.

That was all it took to turn Lexie's fake smile into a genuine one. "Good afternoon, Bob."

He waved at her, and most of the other patients waved and smiled too.

Lexie walked through the ward, checking to see what had changed since she'd been there last. Not much, except that Mo, the alcoholic was gone. He'd been released to go home. Maybe he wouldn't end up back in the hospital. But if he did, she might not see him since he should go to the alcoholics' ward instead. Problem was, that ward filled up too fast and overflowed onto this one.

The bed next to John Doe was empty for now. She checked in with the other patients before going to see him. Although she wanted to see him first, she didn't want to show favoritism. When she finally got to his bedside, he seemed to be sitting up more. "Good afternoon, John. How are you today?"

His eyes focused on her, and she almost jumped back. He blinked as if answering. "Do you remember me?"

He blinked twice.

Heart pounding, she tried to stifle her surprise. "Good." She checked his IV drip, then looked back at him. "Think maybe you'd like to try some solid food today?"

Another blink. Should she accept that as a "yes"? "Maybe some soup or pudding?"

Another blink.

"I'll see what I can do for your dinner tonight."

She adjusted the blinds on the windows so more light came into the room, then checked his head. "That scar is practically gone. May I fluff your pillow?"

Blink.

She lifted his head, removed the pillow, fluffed it, then put it back under his head carefully.

"Would you like me to get you some water?"

Blink.

"I'll be right back."

She didn't usually leave to get one person something since it was more efficient to do it all at once, but she wanted to find a supervisor or doctor before they left for the day and see if they could remove the IV. She hurried out the door and down the hall and found Nurse Addams.

"Is there a problem, Nurse Smithfield?"

"No, ma'am, but I think John Doe is ready to eat real food, and maybe we can remove the IV."

The nurse raised her eyebrows. "You do? And why do you think that? Did he tell you he was hungry?"

"No, ma'am, but he communicated with his eyes. By blinking."

"Hmmm. That so? Can you show me?"

Would John Doe show the same response to the head nurse, or would Lexie look like a fool for saying so? Nurse Addams stood and walked down the hall with Lexie. When they went in, the patients glanced their way but stayed silent and turned back to what they were doing. They reached the foot of John Doe's bed, and the head nurse approached his bedside and studied his face.

"Hello, Mr. Doe. My name is Nurse Addams. Do you remember seeing me before?"

John Doe blinked.

"You blinked. Does that mean 'yes'?"

He blinked again, then his eyes found Lexie standing at the foot of the bed. She offered a reassuring smile.

"Nurse Smithfield here thinks you are ready to have your drip removed. Is that right?"

Blink.

"But to do that, I have to be sure you will eat. Can you open your mouth for me?"

John Doe slowly opened his mouth.

"Very good. I'll go ahead and remove the IV, and Nurse Smithfield will bring you something easy to eat tonight. But if you don't eat, we'll have to put the IV back in. Do you understand?"

Two blinks. Was that an enthusiastic answer? Lexie assumed so, which gave her a thrill of excitement.

"Nurse Smithfield, go get me some Betadine, a bandage, and tape, and we'll get this IV out."

Lexie hurried to the utility room for the necessary supplies and returned with them. She watched as Nurse Addams removed the IV needle from John Doe's arm and glanced at his face to see his reaction. He, too, was watching the procedure.

"Next time, Nurse Smithfield, you can do this yourself." The head nurse nodded to Lexie, then she turned back to the patient.

"There. Your arm is free now. Can you move it?" The arm lifted slightly off the bed.

"Good. Maybe soon, we can get the cast off your other

arm." She turned to Lexie as she stepped back from the bed. "He's all yours now, Nurse Smithfield."

Warmth spread over Lexie's face as she nodded. She glanced at John Doe and thought she saw the hint of a smile on his face. There was progress in his condition, and she wanted to jump for joy but had to maintain her professional demeanor.

"You'll remember to bring him something he can eat tonight?"

"Yes, ma'am. I thought I'd bring some soup … and some pudding."

"Perfect. He shouldn't have a problem getting that down, but I'm not sure he can feed himself yet. I'd say that's up to him and how hungry he is."

She motioned for Lexie to move toward the door. As they stepped outside the ward, she faced Lexie. "Good work in there, Nurse Smithfield. I hope he continues to progress and maybe tell us who he is. We still don't know the extent of the injury to his brain."

"Thank you, Nurse Addams. I'll keep an eye on him tonight."

"Well, it's time for me to leave. I think it's also time for your patients to get some exercise."

"I'll make sure they get it," Lexie said.

First, though, she picked up the phone and called the kitchen and asked for some soup and pudding for John Doe's dinner. Then, she took a few moments to look over the charts to see which patients were supposed to get what type of exercise. The weather was nice, and a good day for some of them to go to the rooftop enclosed area. She called downstairs to see if an attendant was available to accompany the patients upstairs to the ninth floor. Unlike the patients in the other wards—Disturbed, Semi-Disturbed, and Prison ward—her patients in the Quiet Male ward were more trustworthy for the activity. The eight- foot fence that surrounded the rooftop area protected and corralled them.

When Mr. Brown, the WPA attendant arrived, she took him into the ward. Without the government's Works Progress Administration, the hospital wouldn't have enough attendants. Lexie called out the names of the patients who could leave, then said, "Line up in front of Mr. Brown, please. It's a beautiful day to get some fresh air."

The patients complied, falling in line obediently.

"Mr. Brown, would you please take them up to the rooftop area? They can spend an hour there if they behave. You men, follow Mr. Brown and enjoy your time. See you in a little while."

With a few less patients, her job should have felt less overwhelming, but with a twenty-bed ward, she still had more patients than one nurse should have to handle alone. Russell's dimpled smile appeared in her mind, and she remembered he would be leaving tomorrow. If she were a military nurse, maybe she'd get to see him perform with the USO. What a selfish thought. She's seen him perform many times, and the people he was going to entertain had never had the privilege.

"Nurse, aren't you going to hum today?"

Lexie was brought back to the present. "Oh, yes, of course, if you'd like. We sang the song yesterday in church."

She began humming "Amazing Grace" again as she checked on each patient. Ronald, an elderly man, grabbed her hand as she passed by his chair and looked up at her.

"Is that you, Dorothy? Oh, I'm so glad you came to see me. I was just telling Frank about you."

Ronald, a patient diagnosed with senility, sat across from Thaddeus, another elderly patient with the same problem. The two often sat together, though neither knew what the other was talking about, much less each other's names. It didn't seem to matter, though, and at least they had company. And they were safe here. Often, older patients with senility were found roaming the streets lost. Many were brought to Bellevue because their children couldn't or wouldn't take care of them. Lexie's heart went out to the men.

She wouldn't tell Ronald she wasn't Dorothy, his deceased wife. As far as she was concerned, there was no harm in letting him think she was. Patting him on the shoulder, she said, "Hello, Ronald. How are you today?"

"Fit as a fiddle!" He slapped his knee, then pulled down on her hand that was still clasped in his. "Come, sit with me. You must be tired after taking care of all the children."

She gave his hand a gentle squeeze. "Sorry, dear, but I must get on with my work."

Ronald turned to Thaddeus. "That Dorothy. She's always so busy!"

Lexie wriggled her hand free from his and moved on to the next patient. She resumed her humming as she made her way back to John Doe. "How does your arm feel, now that you can move it?"

He blinked and lifted his arm a few inches off the bed, then ran his tongue along his lips.

Lexie stared, not sure what to think of his action before it hit her. "Your water. I forgot to bring it. I'm so sorry. Be right back."

She filled up several pitchers and grabbed paper cups before returning to the ward.

"Anyone care for some water?" She scanned the room, turning the cart toward John's bed. Several of the men came up to her with their hands outstretched. Lexie poured some cups of water and handed them out before proceeding to John's bed.

"Here you go." She held the cup out. "Do you think you can take it yourself?"

A surprised look crossed his face before he reached out with his free arm.

"Here, I'll raise your bed for you." She moved to the end of his bed and turned the crank until the portion behind John was elevated to a sitting position.

"Let's try," she said and placed the cup in his hand, then covered his hand with hers to steady the cup as he lifted it to his mouth. His hand shook as he lifted his arm all the way to his face, but he managed to get the cup to his mouth with her help. He drank all the water before pushing the cup away. "Very good." She put the cup down and straightened his sheets, humming as she worked.

As she was about to leave his bedside, his hand gripped her by the wrist. Lexie jumped, unable to veil her shock. The grip was strong, stronger than she believed he was capable of in his condition. Her heart raced, and she looked into his eyes for signs of trouble. He implored her with his eyes, and for the first time, she realized those eyes were green. But there was no hint of malice there, rather a plea. She took a deep breath, then spoke.

"Did you need something else?"

A soft, raspy voice said, "Sing."

One word. But the first word she'd ever heard him speak. Gathering her senses, she said, "Sing? You don't wish me to hum?"

A slight shake of his head said "no." Oh dear. Her humming bothered him.

"Sing the words."

Her heart leaped hearing him speak. "The words to 'Amazing Grace'?"

He nodded and whispered, "Yes."

"I'll see if I can remember them. I read them in the hymnal just yesterday. I can't promise you the best voice, though."

He gave her a weak smile.

Lexie began singing, recalling as best she could the words to the hymn. "Amazing grace, how sweet the sound." John Doe closed his eyes, but the smile stayed on his lips.

At the other end of the room, Bob spoke up. "She can sing! Come over here where we can hear you better."

Lexie gave a last glance to John Doe, wondering if he had fallen asleep or was still listening, before heading Bob's direction. She sang a little louder, and when she finished the hymn, Bob applauded, and others joined in. They were clapping when the patients who'd left for exercise returned, provoking confused looks on their faces as well as the attendant's. Lexie blushed at all the attention. She was not a USO star, after all.

And just like that, her thoughts returned to Russell. If only they'd had time for one more kiss before he left, but that wouldn't be possible. She wouldn't get off work until midnight, and he was leaving early the next morning. There wasn't even time for a phone call. Her despair must've changed her expression because one of the patients called out to her. "Don't be sad. You're the Happy Nurse!"

She had to be. For their sakes, and for her own. She managed to return a smile to her face, where it stayed as she studied the hopeful faces watching hers.

"Is everyone ready for supper?" Shouts of affirmation filled the room.

"All right then. Wash up over at the lavatory." She pointed to the one sink at the end of the room. "Clear your areas so there's space to put your trays."

Most of the patients did as told, but a few were unable to follow instructions—either they were asleep or not processing the information. She picked up a washcloth and wet it, added some soapy water, then wrung it out. Then she went to the patients who didn't go wash their hands on their own and wiped their hands for them. She also wiped off John Doe's hands the same way.

"Maybe you can sit up on the side of your bed for supper," she said. "Pretty soon, you'll be walking again." He didn't say a word, just watched her and appeared to contemplate what she said.

"All right. I'll go get the food now," she said.

Lexie found the kitchen attendant with the food trays waiting in the hallway. She opened the door to the ward so he could roll the trays in, then he helped her hand them out. The patient "helpers" took trays to other patients as well. Thankfully, only a few patients needed assistance to eat, so she aided them first. When she approached John Doe's bed, he attempted to sit straighter. She put down the tray on his nightstand and adjusted the pillow behind him.

"Okay, good. Now, I'll give you the spoon and hold the

bowl while you feed yourself. Can you do that?"

He took the spoon and brought the clear broth to his lips, only spilling the spoon's contents a few times. After he'd had half of the soup, he put the spoon in the bowl and put his hand up to signal that he didn't want any more. "You're finished?" Lexie asked, and when he nodded, she placed the bowl on the tray. "Would you like any pudding now?"

"No." The words came out in a whisper. "Thank you." He sank back against the pillow.

"You're welcome. I'm glad you were able to get something down tonight. It's been a while since you've had any real food."

He raised his eyebrows. "How long?"

Lexie searched her memory. "I'm not sure. I'll have to check your chart. I don't know how long it's been since you were injured, but you arrived here about ten days ago."

His forehead furrowed. "I don't remember."

"That's all right. The good thing is you're doing better now. Maybe your memory will come back soon."

Chapter Eighteen

"*H*e did what?" Penny's eyes were wide as quarters.

"He left this morning with Artie's Band to play overseas with the USO."

"Russell went overseas? I didn't even know he was planning to go."

"He wasn't, I mean, it just came up. Artie's band had an opening, and the USO needed a band to leave this week."

"Do you know where he was going?"

"England, a base in England to start with, then some bases in Northern Ireland."

Penny plopped down on the bed. "Well, hot diggity dog! He's gonna have a gas being with all those stars!"

Why did Penny have to mention that aspect of Russell's trip? "I hadn't thought of that. I guess he will have a good time."

"You hadn't thought about all those famous people and glamour girls that go with the USO?"

"No, I was just thinking about him being so far away." Glamour girls? Would Russell's head be turned?

Penny's brow wrinkled. She placed her hand on Lexie's

knee and peered at her face. "Lexie, are you worried about him with all those girls?"

Lexie shook her head. "No, I don't worry about Russell's loyalty." But deep inside a tremor of jealousy waved its ugly head.

"Of course, you don't. Russell's the most honorable man I know. Thank God, he's not like all the other guys who would be charmed by all that glitterati."

Penny's comments were meant to comfort, Lexie was sure, but they were having the opposite effect on her. "Yes, thank God, he's not."

"How long will he be gone?"

"I don't know. He didn't know yet."

"Well, I guess he'll be able to write you letters."

Letters? She thought she could still talk to him on the phone. But now, she wasn't sure. Besides, letters came from people who were gone a long time, and she didn't expect Russell to be gone that long. Maybe she was kidding herself.

"Yes, I'm sure he will."

"Of course, he might get a chance to call over here, but it costs an arm and a leg for a phone call. I wonder what the time difference is?"

"Five hours, I think. If it's noon here, it's five o'clock in the afternoon there."

"So, if you get off work at five, he'll be in the middle of a show, won't he?"

"Probably." Why did Penny keep asking questions that made her so uncomfortable?"

Penny patted her knee. "Don't worry. I'll make sure you're not lonely."

How could she do that? She and Penny didn't even have

the same schedule. And even if they did, Penny wouldn't be able to stop her from missing Russell.

"Thanks." Lexie stood and straightened her skirt. "We better go downstairs now."

Penny hopped up from the bed. "Back to the grind! Hey, are you going to work anywhere else but psychiatrics?"

Lexie shook her head. "I don't think so. The psychiatric hospital will be my main concentration."

Shaking her head, Penny said, "I don't see why you're so interested in those people. You can't just put a Band-Aid on them and send them home like you can other people."

"No, you can't. And that's what makes the treatment so intriguing.

We're still trying to figure out what works with mental illness."

Penny shrugged. "Well, I guess it's a good thing there are people like you who care about it, for their sake. Because some of us would rather treat *real* illnesses."

Lexie jolted at the connotation that mental illness wasn't a real illness. She didn't want to argue with her friend, but unfortunately, Penny's attitude was all too common in the medical field.

After class that morning, Lexie had time to kill before she reported to the ward. She skipped lunch, not caring to be around the other nurses and their chatter. Instead, she decided to go to the hospital library to study. But after a few minutes there, her stomach growled, and she felt restless. The hospital cafeteria was closed until supper, but the diner wasn't. Even though she'd have to eat without Russell, it would be good to be where they'd been the day before, even relive the last time they'd been together.

She changed clothes and headed up the street to their familiar spot. The lunch crowd was gone by the time she arrived, so she had no problem finding a seat at the counter. Strange how empty the place felt without the crowd, without Russell. Empty and lifeless. Even her cherry Coke had lost its fizz.

"Mind if I join you?" a familiar voice spoke beside her.

The sound brought her out of her reverie, and she jerked her head toward the source. Cal Miller took off his hat and slid onto the stool beside her.

"Oh, sure." Lexie glanced around to see if anyone else had accompanied him to the diner. Would Russell mind?

"Are you not working at the hospital today?"

Lexie frowned, thinking him too nosy, then remembered that she had told him what she did. "I'm working later—the night shift." Should she tell him that?

Cal looked around the diner. "I guess your fiancé is working, eh?"

"No, I mean yes." Noticing his confused look, she continued. "He doesn't work at the hotel anymore. He joined a band that's playing for the USO … overseas."

"Ah, so that explains it."

"Explains what?" Lexie tilted her head as she asked.

"You look sad, like someone turned off the lights on your face."

Lexie had to smile at his remark. "That's a strange thing to say. But maybe you're right. I do miss him already."

"So he's not a soldier?"

"No, he'd like to be…" She didn't believe she should share Russell's dilemma. "He couldn't pass the physical."

"I've noticed his limp. That must be why."

She nodded but wanted to change the subject. "I thought you were leaving town. Didn't you tell me you were going to work at the aluminum company?"

Cal ran a finger inside his collar like it was too tight. "Yes, that's true." He cleared his throat and took a sip of his drink. "They're not ready for me yet."

"Oh, I see. What kind of work will you be doing?"

He glanced around the room before answering. "Electrical. I'm an electrician."

"Hmm." She turned back to her sandwich.

"And how are things at the hospital?' Cal asked. He turned to the waitress who approached the counter, pad and pen poised, and gave her his order.

"Good, I guess. School's going well."

"At least you don't get any war victims here."

"Actually, we do. Not immediately, of course, but if their injuries are long-term, they're sent back here. The hospitals in Europe would overflow if they didn't."

"Of course. That makes sense." He lifted his glass to drink, then looked at her. "Are you thinking about being an Army nurse or maybe a Navy nurse?"

Shaking her head, Lexie said, "No. We're desperately short of nurses here because so many have joined the military."

"And you don't have to be concerned with bombs dropping on you."

Frowning, Lexie said, "Thank God, that's true. I can't imagine what it was like for those poor people in England when the Nazis were bombing their country."

Cal's smile evaporated as he focused on the hamburger the waitress set before him. He picked up the sandwich and paused, glancing at her before taking a bite. "So when you graduate, will you stay here, in New York?"

She'd asked herself that same question. Where would Russell want to live after they married? Right now, it seemed that marriage was the last thing on his mind.

"I'm not sure. I don't know where we'll live when we get married."

"And when do you get married?"

She didn't know that either. Everything seemed so uncertain now, more than ever with Russell's leaving. Lexie shrugged. "When I graduate, and Russell gets back, whenever both those events coincide."

"Good thing you have your training to keep you busy, right?"

"Yes, I have plenty to keep me busy, with class, studying, and working in the hospital."

"You must find the work fulfilling."

"Yes, I do. I believe God wants me to help people, and I do think I'm making a positive difference in the lives of my patients. Why, just last night, I made a breakthrough with a patient."

"How so?"

"A man who was injured somewhere in the Philippines was brought here two weeks ago. He's been in a catatonic state—nonresponsive but awake—ever since. But last night he spoke to me!"

"And you made that happen? How?"

"I don't know, but maybe it's because I spoke to him. I prayed that I could reach him, and I did!"

"So, do you think it was your talking to the patient or your praying that made the difference?"

Lexie considered the question. "Both. I prayed, and God

used me to answer the prayer."

A smile eased over Cal's face. "You believe in prayer, then?"

"Well, of course. Don't you?"

Cal patted perspiration from his forehead with his napkin. "I'm not sure. When I was a child and my parents took me to church, I did."

"But not now? Why not?"

"As an adult, I've seen things that aren't good, and I wonder why God would allow them to happen."

"Sometimes people turn their backs on God, and they suffer the consequences. And this is not a perfect world. Evil exists—you can see that by the war we're in now. But God wants us to fight evil. Good people must stand up for what is right."

Cal motioned for the waitress to refill his glass of Coke. "You make a good point."

"We certainly can't stand by and let evil people have their way. That's why we're fighting Hitler. And if we can't go fight physically, we must fight in other ways, and prayer is one of the best ways I know to fight."

"I'm sure you will pray for your fiancé while he's gone."

"Yes, and he'll pray for me too. I'm sure of it."

"So, Lexie Smithfield, will you pray for me also?"

She was startled by the request but glad to give an answer. "Well, um, yes, if you'd like. What would you like me to pray for?"

Cal rubbed his chin. "Pray for my family to stay safe and for me to make good business decisions."

"I'd be happy to pray for you … and them. But you can pray, too, you know. I don't have a special connection to

God."

"Oh, but I think you do. You seem to be much better acquainted than I am. I don't think He and I are on the best speaking terms."

Lexie raised her eyebrows. "Well, that can be remedied too. But I'll leave that to you." Lexie glanced at the diner clock. "Oh dear, I better be going, or I'll be late." She put some money on the counter and stepped off the stool.

"I enjoyed our conversation. Maybe we'll run into each other again sometime, as long as I'm in town." Something outside the diner diverted his attention, and he narrowed his gaze.

Lexie glanced over to see the German baker glaring through the glass at Cal. She thought they were friends since she'd seen them together. But they seemed angry with each other now. Well, that was none of her business.

"Goodbye, Cal. See you around, maybe." She headed to the door.

"Don't forget," he called out behind her.

She spun around. "Forget what?"

"To pray for me."

She smiled and waved, then went out to the sidewalk, passing the baker who shot her an angry look.

"Well, good day to you too," she muttered under her breath. As she walked away, she looked over her shoulder and saw Cal leave the diner and the red-faced baker confront him, pointing a finger in his face. They weren't yelling at each other, but they were certainly having a heated discussion. Could their conversation have anything to do with Cal's business decision?

Lexie couldn't believe how much she'd talked with the

man, but she was glad she had. The conversation had been therapeutic for her and made her answer some questions about herself and why she did what she did. Why she enjoyed nursing. Why she prayed. Why things were the way they were.

How strange that he had asked her to pray for him. On the other hand, she remembered not long ago having the same doubts, too separated from God to pray. Well, she could pray for that to change too. Perhaps she should pray for his relationship with the baker as well. She might never know what impact her prayers would have because he was leaving town, and she doubted he'd be back. A sense of abandonment threatened her. Russell was gone, and soon, Cal wouldn't be around anymore either. Not that she had the same feelings toward the two of them. It was just nice to have a guy around to talk to. The truth was, she missed her brother Robert more than she realized. But Pearl Harbor had taken him away from her. She choked back a sob as tears filled her eyes. This stinking war wasn't fair.

Chapter Nineteen

"Why are you still here?" Oscar hissed his question through cigar-clenched teeth.

Karl took a deep breath for self-control. How he despised the way the baker sought to rule over him. He shrugged, a motion he knew would further infuriate the flabby man.

"It is not time for me to leave yet."

Oscar lowered his head, glancing from side to side. "Everyone has left except you. Why is it not time for you too?"

"I'm to report to my new job at the aluminum factory next week. So why should I hurry to that town when I can stay here?"

Oscar walked a few yards down the sidewalk away from the diner, motioning for Karl to come with him.

"Because … you are spending too much time with that woman. This is not a social affair you are here for."

Karl smiled to mask his anger and put his hand on Oscar's shoulder. "Calm down, Oscar, or you might have a heart attack."

The German shook off Karl's hand, scowling. "If I think that woman knows more than she should…"

"Yes, Oscar? What will you do, call the Gestapo? Have her arrested?"

"Do not make fun of me, Karl. This is no joking matter. I will not let you jeopardize the whole operation."

Tired of the man's insinuations, Karl shot back. "Do not threaten me, Oscar. I will be in place for the fireworks."

Oscar's beet-red face trembled with anger. He threw his hands up in the air, turned, and stalked away.

Karl watched him leave and tried to regain his composure. Oscar was right that the others had already left town, heading for their assignments, and Karl could have left too. But he wasn't ready. He wanted to stay in the city and enjoy his time there while he still could, because once he left, he wouldn't be able to come back. There were things to do and places to see he'd not experienced when he lived in the country before, and this would be his last chance to do them.

And then there was Lexie. She intrigued him. Her passion for her work, her patients, and her country were admirable, much like the passion he thought he had for Germany. But the truth was, Germany wasn't the same anymore. Hitler had ruined it, and now Karl was torn between being a patriot and being opposed to the man who controlled the country. He had wanted to help Germany win the war, but now that he was back in the States, he questioned whether blowing up the country he had called home for so many years was the right thing to do.

His conversations with Lexie made him think. Think about his mission and its purpose. Think about himself and his own purpose. She truly believed God had given her a purpose. Had He given Karl one too? If He had, would it be the mission he was sent to do? A mission that might take many lives? He doubted it, but then this was war. Yet, he wouldn't want Lexie to know who he really was and what he was doing here—and not just because it would sabotage the mission. She was becoming a friend, someone who trusted him. Would she still pray for him if she knew the truth?

Attendants and nurses were running down the hall to the ward when Lexie stepped off the elevator.

"What's going on?" she asked the person closest to her as she scrambled to catch up with the others.

"One of the patients just had a violent outburst and started knocking things over."

Who could it be? Claude Graham, who'd had the shock treatments? Or a new patient?

She entered the ward and joined the throng of medical personnel clustered near one of the beds. Not being able to see for the people in front of her, she tapped one of the other nurses on the shoulder. "Which patient is it?"

"John Doe, you know, the wounded soldier with the broken arm." Lexie's mouth dropped open. It couldn't be. Not him. He was too nice, and he was always calm. There must be a mistake, and the nurse was talking about another patient. Edging her way closer, she managed to get a look as attendants strapped down the angry, yelling man. Head Nurse Addams held up the glass syringe, forced out the air, then inserted the needle into the man's arm, held still by an attendant.

Seconds dragged by until the man calmed, and those

holding him released their grip.

"Thank you. You may leave now. The medicine will keep him sedated." The nurse directed her comment to the others who had helped restrain the patient. As they left the room, Lexie moved closer to the bed until she was on the opposite side from the nurse. John Doe gazed at her with eyes beginning to fade as the drug took effect.

"What happened?" Lexie whispered to the head nurse.

"He had an outburst like a temper tantrum. This often happens with head injuries." They both gazed at the patient. "Apparently, when his head was struck, it created an injury that has delayed effects."

Lexie shook her head in disbelief and touched John Doe's arm. "He was so quiet and relaxed the last time I saw him."

John Doe glanced back and forth between the two nurses. He looked sad and apologetic.

Nurse Addams patted him on the shoulder. "You'll be feeling better now, Mr. Doe."

As the other nurse walked away from the bed, Lexie remained standing near it, still gazing at the patient. He tried to lift his hand, but the restraints held it down. She touched it gently, wishing she could remove the straps but knew she shouldn't.

"I'm thirsty," he whispered.

Lexie glanced around his bed and noticed that the water pitcher had been knocked to the floor, spilling water out on the tiles. She walked over and picked it up.

"I'll go get you some water."

She hurried outside to the faucet, filled the pitcher, then found a paper cup. She grabbed a towel out of the utility room before returning to John Doe's bedside.

"I'll have to hold the cup for you." She poured some water into the cup and brought it to the man's mouth, lifting his head slightly with the other hand. He drank thirstily, then his head fell back on the pillow.

"Thank you," he said, his words slurring as the medicine worked through his system.

"You're welcome." Lexie managed a smile, her heart reaching out to the man she thought she had begun to understand.

"I was thirsty."

"Yes, I can see that. Do you want more?"

He shook his head. "Before. Couldn't lift pitcher."

His meaning dawned on her. "You tried to get the water and you couldn't?"

He gave a slight nod. "Made me mad. Sorry," he mumbled before his eyes closed.

So that was why he was angry. He was frustrated when he couldn't get to the water. But why such an outburst? Surely, it was the head wound. Sadness weighed her down as she knelt and mopped up the water on the floor with the towel. Would this kind of outburst happen again?

Lexie left the room and found Nurse Addams. "I found out what happened," she told the nurse. The nurse's brows puckered. "What happened?"

"John Doe. The reason for his outburst. He had tried to get water, but he couldn't lift the pitcher, so he got angry. I believe he reacted out of frustration."

"He told you this?" The nurse crossed her arms, tilting her head.

"Yes." Lexie told her about the man's request for water and what he'd said.

"Do you think his overreaction is from the head wound?"

"More than likely. I've seen this kind of thing happen before. But I think we might see more of it as we get more men injured in battle."

"Does it go away?"

"Who knows? Maybe it will, and maybe it won't."

"So what can we do about it? Do we have to keep him restrained?"

"For now, we do. And we'll have to observe him. If he settles down when the drug wears off, we'll remove the restraints."

"But what about his cast? Shouldn't that be coming off soon?"

"The doctor talked about removing it by the end of the week. But he could hurt himself if he goes into another rage and hits something with the arm."

"And what if these outbursts continue? What will we do then? Keep him in restraints and continue to sedate him?"

"We'd probably administer electric shock therapy. That procedure might take care of his problem."

Lexie's heart sank, hearing what she'd expected to hear but dreading the direction the treatment could take. He'd been making progress, and she hoped to see it continue. But now, she wondered if it would. Tonight was going to be a long night.

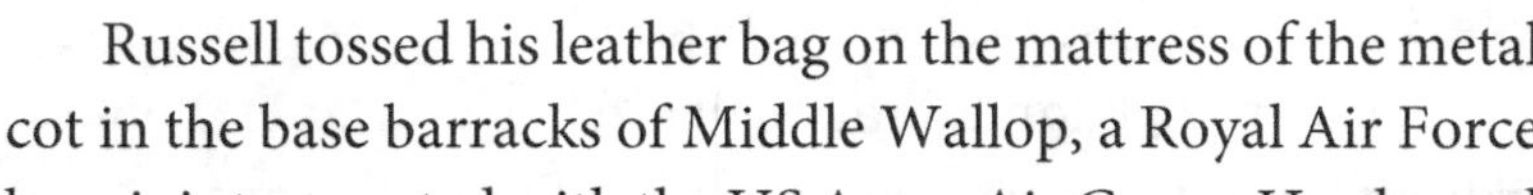

Russell tossed his leather bag on the mattress of the metal cot in the base barracks of Middle Wallop, a Royal Air Force base joint-operated with the US Army Air Corps. He glanced around the long room where identical metal beds lined up in facing rows. Each bed was draped with an olive-drab wool blanket covering white sheets and a pillow. A succession of windows spaced ten feet apart ran the length of the room, though curtains covered them, allowing minimal daylight to seep in. *Well, it certainly isn't the Hotel Martinique.* He rubbed his hands together against the chill of the sparsely furnished space.

The other band members drifted in, scanning the room before selecting their own beds.

"Well, here we are in Middle Wallop, wherever the heck that is! I have to admit, I've stayed in worse places." Harry, one of the trombone players, put his instrument case beside his chosen bed. "At least this place is clean."

"Hey, this isn't bad for Army barracks. Some of them have bunk beds." Artie ambled in and leaned against the wall. "It'll do for the short time we're here. Be thankful we're not in a war zone."

Russell studied the layout of the room, trying to see it through a soldier's eyes. This is where he'd be sent before going into combat. These cots would probably be quite welcoming after a hard day of training.

"Is there a heater in this room?" One of the band members sneezed. "Man, it's cold in here."

"There's a little stove down at the end. Can't imagine it'll warm the whole building, though."

Artie laughed. "Hey, guys. Remember, this is June. We're not supposed to need a heater."

"Yeah, well, I don't think England has a summer. Looks like winter out there to me—gray and damp." Harry nodded toward the outside.

"I hear it's like this all the time," said Artie. "If you want to complain, you should go see the king and see if he can do something about it."

"Think he'd like to come hear us play?"

Artie chuckled and said, "Sure, why not?"

"Hey, maybe we can rustle up some coffee," Louie, a sax player, commented from across the room.

Artie crossed his arms and shook his head. "I think you're going to have to acquire a taste for tea. Coffee's not too popular around here." Artie pulled out a pamphlet from his inside jacket pocket. "According to this *Instructions for American Servicemen in Britain*, 'The British don't know how to make a good cup of coffee. You don't know how to make a good cup of tea. It's an even swap.'"

Harry groaned. "Don't think I'll survive without my morning coffee." He lay down on his cot, putting his hands under his head. "The bed's not bad, long as you don't roll over."

"Say, let me see that. Where'd you get it?" Louie asked, reaching for the booklet.

"The sergeant who picked us up at the plane gave it to me. I guess he thinks we need to read it." Artie handed it to Louie.

"Hey, guys, listen to this," said Louie. "'While in Great Britain, your slogan should be, 'It is always impolite to criticize your hosts; it is militarily stupid to criticize your allies.' Hear that, Harry? Don't be impolite or stupid, okay?"

"Sure thing, Louie. You remember that too."

Sal, one of the trumpet players, strolled up from his cot at the other end of the room. "I saw a pub on the way here. What say we go get a good beer and some food? I'm starving."

"We're invited to eat in the mess hall with the soldiers," Artie said, grinning. "You don't want to be rude, do you?"

"Aw, c'mon, Artie! We don't have to eat in the mess hall,

do we?"

"No, I guess not. Well, not for every meal anyway. We'll check it out for breakfast tomorrow."

"You getting up that early? What time is our gig tonight?"

"Seven. We'll be finished by nine so the boys can get their sleep. Remember to look your best for the *Stars and Stripes* photographer that's here taking pictures of the base and the soldiers."

"You think they'll get a shot of us?" Louie struck a pose like a model, and the rest of the guys laughed.

"Some of us, Louie—the handsome ones!"

Russell sat down on his cot, taking in the banter between the guys. He smiled as they joked with each other, chuckling at some of the comments.

"Say, Russ, you sure are quiet. What's so funny?"

"Oh, I was just reminiscing about my college days when I lived in a dorm. You guys sound like my college roommates."

"That so?" said Nick, the drummer. "Because we're so smart?" The guys all laughed.

"Yeah, Nick, that's it. You're so smart."

"So, Russell, think you can stand being around us all the time? Aren't you gonna miss that pretty young thing we saw you with at the Martinique?"

Russell nodded. "Of course, I will." He looked around at the men. "Didn't any of you leave someone behind?"

Heads bobbed in agreement. "Sure did," said Harry. "I got a girl back home too. But she's okay with me coming over here, you know, doing my part in the war."

Artie spoke up. "That's why we're here. Probably every guy in the Army left somebody behind—sweetheart, mother, sister. If they can do it, we can too."

Russell wondered how Artie's marriage stayed together with all his traveling. "Artie, you have a wife and kids, don't you?"

"Sure do. Jean and I have been married fifteen years. We've got two children, both girls."

"So what's your secret? You travel all over the country. How do you keep your marriage together?"

"Guess you could say we just know each other, understand each other. I've been playing music all my life—was in a band when Jean and I met in high school. In fact, she sang with my band for a few years before we settled down to raise a family. This is the life of a band, and she knows what to expect. Sure, it's hard when I have to miss some special occasion. But I try to make it up when I can."

"He's a lucky man," said Nick. "Some women don't like our kind of life. At least I haven't found one that does yet."

"You're not as good-looking as Artie, though," joked Harry.

"Maybe you just haven't found the right girl." Russell tried to offer encouragement. Not everyone was as fortunate as Artie. Or as he was to have found Lexie. But he wasn't about to credit luck as the reason for him and Lexie getting together. Only God could have put someone like her in his life. And the funny thing was, they'd known each other since they were kids. They certainly knew each other well. Didn't they? Was she happy he was doing this—happy for him like she said she was? Or was she just saying that to make him feel good? He didn't know if she'd be as understanding as Artie's wife over the long haul. But then again, how long was he planning to do this?

Chapter Twenty

*W*ith Russell gone, Lexie spent the whole next day at the hospital. After classes, she went to lunch in the cafeteria with the other girls.

"So you decided to join the underclassmen, Lexie." Penny set her tray down on the table next to Lexie. "I can tell Russell is gone."

Lexie shrugged. "This isn't the first time I've eaten in the cafeteria. I ate here before he left, too, you know."

"Not every day, like the rest of us, though. Guess you don't have a better offer now."

"Oh, Penny, stop. I like hanging out with you and the other girls. I just never seem to have time to socialize with my night schedule."

"Yeah, I know. I'm just kidding you." Penny took a bite of mashed potatoes and scanned the room. She nudged Lexie with her elbow and nodded to her right. "Get a load of that new intern. Not bad on the eyes."

Lexie's gaze followed Penny's to where a young man in a starched white physician's coat stood talking to a couple of other doctors. Black-framed glasses accented his olive skin and matched his wavy dark hair, creating a mature persona that overshadowed his obvious youth. "Do you know who he is?"

Penny nodded. "His name is Dr. Dimitri Kappas. He's from Greece, and he's interning over here."

"That's interesting. I wonder what field of medicine he's going into?"

Penny shrugged and smiled. "Who cares? Isn't he dreamy? And I like the way his name rolls off the tongue— Di-mi-tri-Kap-pas."

Lexie bumped her shoulder into Penny. "Have you met him yet? Wonder if he speaks English?"

"Hmmm. I don't know. Maybe he needs me to tutor him."

"In English?"

Penny smiled wryly. "And a few other things, too, maybe."

"Penny! Watch out, or Nurse Harper will get you. You know we're not supposed to fraternize with the doctors."

"Oh, I have no intention of *fraternizing*. I just want to assist him like a good nurse."

Lexie shook her head at her roommate. "You're impossible."

"Hey, who said we couldn't have some fun in this job? You've managed to squeeze Russell into your schedule."

The mention of Russell's name reminded her where he was, and the feeling of abandonment returned. True, she had an advantage the other girls didn't have, with a boyfriend so near. Most of the nursing students were from someplace other than New York City—upstate or Jersey or Massachusetts—too far away to see their boyfriends very often. Lexie felt guilty being the only one with her fiancé so close. But that advantage was over now, and she was just like the others.

Penny searched her face. "Gee, sorry, Lex. Guess you miss Russell. Have you heard from him yet?"

Lexie shook her head. "No, but he hasn't been gone that long. Besides, remember the time difference? Who knows when he'd have a chance to call?"

"So I guess you won't be going to the diner anymore."

Lexie didn't dare tell her she had gone there the day before, much less talked to Cal Miller. She wouldn't understand. Lexie was sure of it.

"Who knows? I might get a craving for one of Mac's shakes."

"Well if you do, take me with you."

"So, are you going anywhere this weekend?" Lexie pushed the food around on her plate.

"No, hadn't planned on it. Guess I'll just stay here. Oh! I forgot! You got a phone call last night when you were on duty."

Lexie's heart rippled. "I did? Who called?"

"One of those old ladies that lives in East Hampton, you know, the ones you stayed with before. She asked you to call her back."

"I wonder if anything happened. They invited me and Russell to come out for the Fourth, but … they don't even know he's gone." Lexie glanced at her watch. "Hey, I've got time to call them, so I'll go do that now." Lexie stood, picked up her tray, then leaned over and whispered to Penny, "You take care of Dr. Kappas, you hear?"

A grin spread across Penny's face, and she scanned the

room to see where the doctor had gone. When she spotted him, she nodded. "Oh, yes, ma'am, I will be happy to do that. Yes, I will."

Lexie hurried to drop off her used tray before leaving the cafeteria. She rushed across the street to the nurses' residence and found another student on the phone. Lexie tried to wait patiently while the other girl chatted on with meaningless conversation, or so it seemed to Lexie, who couldn't help but overhear. Why did they only have one phone in the whole building? Even if it was a dormitory, the nursing students weren't children, although to tell the truth, some were straight out of high school.

Finally, the other girl noticed Lexie waiting and hung up. The phone at the Maurice sisters' house rang several times before anyone answered.

"Maurice residence," said Jane, the housekeeper.

"Hello, Jane. This is Lexie Smithfield. I'm returning a call from one of the sisters last night. Is everything all right? Are Peg and Marian well?"

"Yes, ma'am, they're just fine. I'll get them for you."

A few seconds passed before Peg's voice was heard on the other end. "Lexie? Is that you?"

"Yes, Peg, it's me. I understand you called last night. Did you need something?"

"Oh no, dear. Marian and I were just talking about you. We haven't heard from you since you left a couple of weeks ago and wanted to see how you were. Did you see any of the parade? We heard it was huge. Too big for my taste, with all those crowds, but I'm sure it was very impressive."

"No, I missed the parade because I had to go straight to the hospital. I heard about it, though."

"So, how is Russell? He left here early too. I think he missed you."

"Russell's fine," she hoped. "He's in England now with the USO."

"He is? Why, I didn't know he was going." Lexie heard her muffled speech as she covered the phone to tell Marian.

"It was rather sudden."

"Well, we want to hear all about it."

"I'd love to tell you more, but I'm sorry, I need to get over to the hospital now."

Lexie heard muffled words again before Peg came back to the phone.

"Lexie, do you have to work this weekend? Because if you don't, we want you to come here and spend Saturday and Sunday with us."

"Actually, I don't think I'm scheduled. I'll double-check today." A picture of the sisters' comfortable cottage sitting next to the ocean filled her mind with longing for the serenity she always found there. "I'd love to come. I'll let you know for sure, but as far as I know, you can expect me Saturday morning."

"Wonderful! We can't wait to see you! Bye now." Peg hung up before Lexie could reply.

What a welcome invitation. With Russell gone, being with the sisters, her "adopted" family, would be so nice and relaxing. Even though her own mother had died last year, she felt like she'd acquired two more with the way the spinster sisters Peg and Marian treated her. And their cottage felt more like a home than any her family had lived in since she was a young child.

The last time she saw the schedule, she was working

tonight, then the day shift tomorrow, and was off Saturday and Sunday. It was hard working a day shift back to back with a night shift, but she'd catch up on her sleep at the cottage. For a moment, she considered inviting Penny. Penny was from a town in New Jersey where her father ran a shoe repair shop. She'd never been to the Hamptons, and Lexie wanted to show her around someday. But not this time. Lexie needed peace and escape from the city and the hospital, as well as private time to talk with the sisters. She'd ask them if they were open to her bringing a guest sometime. Knowing how hospitable the women were, Lexie doubted they'd refuse.

She crossed back over to the psychiatric hospital and reported for duty.

"How's John Doe today?" she asked Nurse Addams, who was seated at the nurses' station.

"Calm. It takes a while for the medicine we gave him yesterday to wear off. Maybe you can work your magic with him today."

"My what?" Lexie's face heated.

"You seem to have a way with him. You understand him. Maybe he'll be able to open up to you."

The compliment flooded Lexie with satisfaction. If only she could have been there to prevent his outburst. Now, it would take some time for him to regain everyone's trust, that is if he had no more episodes.

"I'll do what I can."

"I know you will." The nurse picked up a stack of files and handed them to Lexie. "But first, please take these to Medical Records."

"Yes, ma'am." Lexie forced a smile, hiding her irritation

of being delayed to see John Doe.

Lexie took the stairs to the third floor and crossed over into the administrative wing of the hospital rather than waiting for the notoriously slow elevator. After she dropped off the files, she considered going up to the next floor where the library was. She wanted to explore the shelves to see if there were any books on the effects of head injuries. But that might take too long. As she was standing in the hall considering her options, she heard muted laughter coming from a closet nearby.

A voice with a foreign accent made her listen more intently. She decided to return to her floor instead of going to the library, but she would have to pass the room where the noise was coming from. Curiosity to discover who was in the closet got the better of her, and she eased past the door that was open only a few inches. As she passed, she cast a quick glimpse inside and hitched a breath when she saw the Greek doctor Penny so admired with his arms around one of the nurses in an intimate embrace. She quickly turned away and hurried back downstairs.

Apparently, Dr. Kappas was pursuing other interests while he was at Bellevue, and Lexie wanted to make sure Penny wasn't one of them. She'd heard that some doctors took advantage of their titles to trifle with the staff, but even so, she was disappointed to learn that the young doctor was one of them. Some men just couldn't be trusted, but thankfully, they weren't all womanizers like the doctor. Thank God Russell wasn't like that.

The time on the wall clock read 4:00. Russell was probably in the middle of a performance now. She hoped he was enjoying his time with the band. What other stars were performing in the show? Would Russell hang out together afterward? She sure wished she could talk with him on the phone, but the chances of that happening were very slim.

"You're back. Good. Go ahead and make your rounds in the ward. I'll be here another hour doing paperwork."

Lexie's entrance into the ward brought the usual greetings. Waves from smiling patients hailed her across the room. Even those who didn't smile acknowledged her with a nod. It felt good to be welcomed, but unfortunate that these patients had stayed long enough to become acquainted with her, as well as each other. Surely, some would be leaving soon. To be honest, she'd miss them, but she worried about how they would be treated by the outside world, knowing how difficult it was for them to function normally.

"Good job, Joe," she said to the tall man who held a broom, sweeping the same area over and over. "Thank you for keeping the room clean." Joe had grown physically but never gotten past the age of a child mentally. As a result, he couldn't live on his own and provide for himself, but his parents were now elderly and couldn't take care of him either. Lexie was thankful the hospital provided for people like Joe. Where else would he go otherwise?

At one of the tables, a new patient drew pictures with crayons. Lexie patted him on the back. "What a lovely picture!" The man didn't look up at her but continued to draw. She'd check the charts for his name when she returned to the nurses' station. The game of checkers was still going on, as the men studied the board. Everyone was awake doing something, whether sitting on their beds reading, walking around, or engaging in an activity. Everyone except John Doe. As she approached his bed, he looked at her expectantly.

"Are you feeling better today?"

"Yes, but tired. The medicine they gave me made me tired."

"Yes, but it will help you rest." Lexie smiled to hide the sadness she felt seeing him restrained.

He glanced at the straps that held him. "Can you get these off?"

"I'd like to, and I'm sure you'd like them removed, but I must have permission to do so first."

"I promise I won't hurt anybody."

His imploring eyes twisted her heart. She believed him and didn't think his outburst was meant to harm anyone, but she didn't have the authority to remove the restraints.

"I don't think you would. However, it's not my decision. I'm sorry."

He blew out a breath and turned his head away as if he wanted her to go away. She didn't blame him. What good was she to him if she couldn't provide what he needed?

"Tell you what, I'll ask Nurse Addams before she leaves if the restraints can come off."

He turned back to face her. "Will you please? Tell her I promise I'll behave."

"Yes, I will. In fact, I'll go ask her right now. Let's pray she will agree. Okay?"

John tilted his head. "Pray? About that? I don't think God cares about something so small."

Lexie wasn't sure He did either, but what could it hurt? She patted his arm for reassurance. "Be back soon."

Lexie hurried out of the ward, hoping Nurse Addams would allow her to remove the restraints. She approached the counter at the nurses' station and waited for the supervisor's attention.

Looking up, Nurse Addams said, "Yes?"

"It's about John Doe. Can we remove the restraints now?"

The nurse looked at her watch. "Well, it's been 24 hours since we put them on. Do you think he's calm enough?"

"Yes, ma'am, I do. In fact, I think the restraints only add to his frustration."

"Hmm. Perhaps." The nurse snapped her fingers. "Wait. I think the cast is supposed to come off today. Let me see about that." She found the doctor's notes for John Doe and read over them. "Yes, I'm right. Go ahead and get the plaster shears."

Lexie turned to leave for the utility room just as the elevator door opened as the Greek intern stepped out. She stared at the handsome young doctor, a vivid memory of him with the nurse in the closet.

"Good afternoon, ladies. My name is Dr. Kappas. Dr. Schroeder sent me to remove a cast from one of your patients."

Lexie looked back to Nurse Addams, whose face registered the same surprise Lexie felt.

"Dr. Kappas. I wasn't expecting you." She nodded her head toward Lexie. "However, Nurse Smithfield and I were on our way to remove the cast ourselves."

The doctor's eyes twinkled as he flashed a bright smile. "Then, good. I can save you the job." He aimed a gaze at Lexie. "Nurse Smithfield, would you please assist me?"

Lexie faced Nurse Addams for an answer. "That's fine with me," the head nurse said. "I was ending my shift anyway. Nurse Smithfield was on her way to get the supplies."

"Excellent," the doctor said, clasping his hands. He

looked up and down the hallway. "Where might I find the patient?"

"This way," said Lexie. "In that door. Wait here, and I'll get the supplies and meet you."

When Lexie returned with a tray bearing the plaster shears, a towel, and some alcohol, the doctor flashed her a charming smile. Lexie balanced the tray on one hand while retrieving the ward keys from her apron pocket. She unlocked the door and motioned for the doctor to go in before her.

Lexie led the doctor to John Doe's bed, and as they approached, the patient's brows knit with concern. Wanting to keep him calm, Lexie stepped to his bedside with the doctor following close beside her.

"John, this is Dr. Kappas. He's here to remove your cast."

John looked from her to the doctor, then back to her with questioning eyes.

"Why is this man in restraints?" Dr. Kappas asked. "Is he violent?" To his credit, the questions were asked in a low voice under his breath.

"There was a misunderstanding yesterday," Lexie said. "In fact, we were getting ready to remove them."

The doctor raised his eyebrow. "Before or after the cast comes off?"

Lexie focused on the patient. "John, if we take off your restraints now, you'll lie perfectly still while we remove the cast, won't you?"

Understanding crossed his face, and John nodded. "Yes."

Dr. Kappas didn't seem convinced. "Are you certain?" he asked Lexie.

"Yes, I promise John will behave," she said, steadying her gaze at John. She hoped she could trust him. What if she couldn't?

The consequences were too undesirable—for both her and for John.

"All right, then. Let's proceed." The doctor motioned to the strap nearest her.

Together, Lexie and the doctor unclasped and removed the restraints across the patient, John watching their every movement.

Once they were off, the tenseness in his body subsided, and he relaxed. He wiggled his fingers and moved his feet slightly to restore the circulation.

"Now, we need you to stay perfectly still while we cut the cast off," Lexie said to John.

Dr. Kappas took the plaster shears and, starting at John's wrist, began snipping away at the cast, stopping every five cuts for her to wipe off the blades. Lexie stood ready with a piece of gauze and the alcohol, watching the doctor work. As he leaned across the patient to get at the cast, she noticed a red mark on his collar and presumed it was lipstick from the nurse she'd seen him with before. Would anyone else notice, or would they know what it was?

John fixed his eyes on the process, watching as the cut was made all the way up to the elbow, following as the doctor moved to the section of the cast on the upper arm and began cutting down. Once Dr. Kappas reached the elbow, he opened up the cast sections, then cut the remaining portion apart. The doctor removed the cast and handed it to Lexie to place on the tray. The skin of John's newly released arm was pale compared to the rest of his body.

"Extend your arm. Slowly," the doctor ordered. John complied and straightened out his arm. "Feel any pain or discomfort?"

John shook his head. "No."

The doctor poked and prodded with his fingertips on John's arm. "Tell me if this hurts."

John remained still, showing no sign of pain.

"We'll X-ray the arm to make sure it healed." Dr. Kappas turned to Lexie. "Will you order it, please?"

"Yes, of course."

"Fine. Then we're finished here." He motioned to Lexie. "Nurse, would you please come with me?"

Lexie nodded, then touched John on the shoulder. "I'll be back to check on you later."

Once they were outside the door, the doctor changed his demeanor from professional to personal. "Nurse Smithfield, you are good with the patients."

"Thank you, sir. I try to be."

He peered at her face. "You know this man, this John Doe personally?"

Lexie frowned. "No, not at all. I don't even know his real name."

"Oh? John Doe is not his real name? Why do you call him that?"

Lexie realized the American custom of naming someone John Doe was unfamiliar to the doctor who hailed from another country, so she explained why they referred to the patient by the name.

"I see. Well, he appeared to be fond of you."

Lexie leaned back to look at the doctor. "Fond of me? Why would you say that?"

"The way he looked at you. I saw … how do you say … admiration in his eyes."

Her face heated with the oncoming blush. "I'm sorry, Doctor, but I think you are mistaken. The patient may appreciate my concern—nothing more."

The doctor offered her a charming smile and shrugged. "You don't see it? You should not underestimate your attraction, Nurse Smithfield. I can understand why any man would be captivated by you." He tugged her elbow. "Do you have a few moments to join me for some refreshment?"

Lexie pulled her elbow away. "No, Doctor. I do not. My time is devoted to my patients."

He drew back as if surprised by her reaction. "I see. Well, then, I will not interfere with your devotion. You should know I'm good friends with Dr. Henson, the Chief of Staff. I might be able to help you along with your degree."

Lexie's fingers withdrew the cross necklace she always wore tucked into her collar and fiddled with it while she listened to his suggestion that sounded like a threat and a bribe rolled into one. Dr. Kappas needed to be put in his place.

"Is that right?" Lexie said. "My grandfather was on the Board of Directors for the hospital when they hired Dr. Henson." She didn't like to flaunt her family's background, but now seemed like a good time to do so.

The doctor paled, then crimson raced up his neck, turning his face red. He cleared his throat. "Well, perhaps we'll run into each other in the hospital again."

"Perhaps." But not if she could help it.

The doctor headed toward the elevator and pushed the button, staring at the floor while he waited.

"Oh, Doctor?" Lexie called out.

"Yes?" He turned to her with a look of expectation.

"You have something red on your collar. You might want to wash that off before you *run* into anybody else."

Chapter Twenty-One

"Who was that man?" John Doe pushed himself up in the bed. "I haven't seen him before."

"Dr. Kappas, the doctor who removed your cast? He's a new intern from Greece."

John frowned. "I don't like him."

Lexie bit back her agreement. "Oh? Why not? Did he hurt you when he removed the cast?"

John shook his head. "No. I know his type, and I don't like them."

"His type?"

"Cocky. Thinks he's a hotshot."

Lexie stifled her laughter at John's accurate assessment of the doctor, but she couldn't help but smile. She'd never heard him talk so much. Maybe he was getting his memory back.

"He made a pass at you, didn't he?" John searched her face, which was feeling hotter by the minute.

"Now, John, don't get all worked up about the doctor. I doubt you'll see him again." At least not while she was on duty.

"Yeah? I hope you're right."

"So how does the arm feel?"

He raised and lowered the arm that had been in the cast. "It's kind of weak but doesn't hurt."

"That's good." She extended her hand to his. "Here. Squeeze my hand, but not too hard."

John responded with a firm but comfortable grip, and Lexie sensed warmth in his grasp as if he wanted to convey something more, and she gently slid her hand out.

"I'm very pleased with your progress, John Doe."

His eyes sparked. "No."

"No? No, what?"

"No, that's not my name. I'm not John Doe."

Lexie's pulse quickened. "Do you remember your name?"

He nodded. "John Michael Walker. I knew John Doe wasn't right, and I remembered. It's John Michael Walker."

"Well, it's very nice to meet you, Mr. John Michael Walker. So your name really is John."

"Yes, but nobody calls me John. People called me Mike."

"Mike. Do you know what this means? We can find your family and notify them of your whereabouts. I bet they are worried sick."

"I don't know. I don't remember them."

"It's okay. It'll come to you."

"Will you do me a favor?"

"Certainly. What would you like?"

"Would you sing that song again?"

"'Amazing Grace.'"

"Yes, 'Amazing Grace'. I think when I hear it, it reminds me of something, but I'm not sure what yet."

"I'll be happy to."

Lexie went about her duties while singing the hymn, bubbling with excitement over Mike Walker's realization of his name. She could just picture the happy reunion he would have with his family when they saw each other again. Or maybe with his girlfriend. Would he remember the rest of his history? *Lord, please help him remember.* Maybe hearing the hymn she sang would help. He said it reminded him of something, and that had to be a good sign.

The sun was setting outside, so Lexie began lowering the shades on all the windows, following the government guidelines to darken the city's lights. Each time she performed that task she wondered if it really helped. Would enemy planes come so far to bomb New York City? She found the notion hard to believe, but maybe the people in London hadn't believed they would be bombed either until it actually happened. A shudder ran down her back. If the city's dim-out helped protect them, she was more than happy to comply, along with millions of other Americans doing their patriotic duty.

As she lowered the shade beside Mike Walker, he reached out and touched her arm.

She turned to look as he searched her face. "Yes? Do you need something, Mike?" Saying his real name gave her a thrill of gratification.

"Will they send me back?" His eyes implored her.

She gulped. "Back—home?"

"No, back to war."

"I … I don't know. I hardly think you're well enough to go back to the service."

"But what if I get well enough? What if *they* think I'm well enough?" He was growing more agitated, and Lexie had to keep him calm. She patted his arm.

"Well, first, you'll go home to your family to fully recuperate. Then, by that time, the war will be over, and you won't have to worry about returning to service." She prayed she was right.

He quieted, then said, "My head hurts."

"I'll bring you some aspirin." She offered her most reassuring smile. "You'll feel better tomorrow, I promise. No need to worry." *Lord, please let my words be true.*

Friday morning, Lexie woke with a sense of expectation. Today was going to be a good day, and she looked forward to it. Why not—with Mike Walker's imminent recovery? Plus, she was excited to go back to visit the sisters in the Hamptons and have a whole weekend off for a change. She couldn't wait to share Mike's story with them. A little cloud tried to dampen her spirits, reminding her that Russell wouldn't be there, but she blew it away, determined to make the most of her time.

Her shift at the hospital began early, so she was about to leave just as Penny was waking up.

"Hey. You already up?" Penny stretched and glanced at the alarm clock on the nightstand between the twin beds.

"Yes. I have morning rounds today." Lexie waited by the door as Penny pushed herself up to a sitting position on the side of the bed.

Penny yawned. "Oh, that's right. It's Friday, isn't it? You're going to visit those ladies out on Long Island tomorrow, aren't you? Well, you have fun and be careful."

"Maybe I'll see you later at the hospital. Do you have plans tonight?"

Penny twisted her lip. "Plans? Me? Actually, I might take the ferry over to Jersey tomorrow and see the family since I have the day off."

"You should. I'm sure they'd like to see you. Bye now." Lexie closed the door and ran downstairs. The housemother stopped her before she got to the door.

"Nurse Smithfield, Nurse Harper wants to see you before you start your shift."

"She does?" Oh dear, was she in trouble?

The housemother laughed at Lexie. "Don't look so scared!"

Lexie hurried to Nurse Harper's office and tapped on her office door.

"Come in."

Lexie complied, and Nurse Harper said, "Have a seat, Nurse Smithfield."

A tremor of anticipation quickened her pulse as Lexie eased into the chair and recognized her test papers in the nursing instructor's hands.

"I'll get right to the point. Your test scores are excellent. You have a thorough grasp of the material taught in the second year of nursing school, and you should be very pleased with yourself."

"Thank you," Lexie said, surprised that she had done so well.

"Your instructors are also quite pleased with your classwork, and Nurse Addams tells me you've established good rapport with the patients in the psychiatric ward. I know that is important to you, as it is also important to us."

"Yes, ma'am, it is."

"I've discussed with the faculty your progress, and we all agree you can start the third year's curriculum beginning in August. Assuming you do as well with that part of your training, you should be able to graduate in December. Is that agreeable to you?"

Lexie took a deep breath to calm herself. "Yes, ma'am. That would be very agreeable to me. I really appreciate the opportunity to graduate early."

"Well, you've proven yourself. And since you already have a bachelor's degree, it makes sense that you shouldn't take as long to complete your nursing education."

Lexie couldn't help but smile with the happiness that filled her.

"I won't keep you any longer, but I wanted to let you know what we've decided."

Lexie stood and accepted the hand Nurse Harper extended. "Thank you very much."

"It is my pleasure, Nurse Smithfield, to reward a student who exemplifies such dedication. And don't worry about being late for your shift today. I've already informed Nurse Addams that I would be speaking beforehand this morning."

Lexie practically skipped over to the psych ward for her shift. She could graduate in December! That meant she and Russell could get married soon afterward, maybe even have a Christmas wedding. She couldn't wait to tell him. If only she could tell him in person.

Nurse Addams looked up at her as she exited the elevator. "Good morning, Nurse Smithfield. You look like you're having a good day."

Lexie smiled and nodded. "Oh, yes, ma'am. So far, it's been a wonderful day."

"I understand you might be graduating in six months. Congratulations."

"Thank you."

"I see in your notes here that John Doe's real name is John Michael Walker."

"Yes. He told me that people used to call him Mike."

"I told you that you had a magic touch with him. Did he tell you any more about himself?"

Shaking her head, Lexie said, "No. He couldn't remember anything else. The more he tried, the more frustrated he got—said he was getting a headache."

Nurse Addams gave a quick nod. "That's common for head injuries. You gave him something for that?"

"Aspirin. He was sleeping when I left last night."

"Good. I'm sure he'll be glad to see you again. In fact, they all will." Nurse Addams cocked her head. "So what's your secret?"

Lexie's felt a blush coming on. "My secret?"

"Well, whatever it is, the patients like you a lot. They ask about you when you're not here."

"They do?"

"Yes, they do. And you can check off 'establishing rapport with the patients' on your self-evaluation sheet."

"Thank you." Apparently, Nurse Addams had given Nurse Harper the same information. Lexie had to ask the question that had burned in her mind since the night before. "Nurse Addams, may I ask you a question?"

The nurse laid down the paperwork in her hand and gave Lexie her full attention. "Go ahead."

"If John, I mean Mike Walker, recovers from his injuries, will he be sent back to the war?"

"I can't say. He might. But he has a ways to go before that would happen. We still don't know about the severity of his head injury. Why?"

"I … I just wondered." For some reason, she didn't tell the head nurse Mike had asked the question first.

Nurse Addams leaned forward, crossing her arms on the desk, and directed her gaze at Lexie. "One of the difficult parts of this job is that we're supposed to care about our patients but not get so close that we can't let them go. Do you understand, Nurse Smithfield?"

Lexie affirmed with a nod, a knot forming in her stomach. "Yes, ma'am."

"Nobody said this work was easy, you know."

"I know. I didn't expect it to be." She didn't expect to care so much either. Lexie turned toward the ward, committed to her task.

"Oh, Nurse Smithfield?"

Lexie stopped and turned. "Yes?"

"Are you still singing for the patients?"

"Yes, well, so far, I've only sung one song. I used to hum, but then they asked me to sing it." Her face warmed.

"I see. What was the name of the song?"

"'Amazing Grace.' It's one of the few songs I've learned the words to—I guess because I've heard it for so long."

"Hmm. Well, that's a good choice. I'm glad the patients enjoy it. Give 'em a little religion while they're here."

Lexie hadn't thought about it that way. She was just singing a song that was in her heart. And apparently, many of the patients were familiar with the old hymn. She took a few steps, then stopped again.

"Nurse Addams? You know I'm off for the weekend, don't you?"

"Ah, yes, I see that. Well, better tell your patients, or they'll be looking for you. We don't want to let them down now, do we?"

"No, ma'am. I'll let them know."

The patients were in their regular places, for the most part, doing the same things they always did. She glanced around the room, and her breath caught. Mike Walker was walking slowly toward her.

"Look at you. You're up! And walking!"

Mike smiled, sending warmth through her. She'd never seen him standing and didn't realize how tall he was. Or how handsome. But here she stood, looking up at him, feeling a vulnerability she was unaccustomed to around the patients.

"I'm not running any races yet, though." He stopped and grabbed the nearest bed rail as he caught his breath.

"He wanted to surprise you." Bob's voice rang out across the room.

Lexie smiled, glancing from Bob back to Mike. "And he sure did. Would you like to rest a minute?" She grabbed a metal chair and pulled it over to him. "Your body's not used to exercise."

Mike lowered himself into it. "It sure isn't. Pathetic, isn't it, that I should tire doing so little."

"No, it's very good! You've progressed very well since you've been here—and in a relatively short time."

He blew out a breath, shaking his head. "You might believe that, but I don't. I think I should be much better now. I didn't hurt my legs, and look, my arm is fixed." He lifted his arm, displaying its range of motion.

"I know, but you've been lying in a bed for weeks, and your muscles have to get used to movement again. Don't worry, I'm sure by Monday when I see you again, you'll be getting around much better."

Mike frowned. "What day is today?"

"Today is Friday, June 26th, 1942."

"So you'll be gone tomorrow and the next day?"

"Yes, I have the weekend off. I'm going to visit friends in East Hampton." Should she have given him that much personal information?

"Oh." He pointed to her engagement ring. "Your fiancé going, too, I guess."

The heat moved up her neck. "No, he can't. Not this time." She decided to leave the rest of the information out.

Mike grew quiet and focused on the tile floor. Lexie felt guilty leaving the patients—as if she were going to abandon them.

"Would you like to go back to your bed or maybe join the men over there for a game of cards?"

He glanced from one choice to the other. "Think I'll check on the card game, maybe interest them in a game of poker." Mike gave her a wink, a gesture that surprised her. Who was this man? His newfound boldness was such a contrast to the person he'd been when he first arrived at the ward. Surely, his mental health was better than anyone in the ward—or at least it appeared to be.

He pushed himself up from the chair and walked slowly across toward the card game in progress. Then he stopped and turned. "Say, Nurse Smithfield. Can you do me a favor?"

"I can try." Hopefully, he wouldn't ask for anything

outside of her capacity.

Mike pointed to his hospital gown. "Can you get me some real clothes? I don't need to wear this dress anymore."

Lexie glanced around the room. Unlike "sick" wards, everyone in the room was dressed in street clothes, that is, everyone but Mike. But most of them had arrived in street clothes. Apparently, the remnants of his uniform had disappeared before he reached Belleview. "Yes, I'll try to find you some. I'll have to get your sizes."

One of the other men spoke up. "He looks like he wears a Size 15½ shirt and a Size 30 pants. I used to work in a men's clothing store."

"Sounds good to me," said Mike.

"I'll go write a request for that right now."

Lexie left the ward and told Nurse Addams what Mike had requested. "Well, that's a good sign. He wants to dress normally, so he doesn't see himself as sick."

"No, he doesn't."

"I'll send one of the attendants out to pick up some clothes for him. I'm glad to hear he's interacting with the other patients. If he doesn't have another outburst, he can be transferred to another part of the hospital, at least until we find his family. We don't know who to release him to or where they are yet."

Lexie wanted to be happy for Mike, happy that he would be released soon. But a touch of melancholy threatened her joy, and she realized she would miss him. He didn't act happy to hear she would be gone all weekend either. Nurse Addams was right. She couldn't get so close to a patient and had to let him go. All she could do was pray he'd be all right. And she could be thankful he didn't have to stay in the hospital forever, and that someday he could return to a normal life, whatever that was for him.

Lexie went through her morning routine as usual but looked forward to getting away to Long Island for the weekend. She prepared and administered the midmorning medications, then served lunch to the patients and collected the dishes afterward. When the elevator door opened and two attendants exited, one held a bag from Gimbel's. "Did you need clothes for a man?" he asked, handing her the bag.

"Yes, thank you."

Lexie opened the package and removed the tags and pins from the clothes—a short sleeve white shirt and a pair of gray trousers, plus underwear, socks, and a belt. She held them up and shook them out. Nurse Addams walked up and eyed the clothes.

"They need ironing," said Lexie.

"We keep one in the utility room cabinet if you want to press the clothes before you give them to him."

When Lexie presented the freshly pressed clothes to Mike, he considered them, then nodded. "Not sure if they're my style, but they'll do. Thanks."

"You're welcome. I'll pull the curtain if you want to put them on now."

"Sure."

Lexie busied herself straightening the beds with her back to Mike while he changed. At the sound of the metal curtain rings sliding along the rod, she turned.

"Well? What do you think?" Mike stood smiling with his hands extended to the side.

Lexie crossed her arms and tilted her head. "I think you look quite nice."

"Nice? That's all? Not debonair?"

She gave him a wry smile. "Oh, yes, very. Yes, that's the word, debonair."

"Yeah, well, it's better than that hospital gown. At least now I feel like a man."

And he certainly looked like one too. She could only imagine how nice he'd look in a uniform. But what was his style anyway?

"Okay, well now that you've regained your manhood, I need to leave. My shift is over."

Mike studied her a moment. "That's right. You're going to Long Island. Well, have a good time."

"I will. And I'll see you Monday."

Chapter Twenty-Two

When Lexie returned to the nurses' residence that afternoon, she called the Maurice sisters, and Peg answered the phone.

"Hello, Peg? This is Lexie."

"Hello, dear. Please don't tell me you're calling to say you can't come." Lexie heard her muffled voice say, "It's Lexie" and knew she was talking to her sister.

"On the contrary. I just want to confirm with you that I will be there tomorrow morning."

"Excellent. When will your train arrive?"

"I should be there by ten."

"Good. I'll send Homer to pick you up."

"I hate to put you out. And I really don't mind walking."

"Nonsense! We'll come get you. We'll have brunch when you arrive."

"Sounds great. I'm really looking forward to seeing you."

"And we're looking forward to seeing you, too, dear. You

don't have to go back early this time, do you?"

"No, thank God. I can stay until Sunday afternoon."

"Excellent. Well, you be careful, and we'll see you tomorrow."

"See you soon." Lexie was smiling when she hung up the phone. She couldn't wait to share her news with them. Going to see them was like going home, although she'd never lived there. Perhaps someday, she'd be able to welcome them to her own home, wherever that would be.

She pulled her small suitcase out of the closet and started packing. She wouldn't need much for the weekend—just a couple of casual outfits and a dress for church on Sunday. She threw her gloves, dress shoes, and hat in, then pushed the latches down to close the suitcase, hearing them snap into place. She'd run into Penny during the day and found out that a group of nurses was going to see a movie tonight. Perhaps she'd take Penny up on her invitation and join them later. She glanced at her watch—only 4:30. Maybe she should have taken the evening train to Long Island instead.

Oh well, too late now. She'd already told them she was coming tomorrow. Maybe now would be a good time to write a letter to Russell. She sat down at the small desk, then took a sheet of stationery out of the single desk drawer. But she'd only written "Dear Russell" when a craving for a milkshake set her taste buds on alert. Maybe Penny would be back soon, and they could go together. But it would be another hour before Penny finished work.

Lexie drummed her fingers on the desk. Should she wait on Penny? She didn't really want to go alone. Was it because she was scared? Because Russell wouldn't be there? No, she wasn't afraid. Outside the window, a darkened sky threatened rain. Maybe one of the other student nurses could go with her. She left her room and walked down the hall to see if anyone else was there. Not finding anyone, she went down to the living room and found Nancy, another student, standing by the telephone.

"Hi, Nancy." Lexie didn't know the shy girl well, but they shared a class together. "Would you like to go to Mack's with me and get a shake?"

"Oh, hi, Lexie. Sorry, but I can't go right now. I'm waiting for my boyfriend to call." She looked down at the phone as if willing it to ring. "He said he'd call after work and let me know if he could see me this weekend before he ships out." She lifted her gaze to Lexie. "Maybe another time, though."

"Sure." Now what? The more she told herself not to go, the more the milkshake summoned.

Oh, bother. She'd just run down to the diner real fast and quench her craving, then hurry back. Thunder rolled in the distance when she walked outside, so she rushed down the street, hoping to beat the rain.

Only a few people were seated at the counter, but she chose an empty booth instead, preferring to be alone. When the waitress came over, Lexie decided she was hungry too, so she ordered her regular club sandwich, along with the chocolate milkshake. Waiting for her food, Lexie stared out the glass at the traffic and pedestrians passing by. She sighed, wondering what Russell must be doing. Five hours difference meant it was around 10:00 at night in England by now. He was probably playing with the band before hundreds of servicemen at that moment. She wished she could see him there. Was he enjoying himself? Did he miss her?

"Hello again."

Lexie jumped at the male voice and jerked her head to see Cal Miller standing by the booth.

He smiled. "I didn't mean to scare you." He motioned to the opposite seat with the hat he held in his hand. "May I?"

"Yes, of course. I thought you had left town." She hadn't expected to run into him again, but how could she tell him not to sit with her?

"I'm leaving next week."

"You haven't been in a hurry to get there, have you?"

He shrugged. "Why leave here before I have to? There's not much going on in a factory town."

"I guess not. So, what have you been doing with yourself while you've been here?" She didn't mention seeing him around town when she and Russell were out.

Cal glanced out the plate glass window. "Saw some shows, heard some bands, you know, the things you do in New York City."

Lexie's food came, and Cal just ordered coffee. He looked at her food and said, "Early dinner or late lunch?"

She smiled. "Sort of both, but mainly dinner. I only came in here for a milkshake but decided to eat too. I have to get back soon."

He gave a slight shake of his head. "I promise I won't keep you." Lifting his cup, he stared at the liquid, then took a sip before saying, "How are things at the hospital?"

Lexie nodded. "Good, very good. But I'm glad to get away for the weekend."

Cal lifted his eyebrows. "Where are you going? Isn't your fiancé overseas?"

She squirmed a little in her seat. Wasn't that question a

bit too personal?

"I'm going out to the Hamptons. I believe I told you I had friends there." At least he knew she wouldn't be available if that's what he was hinting at.

"Ah yes, the people you had been visiting the first time I saw you."

"Yes, those people."

"Are you planning to stay there for the Fourth of July and watch fireworks?"

She frowned at his remark. "No, well, I can't stay all week, but I might go back for the Fourth. Of course, you know there won't be any fireworks, don't you? The government has banned them because of the blackout." Didn't everyone know that?

"Oh yes, I forgot. That's too bad, isn't it? Won't you miss them?"

Shaking her head, she said, "No, not really. When the war's over, we'll go back to things the way they were before."

He cocked his head. "Will we now?"

Cal was acting strange, not as carefree as he'd been before. She took a bite of her sandwich and ate quickly, trying not to choke. Grabbing her drink, she took a sip before replying. "You don't think so?"

"How can things ever go back the way they were before the war? So many things have changed."

His morose tone was alarming. Did she hear a tinge of regret in his voice?

"I think we can change what we want to change, whether for good or for bad. And what we can't change, we learn to adjust to."

"You always look on the bright side, as they say."

"Why not? I prefer to be happy, so I try to focus on the good things, not the bad." Wasn't that what the minister had said in church?

"But is that realistic? Are you pretending bad things don't exist?"

"No, not at all. In the hospital, I deal with bad things all the time—people sick, injured, or dying. But we do the best we can to help them. And we hope and pray for a favorable outcome."

He chuckled. "There you go again, praying. So, did you remember to pray for me?"

Was he making fun of her or was he serious? Although his tone of questioning was irritating, she answered him truthfully. "Yes, Cal. You asked me to, so I did. May I ask you a question?"

He lifted his eyebrows. "Go ahead."

"Has something happened to make you sad? You're acting different today."

His gaze returned to stare outside the window at the black sky. "No. Nothing's happened—yet. I've just been doing a lot of thinking." He returned his gaze to her. "Sorry to bother you."

Lexie shook her head. "It's no bother. I just wish I could help." Maybe he was just lonely. "Are your friends gone?"

"Friends? I have no friends here—unless you allow me to call you a friend."

Lexie's face warmed. Was it safe to be his friend? "Oh, I saw you with a couple of other men, and I assumed you were friends."

His brows knit together. "No, they're not my friends. Just business associates."

"I see." Lexie finished her sandwich, then picked up her milkshake, wanting to savor the rest. But the conversation had taken some of the enjoyment out of the concoction.

Outside the diner, the clouds gave a premature appearance of nightfall. Lexie's mood had darkened as well. She fought the feeling of doom that Cal emitted and sought a way to cheer him up. It was her turn to ask a personal question. "Have you talked to your family?"

His face fell in answer to her. "No. Why do you ask?"

"I remember you said you hadn't seen them for a while. I thought you might call them."

He lowered his gaze to the coffee cup cradled in his large hands.

Had she overstepped her bounds? When he didn't answer, she assumed she had. "Well, I better go. I want to get back before the rain starts." She grabbed her purse and slid out of the booth. "I hope things go well for you in your new job, Cal."

He slapped two quarters on the table, then exited the booth also. Standing beside her, he set his fedora on his head. He searched her face. "Lexie, you said you wished to help me."

Her body tensed. What was he going to ask her to do? "Yes, I did."

"You have. You have helped me."

Lexie angled her head as she looked up at him. "I have? Well, I don't know what I did, but I'm glad."

He took her free hand and enclosed it with both of his. "Be careful, Lexie. I hope God protects you from all the bad things in the world."

What a strange thing to say, and the third time today

someone told her to be careful.

"He will, Cal. He will. Goodbye."

"Goodbye, my friend."

Lexie left the diner, glancing back over her shoulder at Cal, standing outside the door. He gave her a little wave, and she turned back around. As she hurried back to the residence, she could smell rain. And something else. Her skin crawled with a sense of being watched. Was Cal still watching her? She jerked around, but he was nowhere in sight. Everyone else had their heads down, scurrying down the sidewalk as fat raindrops fell from the clouds. Why did she have that feeling? Who else would be watching her? A loud clap of thunder made her jump, and her heart raced. She chastised herself. *Lexie, why are you so suspicious?*

She jogged the rest of the way to the residence just as the storm commenced.

Karl watched Lexie hurry away, then turned around and bumped into Oscar.

"You are still here. Are you abandoning your mission or just sharing secrets with the woman?"

The obnoxious baker was tailing him. "I do not answer to you, Oscar."

"I warned you about the girl. She is a problem." Oscar growled.

Karl pierced Oscar with his gaze. "Leave her alone, Oscar. She knows nothing."

"I don't believe you, or you would have already left."

Karl clenched his teeth. "I don't care if you believe me

or not, but leave her alone. She is innocent."

"Like all Americans, yes?"

Karl shoved Oscar aside. "Get out of my way, Oscar."

As he walked away, he heard Oscar's voice. "Remember, I warned you."

Karl's decision was made.

While the band took a break, Russell stood and stretched. Too bad he didn't play a horn. Those guys got to stand up during the performance. Wasn't quite feasible when you played the piano.

He sauntered over to the back door where the other guys had gone outside for a smoke. A blast of chilly, damp air hit him as he opened the door. The weather in England took some getting used to. He decided against going outside, so he turned around and went to get a drink from the refreshment table. Gloria Bentley, one of the Hollywood starlets who had come along with the USO tour, stood by the table.

She gave him a gleaming smile as he approached. "Hey, sailor. What brings you here?"

Russell glanced around to see who she was talking to, and she laughed.

"I'm talking to you, Piano-man. I haven't seen you with Artie's band before. You must be new."

"Is it that obvious?" Russell picked up a glass and took a sip, the cold beverage refreshing after the long set of songs.

She angled her head toward him. "Oh, just a little—like a fish out of water."

Russell's face warmed, and he ran his finger around his collar and attempted to loosen his tie. "I've played with Artie's band at the USO dances in New York when he needed a piano player. But I have to admit that this is my first gig overseas."

"So why aren't you hanging out with the band? You don't like their company?"

Attempting to appear casual by laughing, he felt like a teenager around a girl he had a crush on. Gloria was one of the most beautiful women he'd ever seen, and she oozed "star." Her jet-black hair gleamed in waves that perfectly framed her ivory skin. Green eyes glittered when she spoke, lighting up the room around her. She wore a shimmering gold, form-fitting evening dress with exposed bare shoulders, a total contrast to the olive drab Army uniforms of the audience who were completely captivated by her presence. Russell had been around a lot of wealthy, famous people in his years at the Jekyll Island Club, but associating with celebrities in her realm was new to him, especially one so breathtakingly gorgeous. He was on unfamiliar ground, and she had read him like a book.

He swallowed the lump in his throat. "No, that's not it. I really like Artie and the boys. Most of them went outside to cool off and smoke, and I was planning to join them, but I don't care for the weather outside, and I don't smoke either." Russell affirmed the promise he'd made to Lexie. True, she wasn't there to keep an eye on him, but he knew he'd made a promise, and that was enough. Besides, he felt better since he quit and didn't have a stale taste in his mouth all the time like he used to.

"Well, if you're lonely, I can keep you company." She

opened her arms out to the side. I'm alone too." Russell's gut churned. What was she offering? There were a million guys that would drop to their knees if she made that offer to them. He didn't mean to stare but wondered if he looked bug-eyed with his mouth gaping open at her suggestion. But his eyes wouldn't move away from her as if they were magnetized to her lovely face, not to mention her perfect hourglass shape. He picked up a napkin and mopped his brow with it. How did it get so hot in here?

Her playful laughter broke the tension. "So what's your name, Piano-man?" She no doubt knew the effect she had on men and enjoyed every moment of it.

Russell blew out a breath before answering. "Russell. Russell Thompson." He didn't ask hers. Everyone knew who she was.

She extended her hand. "Hi, Russell. I'm Gloria."

As if she needed to tell him. He took her hand, planning to give it a masculine shake, but she squeezed his hand like she was molding clay. "Nice to meet you, Gloria." He eased his hand out of hers, but the heat she'd transferred continued to travel up his arm. *Control, Russell. Pull yourself together.* He glanced toward the bandstand, hoping the rest of the musicians had returned.

"Where are you from, Russell? Did I detect a Southern accent?"

He chuckled, pretending to be composed. "Maybe you did. I grew up in Georgia."

"Ah, so that's what I heard." She eased closer to him. "Ever since *Gone with the Wind*, I've thought southern accents were sexy."

A flash blinded him for a second as the light on the

photographer's camera popped. "You two get a little closer together!" The *Stars and Stripes* reporter motioned with his hand.

Gloria smiled and slid her arm around Russell's neck before he knew what was happening.

Another pop and flash. "There. Got it." He grinned and gave a thumbs up before scurrying away.

"Hey, Russ! We're going back on!" Nick's voice couldn't have been more welcome at the moment.

He glanced at the stage and stepped away from her. "Time to go back to work."

"I'm right behind you," she said.

Russell hoped she'd stay there and keep her distance. In the first half of the show, her rendition of "Chattanooga Choo Choo" had gotten rousing applause from the male-dominated audience. Thankfully, he couldn't watch her while he played. Otherwise, he'd surely miss a chord. As he took his seat on the piano bench, one of the trumpet players leaned over to him and said, "Hsss! Hot stuff!" and shook his hand like he'd touched a hot stove. Russell focused on the keyboard and waited for Artie's command to begin playing. The first number was orchestra-only, then Artie introduced Gloria again. She slinked across the stage to thunderous applause, hoots, and whistles, displaying her sparkling smile as she scanned the room. After several peppy tunes, the band began the next number, "I'm in the Mood for Love."

Gloria's throaty voice began to sing the song while soldiers waved and called out, "Me too!" She stepped off the stage and strolled along the front row of soldiers, grabbing a soldier by the chin as she sang directly to him. More hooting continued while she sang and played the crowd. Russell focused on the piano keys but was aware of her movement. He was unprepared for her return to the stage when she walked over to the piano and put her hand on his shoulder. He looked up at her and smiled like a good showman should. The *Stars and Stripes* photographer snapped a picture of them as he made his way through the room.

Finally, the song and the set were over. Artie told the crowd "Good night," the band stood and bowed to a standing ovation, and Gloria waved goodbye to the crowd. The soldiers filed out as the band members put away their instruments. Louie yelled, "Who wants to go to the pub with me?"

Everyone else in the band chimed in, saying they'd go. Russell decided to join them, too, because he was hungry and had no idea where else he could grab a bite to eat. He glanced around and didn't see Gloria. Thank God, she was gone. He wasn't interested in fending her off anymore. When the guys got all their things packed away, they headed out the door and through the gates of the base, then walked three blocks down the street to the pub on the corner. The guys spread out in the small room, grabbing chairs where they could find them. Some of the locals played darts in the back corner and eyed them as they settled into their seats. Russell got the idea that they weren't completely welcome.

"Pints for everyone!" said Harry as the waitress came over to his table. She took food orders from all of them and returned to the bar to turn them in. Russell sat back in his chair and took in the pub surroundings.

Sal leaned over to him. "Say, Russ. That Gloria doll was making a move on you. What you got that I don't have?" He bumped Russell with his shoulder and laughed.

Nick sat across the table from them and chimed in. "Yeah, man, I thought she was going to sit in your lap." The guys guffawed, and others made comments.

"She can sit on my lap anytime she wants to!" Louie said.

Nick lowered his voice and motioned toward the door. "Here's your chance, then."

Heads turned to the entrance where Gloria had just arrived. She had exchanged her evening gown for wide-leg trousers and a plaid jacket, but she was no less lovely. In Russell's opinion, she was even more so with her natural beauty coming through. And her ordinary clothes made her less threatening than the body-hugging evening gowns she wore on stage.

She waved to the guys and came over to Russell's table. Nick jumped up and said, "Here, take my chair." She smiled and accepted, sitting across the table from Russell.

"What are you guys having?"

"Ale. You want me to order you one?" said Harry.

"Sure. Sounds good. A girl can get pretty thirsty singing."

Harry waved the waitress over and ordered the drink for Gloria.

"It was a good show," said Artie. "And of course, you were fabulous, as always."

Gloria smiled, scanning the faces around the table. "Couldn't do it without a great band, though." She lifted the heavy glass of ale and chugged, her eyes wide in surprise.

"This stuff is warm," she said.

"That's the way they like it here," said Harry. "Maybe it's because the weather is cold so much."

"Only one more night here, then we go to another base,"

said Artie. "I believe the next one is in Northern Ireland."

"I always did want to travel," she said. "Just didn't expect to be doing it during a war."

"Yeah, me too," said Louie. "Where are you from, Gloria? I mean, originally."

"Iowa. I'm a long way from there now!"

The guys laughed with her, and Russell chuckled as well. Dressed as casually as she was, picturing her in Iowa was not difficult. She behaved much more natural and believable than when she had on her glamour-girl get-up. Was it all an act? His mind shifted to Lexie. She was always natural, even when dressed up. He loved the way she was the same sincere person to everyone and everywhere. He smiled, as memories of Lexie drifted through his thoughts. Funny how being around another beautiful woman made him appreciate Lexie even more. He checked his watch, noting the local time as 10:30. Was Lexie working tonight, or was she at the residence? It sure would be nice to hear her voice, but getting a call to the U.S. was difficult, and now wouldn't be a good time to try anyway.

As Russell finished his shepherd's pie, he eyed Gloria, who'd already consumed a pint of ale and had started on a second one. She giggled and joked, her voice becoming more slurred. If she didn't stop soon, she'd feel pretty bad tomorrow, if not later tonight. He pushed away from the table, pulled out his wallet, and put some money down.

"Leaving so soon?" Nick asked.

"Sorry to break up the party, but I think I'll head back."

"Man, it's early!" one of the band members called out.

"He's not used to our hours, you know. He had regular hours before," said Harry.

Russell smiled and nodded. He was indeed used to working different hours.

Artie stood and shook Russell's hand. "Great job tonight, Russell. Go on and get some rest. We'll try not to wake you when we get in."

Russell doubted they would be quiet after a couple more hours drinking in the pub, but such were the disadvantages of sharing one room with a bunch of guys who were used to staying out late. Russell said good night to the guys and was about to leave when he was pressed to get Gloria out of there. Fresh air would do her good.

"Gloria, would you like me to walk you back to your barracks?"

Her eyes sparkled from the effects of the alcohol, and her smile widened. "Why sure, Piano-man. I'd love for you to walk me home." She wiggled out of her seat and stood, swaying a bit before one of the guys reached up to steady her. Russell hoped she'd be able to walk all the way back. He would rather not carry her.

The other band members laughed and called out suggestive remarks, which Russell ignored. He waved goodbye and took her arm, but she turned and blew an exaggerated kiss to everyone in the room. He opened the door and gently pushed her out.

She was unsteady on her feet as they started walking, and she clung to Russell's arm. After they'd walked a few yards, she gazed over at him and said, "Polio?" She motioned to his foot, the one that had rendered him unfit for military service. The one that was hurting right now, thanks to the chilly damp weather.

He shook his head. "Nope, hunting accident when I was

a kid."

"Oh, sorry. My dad had a limp like yours, and his was from polio." She squeezed his arm. "Hey, I hope I didn't embarrass you."

"Don't worry. I've lived with it a long time, so I'm used to it now." But he preferred no one noticed. However, sometimes it was hard to disguise it.

"You're a handsome guy, you know. The limp doesn't bother me at all."

So why did she mention it?

"You're different, I mean, not just the limp, but the way you act. You're not like the other guys."

"An oddball, huh?"

"No, not different in a bad way," she slurred. "You're a good guy—I can tell. I've been around enough men to tell the difference."

"So I guess that's a compliment?" He didn't mind being pigeonholed as a good guy. Unfortunately, there were plenty of men who didn't fit that category. And she'd apparently known many of them.

"Sure. That's why I like you." She snuggled closer to his side like she was trying to get inside his jacket.

"I heard your boyfriend was Blake Johnson." The movie star had been linked to several actors, to his knowledge. Russell hoped the mention would tear her focus away from himself.

Gloria waved her hand like she was shooing a bug away. "Blake is a dear friend, but we're not ... like that. I'm unattached, in case you're interested."

She clung to him tighter still when they stopped at the guard gate and showed their IDs. The serviceman on duty ogled Gloria before he let them pass, no doubt drawing an incorrect conclusion about their association.

"Where are your barracks? I'll walk you to it." His father taught him to be a gentleman, even though Gloria wasn't behaving like a lady.

"Over there." She smiled demurely, pointing down the road.

He nodded, then walked her to the building. When they reached it, she turned to face him and leaned into him, gazing into his eyes with lust in hers.

Russell placed his hands on her shoulders and gently pushed her away. "Gloria, I'm flattered that you're attracted to me. Any man would be. However, I have a fiancée, someone I love very much, and she's the only woman for me."

Gloria stepped back, her face turning crimson. "So that's it. You've got a girl. Well, she's a lucky one." She waggled her finger at him. "You tell her she's got a good man, and good men are hard to find."

"Depends on where you look."

A look of surprise crossed her face. "Yeah? Maybe you're right." She extended her hand. "Well, good night, Piano-man. Thanks for walking me back."

"You're welcome, Gloria. Hope you get a good night's sleep."

She responded by planting a kiss on his cheek. He sure hoped it didn't leave a lipstick mark. That would be difficult to explain.

She wrestled with the door handle, so he reached out and opened it for her, shoving the door open and motioning for her to go inside. She took a step, turned, and gave a little wave before going in.

Russell breathed a sigh of relief. A man could easily be tempted by a woman so beautiful, even a "good" guy. But why did she throw herself at men? Why would someone with her looks feel like she had to work so hard to get attention? He shook his head. What a shame.

Thank God, he had a good woman waiting for him back home, and right now, he needed to write her a letter.

Chapter Twenty-Three

*L*exie walked under the huge Victory banners hanging at Penn Station, eager to board the train to Long Island. A relaxing weekend was on her agenda with no responsibilities until she returned on Monday.

The thunderstorm last night had been brief, so she'd taken Penny up on her invitation to join the other girls for a movie. Scenes from *This Above All* flashed through her mind as she rode the train out of the city. Tyrone Power portrayed a British soldier who was a conscientious objector, but he'd fallen in love with a wealthy woman played by Joan Fontaine who had joined the WAAF, a British women's auxiliary of the Royal Air Force. Lexie couldn't help but compare her and Russell's relationship to the onscreen couple. In the end, the hero changes his mind, but it might be too late, and the last scene is of the couple getting married in a hospital.

Of course, the other nurses had plenty to say about the last scene that ended with an air raid alarm going off as the screen went black. Lexie ached for the movie couple who had such a difficult time getting back together. But the ending had shocked them all. No one knew if the couple survived the attack. And the fact that the movie took place in Britain did little to comfort her. Even though the Nazi flyover bombardment had ended, occasional random air raids over London and other targets still happened. Would the military bases where Russell was going have a chance of being bombed? Her heart pricked with the possibility that he might be hurt.

When she arrived at the Amagansett station, Homer was there to meet her and take her back to the Maurice sisters' summer cottage. The weather was lovely, and she hoped to spend some time at the beach. The sight of the cottage always made her smile with its gray wood-shingled exterior, its windows and wide front porch painted a contrasting white. Window boxes on the balconies were planted with cheerful red geraniums, so befitting the personalities of the sisters. Homer stopped the car on the driveway near the front door. Lexie walked toward the porch, while Homer retrieved her overnight suitcase from the car.

But as she reached for the front door, she heard Peg's voice call from outside. "Lexie! We're back here!"

Lexie followed the sound of the sister's voice to the backyard and halted when she found the two women. "What on earth are you two doing?"

Marian was kneeling on the ground, her straw sunbonnet covering her head while she poked her fingers in the dirt. Peg stood nearby leaning on a hoe. Both women wore men's dungarees rolled up to mid- calf and casual shirts also rolled up to the elbows. Lexie gaped at the unusual sight of the two women in working-class clothes.

"Why, we're making a Victory garden." Peg beamed with satisfaction.

"But … why? Doesn't the Maidstone Market have everything you need?"

Marian looked up from under her hat brim. "Most the time it does. But that's not the important thing. We want to do our part for the country and supply our own needs—not take food away from the soldiers."

Lexie doubted the sisters would ever eat enough to take food away from the military, but then everyone was being asked to do what they could.

"Would you like to help us, Lexie? If you don't have gardening clothes, we have an extra pair of dungarees you can use," said Peg.

How could she turn them down? If these women could get their hands dirty, so could she. "Sure. But you'll have to tell me what to do. I've never done any gardening before."

"We used to help our grandfather in his garden a long time ago, didn't we, sister?" Marian nodded to Peg.

"Yes, we did. He was what they call a 'gentlemen farmer.' He enjoyed seeing things he planted grow." Peg opened a seed packet.

"Like his investments." Marian winked at Lexie.

"Sister! That's a good one." Peg chortled. "But I must agree with you. He did like to see everything grow."

"So what are you planting?" Lexie asked.

"Tomatoes, cucumbers, beans, radishes, and carrots to start. Homer says he wants to plant some corn too. Good thing he's helping us. He's more experienced growing things than we are." Peg pointed to various sections of the marked-off area.

"And Peg, don't forget we're planting squash and peppers too," Marian added.

"Oh, yes, I forgot about those."

The sisters' enthusiasm was contagious. "Well, I look forward to your harvest. I'll go inside and change. Be right out to help you." This weekend might not be as relaxing as Lexie had expected, but it would be invigorating, no doubt.

After a couple of hours of hoeing and planting, the women stood back to assess their progress. The work had been exhilarating, not tiring as Lexie first thought. They had chatted about the war and its effects on the local area while they worked.

"I think that will do just fine!" said Peg, brushing her gloves together to shake off the dirt. She handed her hoe to Homer. "Thanks, Homer. You can put these things away now."

"We did good work, didn't we?" Marian nodded.

"We make a good team. Thanks for letting me join you. This was fun," Lexie added, picking up the shovel and giving it to Homer.

"I'm hungry. Let's get some lunch," Peg said, then led the way inside. After washing up and changing clothes, they rejoined each other on the front porch for lunch.

As the women sat in an alcove created by one of the towers that flanked each side of the house, they were fanned by a light breeze off the ocean. Jane carried out a tray with plates of chicken salad finger sandwiches and cups of vichyssoise, while the women helped themselves to tea from the serving cart.

"Have you heard anything from Russell, Lexie?" Peg asked, helping herself to one of the sandwiches. A gust of wind blew across the lawn, tempting their linen napkins to fly away. Peg tucked hers between her knees for safekeeping.

Lexie shook her head. "No, not yet. He hasn't been gone long enough for me to receive a letter. And it's pretty difficult to make a phone call."

"I'm sure you miss him." Marian sipped some tea between bites. "And I'm sure he misses you too."

"I do, and I miss being able to talk to him every day. Oh, I forgot to tell you. I have news."

"Yes? Well, don't keep us in suspense! What's your news?" Marian leaned forward.

"If all goes well, I should be able to graduate in December!"

Peg clapped her hands. "December? How wonderful! I know Russell will be glad to hear the news."

"I think so too. But I had to write a letter to tell him, and I don't know how long it will take for him to get it."

"Lexie, maybe you could get married in December!" Marian's eyes gleamed with excitement.

"A Christmas wedding! Is that what you're thinking, sister?" Peg clasped her hands.

"Wouldn't it be wonderful?" Marian exclaimed, then glanced at Lexie. "Would you like that, Lexie? Do you think Russell would like a Christmas wedding?"

"I love the idea, and I bet Russell would too."

Peg grew serious. "I hope he doesn't stay overseas very long. I don't like the idea of you being in the city by yourself."

"Don't worry, Peg. I'm seldom by myself. I'm usually surrounded by other nurses." The sisters would be upset to know she went to the diner by herself, much less talked with strange men.

"Well, I'd feel much better if he were there to be your escort."

So would she, but she was getting more confident about getting around without him.

"I hope he's happy over there. We knew how unhappy he was about not being able to join up," Marian said, looking at her sister.

"You did? He told you this?"

"Not in so many words, but we could tell he was frustrated. With the paper talking about all our boys in the service, he's been feeling left out, kind of useless," said Peg.

"I wish he didn't feel that way." Lexie sighed as she stirred her soup. "What he does with the USO *is* important."

"We believe so too, but he doesn't think it's enough. After all, he's not putting himself in any danger when he performs here in the States." Marian lifted her teacup and took a sip.

Lexie looked up, eyes widened. "Do you think that's why he went overseas? To put himself in danger?" And she thought he was safe there.

"No, I don't think the USO goes places that are dangerous. Thank God, the Nazis' bombing blitz of England is over. But maybe he did want to be closer to the action," Peg said.

"I guess I never realized he was that unhappy being here. He's always so upbeat, and he acted as though he liked his job at the hotel." But Lexie remembered the conversation they'd had about pretending to be happy. Maybe she hadn't paid enough attention to what he said.

"Russell's spent his life catering to other people. In his business, he has to be pleasant to people, even those that are difficult." Marian pointed her spoon at Lexie.

Peg nodded as she cradled her teacup. "Oh, isn't that the truth, sister? I can remember several times at Jekyll when he had to diffuse a club member. I'm afraid they could be very demanding, even unreasonable."

"That's right. Remember that time Sebastian Cromley got so fired up about a waiter that spilled soup all over him? As if it were the poor man's fault for tripping over Cromley's cane that was lying on the floor. Russell came to the poor waiter's rescue and was able to calm Cromley down. But Cromley wanted the waiter fired to begin with. Russell never lost his patience, though, and smiled politely the whole time." Marian chuckled. "That Cromley could be such a curmudgeon!"

Lexie smiled, picturing Russell in that situation. His positive attitude was one of the things she loved most about him, and it helped keep her own attitude in check.

"And you'd never know his foot bothers him," Peg said. "He acts like it's not an inconvenience, but I know it is."

"Such a shame that had to happen to him, and so young too." Marian shook her head.

Lexie's heart pinched hearing about Russell's foot. She knew it had kept him out of the military. "It made him 4F," she said.

"But I've never heard him complain about it, have you, Peg?"

Peg shook her head. "Not a whit."

"You know, Lexie, I think he wanted to make you proud of him," Marian said.

Lexie drew back. "You do? But why do you think that?"

Marian set down her cup and faced Lexie. "Well, look at you. You've got a passion to help others, and you're doing something about it by becoming a nurse. He doesn't have anything like that. He's just as passionate about serving his country, but he can't serve the way he wants to."

"But why impress me? He knows I love and respect him like he is."

"Lexie, you're a beautiful woman, and you could have your pick of many affluent young men. Russell's not wealthy, so maybe he doesn't feel like he deserves you," Peg added.

"That's nonsense," Lexie asserted. "I've never been interested in any of them."

The sisters exchanged glances. "Never?"

Lexie's face flamed when she remembered the crush she'd once had on a wealthy boy when she was in college, a boy who'd turned out to be an insensitive playboy. Thank God, she'd realized his true character before she'd made a terrible mistake and really fallen for him.

"No, not seriously. Russell's the only man I've ever been in love with—the only man I ever will be."

"We love Russell. He's a fine, upstanding young man, not to mention handsome, and there are many women that would like to be in your shoes," said Marian.

Scenes of women flirting with Russell played in her mind. He was always polite to them, but he assured Lexie he only had eyes for her.

"I know, and I'm thankful he is loyal to me." She tucked a windblown curl back into the scarf she'd tied around her hair. "I'm afraid I haven't been as aware of his anxiety as you are. I've been so wrapped up in my studies and patients at the hospital. Maybe I haven't been a good listener."

Peg leaned forward and patted Lexie on the knee. "Don't worry, Lexie, you'll have plenty of time to listen when he comes back."

Would she? When would that be?

"Sometimes I wonder if we should have gotten married as soon as we came back from Jekyll Island. But I started school right away and didn't think it would be fair to try to start a marriage while I was studying and spending so much time away from home."

"Honey, it's not your fault. I'm not sure Russell was ready yet anyway. I think he wanted to make sure he'd make a suitable husband for you first," said Marian.

Lexie shook her head. Why would he ever doubt it? And how could she ever assure him he was perfect for her already?

Homer walked up to the group of women. "Excuse me."

"Yes, Homer?"

"I wanted to tell you I've gone through the attic in the main house and the carriage house and found all the rubber you have."

Marian smiled at the man. "Thank you, Homer. Where did you put it?"

"It's piled up there by the garage. Where do you want me to take it?"

Peg pushed herself up from the lawn chair she was in. "Let's see what you've got."

Lexie and Marian stood, too, and followed Homer over to the garage. A collection of rubber boots, bike tires, rubber gloves, and garden hose were stacked high. "You know, I also have a rubber raincoat. Don't you, Marian?"

"Sure do. I'll go get them." Marian strode over to the house and disappeared inside. She reappeared moments later holding two raincoats, as well as a shower curtain draped over her arm.

"We can do without these." She carried them over to the pile and dropped them on top.

Peg pointed to the pile. "Well, there. That's a good assortment. Yes, Homer, go ahead and take it over to Sherman's Sinclair Gas Station. That's the nearest collection point to us."

"I'll help you load it into the trunk," said Lexie, and she picked up some items from the stack.

"Thank you, Lexie. We can help too," Peg said.

With all of them helping, it only took a few minutes to load the items into the car. Lexie chuckled when she found a girdle in the heap and held it up for the others to see.

"What's so … oh, yes, I see. Well, we all have to make sacrifices for the war!" Marian snatched it out of Lexie's hand and tossed it into the trunk.

Lexie burst out laughing. "You are so patriotic, Marian!"

"And think of all the money we'll make! At a penny a pound, we might make a whopping $20.00!" Peg swept her arm over the collection of rubber items. "Good thing we're not doing it for the money."

After the car was loaded, Homer left to deliver the donations. Marian motioned to three bikes parked in the back of the garage.

"Lexie, there's a bicycle scavenger hunt today. Everyone's meeting at the village green at three o'clock. You still have time if you'd like to participate. It should be fun."

"Are you two going to do it?" Something like that would be so much fun with Russell, but without him, she didn't have much interest.

The sisters glanced at each other, then Peg answered. "After today's gardening, I'm not sure this old body is up to it."

"Mine either," said her sister.

"You know, it sounds like fun, but I think I'll skip it and just relax here with you two."

Peg shook her head. "Please don't feel you have to keep us company."

"No, it's not that. I just wasn't planning anything like that this weekend."

Marian crossed her arms. "You'd feel differently if Russell were here, wouldn't you?"

Lexie's heart squeezed at the truth. She nodded. "Maybe so."

"That's perfectly understandable," said Peg. "But you know Russell wouldn't want you pining over him while he's gone."

"It never occurred to me to pine for him. In fact, I never thought I'd miss him so much. I guess I just thought he'd always be here."

Peg smiled. "Sometimes we just don't appreciate people until they're not around anymore."

The women walked back to the house and resumed their seats on the porch.

"You know, the Maidstone Club's season-opening is tonight. They're having a dinner-dance as a fund-raiser for the war effort. Russell had spoken to the manager about playing there this evening." Marian picked up today's copy of the *East Hampton Star*.

"I remember him telling me about that. I hope they found another piano player. Are you going?"

Peg shook her head. "We thought about it but decided against it. We don't like being out on the roads at night. It's so dark, you can barely see the other cars, and you can't tell where you are, with all the houses having their blackout shades down."

"That's right, and even though everyone's supposed to keep their speed under thirty-five miles per hour, some of the young folks out here don't keep the rules. The police have been busy handing out violations to the speeders, but it's still dangerous." Marian waved at a neighbor driving by in a white convertible. "We decided to just have a nice dinner here instead."

"Sounds good to me," said Lexie. "I don't feel like partying tonight."

"That's perfectly understandable. We can stay in, play cards, and listen to the radio. You can turn in early and get a good night's sleep," said Peg. "I bet you're not getting one with your busy schedule."

"Not really."

"So we'll have dinner here, then get to bed early and be rested for church tomorrow," said Marian.

"Perfect." Lexie picked up the book she'd brought with her. "If you don't mind, I think I'll walk down to the beach and read a little."

Peg looked out toward the sparkling water of the ocean. "Sure. Go ahead. The beach is a great place to relax and clear your mind."

Clear her mind? Lexie doubted that was possible. On the other hand, the beach was also a great place to pray.

Chapter Twenty-Four

Russell pulled the strap across him and buckled into his place along the interior of the RAF cargo plane for the three-hour flight to Northern Ireland. Artie's band would be entertaining the growing number of American troops sent there since January.

The band members were lined up against the walls facing each other with their equipment secured between them in the center of the plane.

"Hey, Russell. Where's your piano?" Louie yelled over the drum of the airplane's engine.

Russell shrugged and smiled. "Oops. Guess I forgot to bring it."

"Lucky for you, there are pianos wherever we go. The rest of us have to haul our instruments."

"Yeah, you're right. They'd be pretty hard to carry."

The guys laughed, then settled back on their canvas seats, restricting their conversations to their neighbors as the plane lifted off the ground. Through the open cockpit door, Russell could see Gloria strapped into the center seat behind the pilot and co-pilot. He breathed a sigh of relief that she was not sitting beside him. Since his last conversation with her, she'd withdrawn her attention and kept a cool distance from him. He hadn't meant to hurt her feelings or insult her, but he had to let her know where he stood.

The loadmaster was seated in the cockpit in a small area behind the crew and Gloria so he could keep an eye on the load inside the plane. After they'd been in the air about thirty minutes, he came to the entrance of the door and shouted out at them.

"You can move around and stretch your legs now if you want to. Those seats aren't the most comfortable."

Indeed they weren't. They hadn't been designed for passenger comfort. Rather, they'd been placed inside the plane for paratroopers to sit on until they made their jumps. Russell was thankful the trip wasn't any longer. After talking with the guys on either side of him a while, he unbuckled and stretched, then walked over to peer out one of the plane's small windows.

The June day was unusually clear for England so he could see the ground below them. Rolling green pastures stretched beneath them dotted with occasional farmhouses. He spotted what must be sheep in some of the fields and marveled at the peaceful scene. Who'd think the country was at war?

"Hey, what's that up ahead? A city?" One of the guys pointed at the scene outside the window where he stood.

The loadmaster had joined them in the hold and was checking the straps and buckles holding down the equipment. "That'd be Birmingham, sir."

Russell's gaze followed the direction the plane headed. The closer they got to the city, the more blackened areas were visible in the landscape. Large areas of gray rubble pocked the city between what appeared to be factories and homes.

"Man, would you look at that!"

"Gee, they got hit hard!"

The band gathered in groups of two or three to peer out the window, eyes wide with disbelief at the scene below. The men shook their heads and gaped as they looked.

"Them German planes dropped their bombs on Birmingham and hit them pretty hard," said the loadmaster. "Not as hard as London, but enough to do a lot of damage and kill many of our citizens."

Russell shuddered to think about the innocent people who were victims of the bombing—families, children, people just doing their jobs. More evidence of the German blitz was displayed when they flew over Manchester as well.

The loadmaster came to stand beside him at the window. "The Nazis thought they'd done us in, but they didn't know we Englishers wouldn't go down easy. Once Hitler knew he wasn't going to beat us, he turned around and started hitting the Soviet Union instead. Most of our factories are up and running again. Instead of beating us, he just made us mad and more determined to fight back."

"Thank God," said Russell.

The loadmaster nodded. "Yes, we do. And we're thankful you Yanks are here now too."

"So am I," said Russell. "We need to stop that madman." It was nice to feel welcome to the country, even though his presence wouldn't help fend off an enemy attack. But if being a Yank was a good thing, he'd take it. He smiled, recalling his southern grandfather's disapproval toward all things considered "Yankee." But times had changed, and thankfully, now the whole country was united against the same enemies.

As water came into view, the loadmaster pointed out the Irish Sea that separated England from Ireland. "Out that side there, you can see the Isle of Man." The plane began descending toward its destination, and Russell was able to spot a lighthouse in the water just off the shore of the island.

"What lighthouse is that?" he asked the loadmaster.

"Chicken Rock," the man replied.

"That's a funny name for a lighthouse," said Sal.

The loadmaster shrugged. "Some of the lighthouses are shut off now to keep the Germans from using them as landmarks. Heard some lighthouses up north even got shot at, and some people in them were killed."

The plane nosed downward, and the loadmaster told everyone to get back into their seats and buckle in for the landing. Soon they were on the ground in Northern Ireland where they'd be for at least two weeks, according to Artie. He told the band most of the American soldiers who were sent to Europe since the first of the year had been sent to bases in Northern Ireland.

As they got off the plane, they and their instruments were reloaded onto waiting army trucks which took them to the barracks where they'd be staying.

"Welcome to Langford Lodge." The soldier in charge of their escort addressed them upon their arrival.

"Sounds like a cabin in the mountains," muttered Nick. "How cozy."

"Doesn't look like a cabin," said Sal. "In fact, it looks a lot like the last place we stayed, just bigger."

"I'll give you men time to get settled, then I'll come back to take you to the dining hall for lunch."

After he left, Artie, who'd been outside talking with an

officer, came inside and scanned the room.

"Hey, Artie, where exactly are we?" Harry asked.

"We're about twenty-five miles west of Belfast, I understand."

"Wonder if there's any pubs around here," said Louie.

"Not in walking distance. Sorry."

"Not as sorry as I am."

The band stowed their belongings, then were driven to lunch, passing hundreds of soldiers on the way.

"Gee, feels like we're back in the States with all these American uniforms," Nick noted, craning his neck to see from his seat in the back of the truck.

"Man, look at all the tanks!" said Sal, as they drove past rows of armored vehicles.

While they were at lunch, the base's chief information officer briefed them.

"Hello. I'm Captain Steven Parker, and I'd like to welcome you to Army Air Force Station 597. We are glad to have you here. As you have seen, there are many American soldiers here—at last count around 5,000."

"Wow," muttered Nick, voicing what the rest were probably thinking.

"You may have heard that Major General Dwight D. Eisenhower has taken over control of the European Theater of Operations. We have been building up our forces here over the last five months for a major campaign that will begin soon. As a result, most of the troops we have here will be leaving to participate in that campaign. For many of these soldiers, this is their first time away from home, for most, the first time away from American soil. They are eager to serve their country but are homesick.

"That's why we wanted to bring you here. It will be a long time before they have any other contact with familiar surroundings, and we'd like to send them off with some entertainment that will take their minds off their worries, at least for a little while, and give them something good to remember when they leave here." He paused, then added, "So you see how important your being here is. Thank you again for coming, and please let us know what we can do to accommodate you."

Artie spoke up. "Where will we be playing? I didn't see a place large enough to hold that many soldiers."

"You won't be performing for all of them at once. We've divided them up by divisions, and you'll be playing in one of the airplane hangars where there's plenty of room."

"Where is this campaign going to happen?" asked Nick.

The officer steadied him with a blank look. "I'm not at liberty to divulge that information yet."

The band members glanced at each other, questions evident in their eyes.

Artie nodded. "We understand. Is the hangar near here? We'd like to practice this afternoon before the show tonight."

"Yes, of course. Come with me, and I'll show you." Artie and Russell followed Captain Parker outside where he pointed across the way to tall roofs rising above the barracks. "The hangars are over there. You may walk if you wish, but we can drive you whenever you're ready."

"Fine. Give us an hour to finish up here, and then we'll be ready. Our instruments are there already?"

"Yes, sir. They should all be there."

"And you've rounded up a piano for us?"

"Yes, we borrowed it from the base chapel."

Russell was encouraged to know there was a chapel on the base, but sorry it would be minus its piano for the time being. He and Artie went back inside and returned to their tables to finish their lunch.

At that moment, Gloria strolled in. "What's a girl got to do to get invited to dinner?"

All the men shoved their chairs back quickly from the long table and stood to their feet.

"At ease, men!" She giggled. "I've always wanted to say that." She glided across the room to Captain Parker, extending her hand to the young man, whose jaw had dropped open. "I'm Gloria Bentley. Are you our escort?"

Russell sympathized with the flustered young man who grappled with words to speak, knowing he'd love to be her personal escort.

The man cleared his throat. "Yes, ma'am." He jerked a chair back from the table and motioned for her to sit down. "I'll tell the cook to get you a meal."

"Thank you, dear." The words oozed out of her mouth.

"Can you take us back to our barracks now?" Artie said, breaking the trance Gloria had cast over the officer.

"Yes, sir."

"But who's going to stay and keep me company?" Gloria pouted.

The man appeared confused by the question and unable to make a decision. Three men in uniform walked into the room and made their way to the group. "Captain Parker, we're here to transport the USO band back to their barracks."

The officer's face relaxed. "Good. They're ready."

The band members followed the soldiers out the door,

leaving Captain Parker alone with Gloria. Hopefully, he'd be able to fend off her advances. Russell noticed he was wearing a wedding ring.

What was that delicious smell? Lexie opened her eyes and remembered she was at the Maurice cottage. The clock on the bedside table showed 8:00. She sat up quickly. Was she late? *Oh, it's Sunday.* When was the last time she'd slept so late? A sense of panic made her heart beat faster. She hoped she hadn't made the sisters wait on her.

She scrambled out of bed and dressed quickly for church. But when she entered the breakfast area, the sisters were sitting in their housecoats drinking tea and eating scones.

"Oh. I thought I was late. I didn't want to make you late for church." The sisters exchanged glances and chuckled.

"My goodness, no," said Peg. "We have plenty of time to get ready. The service doesn't start until ten forty-five. Why, we still have a couple of hours to kill."

Jane walked into the room with a plate full of steaming scones. "These are fresh out of the oven, Miss Lexie. Just for you."

"Lemon? Jane, you are so thoughtful to make my favorite."

"Well, Miss Peg likes blueberry, and Miss Marian likes raspberry the best, so I had to make everybody's favorite."

"Thank you, Jane. What a treat." Lexie settled into one of the padded mauve velvet cushions in a white French Provincial chair that matched the dining table. Mauve-and-ivory floral-striped wallpaper covered the room with a bay window that faced the ocean. She lifted a lace-trimmed linen napkin and placed it in her lap before transferring one of the scones from the platter to her plate.

Homer walked in with the newspaper. "Here's the *Times*. Some pretty interesting stuff about our area in today's news."

"Oh?" Peg reached for the paper. "Let's see."

Peg scanned the paper, her eyes growing wide. "My stars! Would you look at that?" She held up the paper and pointed to the headlines.

Lexie leaned forward and read out loud. "*FBI Seizes Saboteurs Landed by U-boats Here and in Florida to Blow Up War Plants.*"

Marian said, "Here? What do they mean by 'here'?"

"It says they landed in rafts, and one of them right here on Long Island!" Peg said.

Lexie's stomach tightened. "When did they land?'

"It says 'in the last fortnight,'" said Peg. "That's two weeks."

"How is that possible? I mean, with so much military here?" Lexie shuddered to think that Nazis had really come ashore, so near where they were.

Marian looked over Peg's shoulder to read the paper. "Oh, my. It's even more unbelievable. Listen to this. 'A young coastguardsman from Amagansett saw them the night they landed and says they gave him money to keep silent.'"

"Amagansett?" Lexie's mind raced back to the last time she'd been in East Hampton and the train ride back to the city. She pictured the four men she'd seen at the train station. Surely, they weren't the spies. Why, if that were so, Cal was one of them!

Lexie's appetite was gone. Was it possible the man she'd

been talking to at the diner was a Nazi spy? And he had been so nice and friendly. She had to know.

"Are there any pictures?"

"Let's see. The story's continued on page thirty." Peg turned the pages, then held the paper so Lexie could see. "Yes, here they are."

Lexie stared at the photos of the men who had been arrested. She recognized three of them, including the man she'd seen Cal with, the "nervous Nellie," as Penny had called him. But there was no picture of Cal. At first, she was relieved, but then the shock of his true identity hit her. He had to be one of them too. She'd befriended him and trusted him, the enemy. Her anger about being deceived fought with disappointment. She'd shared so much information with him, but he wasn't the person she thought he was—a nice, friendly gentleman. How could she be so stupid? Why didn't she realize something about him was suspicious? Sometimes she was too suspicious of others, but to find out she'd trusted someone she shouldn't have was infuriating. What a fool she'd been!

"Are you all right, Lexie?" Marian eyed her with concern. "You seem quite shaken."

"It's just … such a shock." She wasn't about to tell the sisters she'd had conversations with one of the spies. Their concern for her welfare would be confirmed, perhaps rightfully so.

"It certainly is. Just when we think we're safe here," Peg said.

"Well, we are safe, sister. They were caught, and there's no harm done," asserted Marian.

"What will happen to them?" Lexie asked.

"The paper says they'll get the death penalty, even though two of them were US citizens."

Lexie gulped. These men were her enemies, but she almost felt sorry for them, especially the nervous man. No wonder he was so nervous. But what had happened to Cal? Had he not been arrested too? And if he hadn't been, where was he? Maybe he really wasn't one of them, she tried to convince herself. After all, his picture wasn't in the paper. But the lump in the pit of her stomach told her he was a spy. He had been at the train station with the others in the picture, and she'd seen him with one of them at the diner.

And what about the German baker? He was obviously an acquaintance of Cal's too, but his picture wasn't in the paper either. Did the authorities know there were more spies than the ones caught? Should she tell them?

Chapter Twenty-Five

*K*arl glanced up at the tall bell tower beside the entrance of St. Luke's Lutheran Church, hearing its bells ringing, calling parishioners to worship. He trembled as he stepped forward, afraid he wasn't worthy to walk inside. But he had to do this. He moved with leaden feet into the nave of the vast stone sanctuary, removed the fedora from his newly dyed black hair, then held the hat over his heart. Stained glass from the large window over the entrance illuminated and colored the rear of the church as he found his way to the nearest pew.

It had been a long time since Karl was in church. Too long, even though his parents had raised him in the faith. Karl focused on the figure above the altar, the carved wooden statue of Christ, and sank onto the seat. On each side of the figure were the Greek letters for Alpha and Omega, the beginning and the end. How fitting.

He bowed his head, his heart constricted by remorse.

He never meant for things to go so far. He never intended to follow through with the mission. And he especially never intended to hurt anyone. But he had been living a lie. "Father, forgive me for I have sinned," he prayed. He lifted his eyes with tears streaming down. Finally, he had done the right thing. The others would pay the price, but innocent people would be spared. Innocent people like Lexie. What would she think when the news came out, when she realized his deceit? Would she think him an enemy, or would she forgive him?

Whether she did or not, he knew Christ would. That He already had. He sighed and wiped his face. When he stood again, his burden was lighter. He had more to do to make things right for everyone else, though. And Lord help him, he'd be able to.

"Man, would you look at this." said Nick when the band entered the cavernous metal building, normally housing airplanes for maintenance work. A temporary stage had been set up at one end of the hangar.

The band members walked in, their shoes echoing through the room as they gawked at the expansive area around them. Louis let out a low whistle.

"Holy Toledo!" said Vince, one of the trombone players, his head rotating to see the hangar.

"I can only imagine the acoustics in here," said Louie, as he took the stage.

"Wonder how many planes they can fit in here?" said Sal.

Russell stepped up to the piano, running his hand along the top of the keys. The ivories were worn from years of service, a testimony to the piano's importance in the worship service. He doubted it'd ever been used for jazz numbers but hoped it didn't mind the change in genre. Russell played a scale, finding most of the keys in tune. Thankfully, those that weren't wouldn't be noticeable with all the other instruments playing alongside. Good thing he didn't have a solo.

"Everybody ready?" said Artie, scanning the group. They all nodded, then Artie, with his trumpet in his left hand, lifted his baton in the right and marked, "One, two, three."

They played through their whole set, including numbers from Artie Shaw's band and Glenn Miller's, finishing with "Yankee Doodle Dandy" from the new movie that had recently come out. The sound echoed off the metal walls of the hangar, magnifying the sound.

"Hey, Artie. Isn't Gloria going to rehearse with us?" Louie asked between songs.

"Guess not," said the band leader. "She must not need to practice."

When they'd played through the whole set, Artie spoke to a few about their specific parts.

"All right, guys. Let's wrap up here and go get some rest before the show," he said. The men cleaned off their instruments, set them down, and then they headed out, but Russell decided to stay behind.

"Russ, you're not leaving?"

"No, I'd like to stay a while longer and practice a little more."

"If that's what you want to do. I just don't want you to be too tired tonight."

"Don't worry. I'll be fine." Russell smiled at the band leader for assurance.

"See you tonight then."

Artie went out the side door, leaving Russell alone.

He closed his eyes and prayed silently. *Lord, what am I*

doing here? I don't fit in with these guys, but what else can I do to be of service? Show me how I can help others. Show me what you want me to do.

His hands moved of their own volition and began playing "Amazing Grace." The song carried him back to his childhood on Jekyll Island when his mother was still alive. She'd always told him it was her favorite song. He remembered playing the hymn in more recent years when he was the club manager on the island and played for the chapel worship services. And most recently, he'd heard the hymn played when he and Lexie had attended church together at the Marble Collegiate Church in Manhattan.

How remarkable that this hymn he played was such a part of his history. Such a part of church history. When he'd studied music in college, he learned that the song was written by John Newton, an Englishman who'd called out to God in the middle of a storm at sea off the coast of Ireland. And here Russell was in Ireland. Centuries apart and continents apart, yet the message of God's amazing grace was universal, giving comfort to all who heard it.

"Hello?" A male voice took Russell out of his reverie.

Russell turned to look at the man who'd entered wearing the traditional olive-drab Army dress uniform with a cross on each lapel.

"Hello," Russell replied, his eyebrow lifted.

"You're playing my song," said the man, smiling. "Well, actually, one of my favorite songs." He walked across the floor to Russell, extending his hand. "Captain Mark Carter, I'm the chaplain here."

Russell stood up from the piano bench and walked to the

edge of the stage where he leaned forward to shake the chaplain's hand. "Nice to meet you, Chaplain. I'm Russell Thompson. Thanks for letting me borrow your piano."

The chaplain laughed and spread his arms to the side. "Oh, it's not *my* piano. It belongs to the base. Besides, we used it yesterday, and you'll be gone before we need it again."

Russell stuffed his hands into his pants pockets. "So how long have you been a chaplain here?"

"I've only been here since May. I'm assigned to the Fifth Corps—that's two combat divisions."

"I see. Where do you hail from, Captain?"

"St. Louis, Missouri is my home."

Russell had never spoken to a military chaplain before. "I'd like to talk with you some more if you have time. Is there someplace we can go—get a cup of coffee maybe?"

"Sure. My vehicle is right outside. I'll take you to the chapel. We have a coffee pot in the office."

"Sounds great. I have a couple of hours before we go on." Russell stepped off the stage and followed the chaplain out the door to a jeep. They drove to a modest chapel, hardly big enough for all the troops stationed there at the time. Captain Carter unlocked a side door, and they went into a small office, just big enough for a plain desk and two straight-back wooden chairs—one behind the desk and one in front. The chaplain walked over to a coffee pot sitting on a two-burner camp stove and poured two cups of coffee. He handed one to Russell as he came back to the desk and sat down behind it.

"Have a seat." He motioned to the other chair in front of the desk. "Sorry I don't have something more comfortable for you to sit on. The coffee's palatable, the best I can do around here."

Russell held up his hand. "Please, don't apologize. I appreciate the hospitality, Chaplain."

"Please call me Mark." He drank some coffee, then put his cup down. "Russell, something tells me this is the first time you've traveled with the band."

Russell nodded, holding the cup with both hands with his elbows on his knees. "You're right on the money. I'm greener than some of the servicemen out there."

"So how is it so far? Seems to me like a pretty exciting life."

Russell raised an eyebrow. "Exciting? I guess you could say so, but not exciting like going into a war zone. Pretty tame by those standards."

"Would you rather be going into a war zone?" Mark leaned forward. Russell paused a moment before answering.

"I don't know. Maybe. I mean, if all those guys can do it, I should be able to go too."

"So why don't you join up?"

Russell hung his head, then raised his eyes to meet Mark's. "Can't.

Guess you didn't notice the limp."

"I did, but it was barely perceptible. I thought maybe your foot was just sore."

"No. Lost part of it in a hunting accident when I was a teenager. Now I'm 4F."

"But if you weren't, you'd join?"

"Yes, I would. It's so frustrating not to be able to. Makes me feel kind of worthless."

"Hmm." Mark rubbed his chin. "Do you think the rest of the band feels that way?"

The question startled Russell. "Why, I don't know. Never asked them."

"Why don't you? It might be interesting to hear what they have to say."

Russell sat back and blew out a breath. "Guess I sound pretty selfish, huh?"

Mark chuckled and shook his head. "Selfish? Because you want to join the Army and can't? Hardly."

A small picture frame sat on the desk. Russell nodded toward it. "Your family?"

"Yes." Mark picked up the frame and handed it to Russell. "My wife Debbie and my son Tim."

"Nice family," Russell said, handing the photo back to Mark. "So what made you want to be a chaplain?"

"Well, I was already a minister. Served in a small church in Indiana for the past two years, then I heard about the chaplain ministry and decided to join it. I'm doing pretty much the same thing now I was doing then, just to a different congregation."

"Your wife didn't mind?"

"She wasn't crazy about the idea, but she understood. After all, everyone wants to do something for our country, don't we?"

Studying his coffee, Russell said, "You know, my mother always wanted me to be a minister."

Mark sat back in his chair. "That right? Did you ever consider it?"

"Kind of. I wasn't sure if I would be doing it for her or for me. So I studied business and music in college."

"That's an odd combination."

"I figured I could get a job with the business, but I took

the music for myself."

"And you've been playing in a band ever since?"

Russell laughed. "Oh, no. I managed a private club in Georgia, the Jekyll Island Club before the government told everyone to leave in March. I also served as the pianist for our small chapel. Then I moved to New York and took a job as assistant manager at the Martinique Hotel in Manhattan. Until last week, I only moonlighted with the USO. Then this opportunity came up"—he spread his arms out—"and here I am!"

"So that's how you ended up here. But why did you move to New York?"

Smiling, Russell envisioned Lexie's face. "My fiancée is from New York. She wanted to attend nursing school at Bellevue, so I decided to move there too and find a job in the area."

"When do you plan to get married?"

Russell shrugged. "We haven't set a date yet. We don't know when her training will end."

Mark folded his hands on his desk. "Nurses are so greatly needed now. Does she plan to be a military nurse?"

Shaking his head, Russell said, "No. She's never indicated an interest in that. However, she is interested in treating soldiers who've suffered shell shock. Apparently, doctors aren't sure how to treat the condition. After the last war, some returning soldiers were put in mental hospitals."

"Ah, yes. I've heard about that." He fixed his eyes on Russell. "Do you think her vocation is more worthy than yours?"

Russell's stomach tensed. The man could see right through him. "I suppose I do. After all, she's helping people.

And she's filling a void caused by the war, so she's serving her country."

Mark pushed away from the desk and stood, then walked to the small window in the office and pointed out. "See those soldiers out there? They have no idea where they're going next. They're scared and homesick. But one thing they do know is that they're looking forward to your show tonight."

Russell joined him at the window and watched scores of soldiers in army drab uniforms marching in formation. The chaplain's comment echoed the public information officer's. These men were glad he was there. A sense of satisfaction warmed his heart as he let that idea sink in. He was happy to be part of cheering them up, bringing something of their home to them in this place. But was that enough?

Mark faced him with a smile. "I'd say you're doing something useful for the cause. You know, Russell, we can't all be soldiers. I'm not. God gave us each a purpose, and being a soldier isn't yours. But maybe ministering to the soldiers' morale is your purpose."

"Maybe you're right. Mark, can I ask you a question?"

"Of course. Go ahead."

"Did you have to pass the military physical to be a chaplain?"

Mark nodded. "Yes, I did. Same drills."

Russell blew out a breath. He couldn't even pass a physical to be a chaplain.

"Look, Russell. You know God has a plan for you. How do you know this isn't it?"

Russell shrugged. "I don't know. I felt like I should come on this trip, that I would find the answer if I did. But I think there's something more, something else for me to do."

"I'm sure you'll find out what it is. If you're seeking God's will, He's going to reveal it to you. Just keep following one step at a time, and you'll find your answer."

Russell stared out the window at the troops, then turned and shook Mark's hand.

"Thanks for your time, Mark. I'll be thinking about what you said."

"Maybe you need to pray about it too."

Chapter Twenty-Six

Lexie wanted desperately to listen to the sermon, but she couldn't. The events of the last two weeks kept going through her mind. Why didn't she realize something wasn't right about Cal? Maybe subconsciously, she did. After all, she did have some uneasy feelings, but she'd dismissed them, telling herself she was too suspicious. And yet, she'd enjoyed his company, and he'd been a willing listener when she talked about her work at the hospital.

She wanted to kick herself. Was he just acting the whole time? Playing the role of a normal American? She replayed their conversations, looking for clues about his true identity. He said he grew up in the States, didn't he? But his mother and sister lived in Canada, and he'd said he hadn't talked to them for a while. Did they know he was a spy for the Nazis?

Lexie imitated the motions of the service, standing and sitting when everyone else did. She scanned the sanctuary as the minister spoke, the other congregants in rapt attention. What did they think about the enemy being so close to them at one point?

Cal had asked her to pray for him. Was he just

pretending to be a God-fearing man too? He'd questioned her faith, so maybe it was because he didn't have any. Where were his principles? She couldn't believe he followed that despicable Hitler. She shuddered at the thought. How could he fool her so much? A tremor of fear flashed through her mind. Had she ever been in real danger from the spies, from Cal? After all, they came to America to destroy the country and obviously didn't care about any casualties. The last time she'd seen him, he'd acted strangely, and she'd been more nervous going back to the residence, like she was being watched. Was there a valid reason for her fear? Why, even Cal had told her to be careful. Did he know she was in danger? From what or whom?

She trembled with anger, and tears came to her eyes. She'd been betrayed by someone she trusted. And all she'd done was be friendly and give others the benefit of the doubt, treat them the way she'd like to be treated—the Golden Rule—Russell called it. Russell. What would he think when she told him about Cal? Cal had even stayed at the Martinique. Had Russell noticed anything suspicious? And would he think she was a complete fool? She shook her head. How embarrassing. She could just see it now, imagining the shock on his face. "Welcome home, Russell. Did you know I was friends with a Nazi spy?"

Anger boiled up again. Boy, if she ever saw that Cal Miller again, she'd give him a piece of her mind! She wanted to look him in the face and give him what for. But no, she didn't want to see him again. Knowing what she did now, the prospect of running into him again would be very dangerous. One thing she knew, she'd never be able to forgive him, whether he knew it or not.

Peg nudged her elbow and motioned to the hymnal. They stood to sing "Amazing Grace." A lump formed in Lexie's throat as she tried to sing. If only Cal knew this song. If only he believed the words that God's grace could save him. But it was too late for that now. Wasn't it? She'd told him she'd pray for him. Maybe he was a liar, but she wasn't, and if she said she would pray, she would, even though she wasn't sure what to pray for. *Lord God, Cal, or whoever he is, needs you. Help him to do the right thing, and please help me to forgive him for not being honest with me.*

It was almost showtime. Hundreds of soldiers filed in and sat cross-legged on the floor of the hangar, laughing and joking with each other, while others stood around the side and rear of the hangar.

Russell scanned the room full of fresh faces as the building reverberated with anticipation. These guys deserved a good show, and he'd do his best to give them one.

Artie edged over to the piano and muttered, "No sign of Gloria. Got any idea where she might be?"

"Not a clue," said Russell. "Last time I saw her was at lunch, same time as you probably."

"Yeah, that's right. Just wondered if you'd seen her since because you disappeared. Oh, well, guess we have to play without her." He glanced at the waiting crowd. "But those boys were looking forward to seeing her."

The side door opened, and Gloria stumbled in. Immediately, the guys up front started whistling, and she threw them a kiss as she tottered on her high heels to the stage. She looked like a million dollars as always in her pink satin, low-cut gown, but she was obviously tipsy. Boy, Russell hoped she could pull it off.

Artie frowned at her, then pasted on a smile and walked to the mike at the center of the stage while Gloria waited on the side.

"Hello, guys! We're happy to be here and bring you our show!" A chorus of hoots and hollers went up from the crowd.

"And I know you're really here to see Miss Gloria Bentley!" Artie extended his arm, and Gloria made her way slowly across the stage. He stepped away from the mike so she could get to it.

"Hello, boys," she purred, and the audience went wild with whistles, and catcalls rang through the room.

Artie gave the signal, and the band started playing. Gloria began to sing, posing for the men as she strutted about the stage. Although she slurred some of the lyrics, the men didn't seem to notice, mesmerized by her feminine charm. She crooned "I Hear a Rhapsody," and the audience sat spellbound, then they came to life again when she sang "Don't Sit Under the Apple Tree."

By the time the band took their break, Gloria was ready to collapse. She strolled over to the piano bench and sank down beside Russell.

"Are you all right?" Russell was afraid she'd lie down on the bench if he moved.

"I need a drink," she muttered, leaning her head against his shoulder.

"You need some water is what you need." He waved at one of the guys in the band. "Hey, can you get the lady a glass of water, please?"

The man made the okay sign with his fingers and ran over to a jug of water sitting on a small table by the stage and poured her a glassful. When he brought it to Russell, he winked when handing it out.

"Here, drink this." Russell pushed her up off his shoulder, holding the glass to her lips. She sipped the water, then waved him away, shaking her head.

"Not that kind of drink! A *real* drink!"

"I think you've had enough of those." He made her drink more water. "Are you going to be ready for the second set?"

"Sure. As long as you take me home afterward and tuck me in."

Not this again. Guess she didn't think he was serious about not being interested. Or maybe it was just the liquor talking. But he might have to take her home because another man might take advantage of her vulnerability.

The other band members came back to the stage and went to their regular places, picking up their instruments. Artie approached the piano and glanced from Russell to Gloria, then back, motioning with his head toward her. "She gonna be all right?"

"I think so." Russell looked down at Gloria who had fallen back against his shoulder and appeared to be sleeping. He nudged her with his shoulder. "Gloria, time to go back on. Come on, you can do it."

"Hmm?" She opened her eyes and glanced around.

The audience started clapping as Artie walked back to center stage, faced the band, and directed them to begin playing "Jersey Bounce," letting the instrumentals take the lead in the second set. Gloria regained her composure after her brief nap on Russell's shoulder. She stood in front of the piano, swaying to the music. When the first notes of the next song played, she took the mike and began singing "Johnny Doughboy Found a Rose in Ireland."

The crowd showed their appreciation in characteristic fashion, and Gloria flashed her widest smile. She made it through the second set with barely a hitch, but the guys in the audience wouldn't have minded if she'd really screwed up. They were happy just to feast their eyes on her, and she did an expert job working the crowd—winking, smiling, and slinking across the stage. When the band played the last song, Artie said good night and wished the guys well. Many hung around to get autographs, making for a long evening. When the commanding officer finally took over and told the remaining soldiers it was time to go, everyone in the band was exhausted.

Gloria turned around to face the band with her hands on her hips and said, "What I wouldn't do for a cold Coca-Cola right now."

"If you'd asked sooner, I bet one of those guys would've swum to the States to get you one," Louis said.

Gloria smiled and said, "I wouldn't want to put someone out *that* much!"

Artie stepped up to her and pulled her aside. He kept his voice low, but Russell was pretty sure he knew what Artie needed to talk to her about. Arriving late and drunk was not helpful to the band and jeopardized the performance. Gloria lifted her hands and shrugged during the conversation but appeared apologetic. When they finished their conversation, Artie came over to Russell.

"I want you to keep an eye on her and make sure she

doesn't mess up again."

Russell's eyebrows shot up. "Why me?"

"You're the only guy I can trust to stay straight yourself."

So he was going to be Gloria's chaperone? He hadn't signed up for that job. He doubted Lexie would approve of the assignment either.

"I'll try, Artie, but I can't promise to watch her all the time."

"Just do your best. Talk to her or something. We've got more bases to go to, and we can't deal with a drunk performer. The USO would not be happy if things went wrong because of it."

"Sure, Artie. I'll talk to her." Good Lord, what had he gotten himself into?

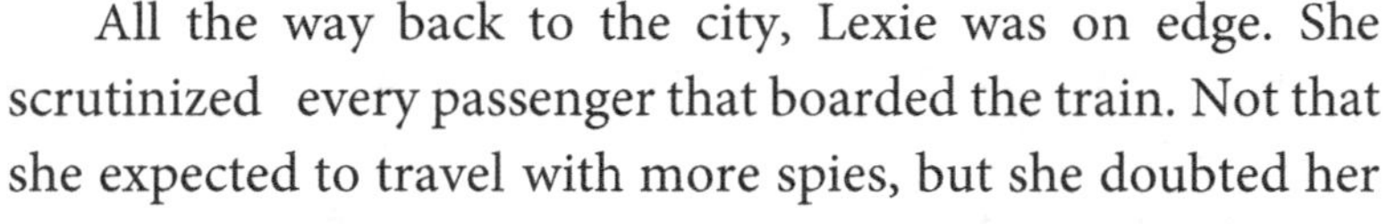

All the way back to the city, Lexie was on edge. She scrutinized every passenger that boarded the train. Not that she expected to travel with more spies, but she doubted her ability to judge people anymore. The faint possibility that she might see Cal only added to her paranoia.

At Penn Station, her head revolved like a top as she tried to get a look at every person she saw. She studied their faces and imagined who they were and why they were there. Stepping outside, she watched every person on the sidewalk, observing mannerisms and listening to their speech for anything unusual. She'd missed the clues before, but she wouldn't miss them again.

Someone bumped into her, and she spun around, eyes wide, ready to meet her attacker.

"Sorry," the gentleman muttered as he went on his way.

Her heart raced, and she took a deep breath to calm down. Where once no one had been a threat, now everyone was. She stepped off the curb and a car honked. She jumped back out of the way. She was paying so much attention to the people that she hadn't even considered the traffic. But something made her move into the street. Was she pushed? With so many people crowding the curb, how could she be sure? She glanced around, a little embarrassed, yet looking for a guilty party. But no one was looking at her. They were all focused on getting across. She must be imagining things.

After waiting for traffic to clear, she crossed the street with other pedestrians, constantly looking over her shoulder to see if she was being followed. She walked two blocks briskly before reaching the corner where the Martinique Hotel stood. She paused and looked up at the tall building where Russell used to work and where Cal and his co-conspirators had stayed. Was this where they made their dreadful destructive plans? If Cal wasn't staying here anymore, where had he gone? How had he avoided capture when all his friends were caught? A wry smile crossed her face remembering that Cal insisted the other men weren't his friends. But that was another lie, now that she knew they were his associates.

She walked two more blocks before she got to Mack's Diner. Was Mack aware that the spies had eaten in his establishment? She had half a mind to tell him, but what would Mack think about her, having seen her with Cal? Would he think she was a spy too? Her stomach knotted. She had been completely naïve, yet she could be considered suspicious too by association. Now she had something else to worry about. But maybe they weren't aware that he was a spy since his picture wasn't in the paper, even though his nervous pal's was.

Anger toward Cal surfaced again as she realized that he had put her reputation in jeopardy, too, whether he knew it or not. Not that he would care.

She quickened her step as she passed the diner, afraid to look in but not sure whether she wanted to keep from seeing someone inside or to keep from being seen. The sun was setting, and shadows were lengthening as she continued the final blocks to the residence. There were fewer people out now that rush hour was over, and she felt conspicuous walking alone. Every sound she heard sent her body a warning. Every sign of movement drew her attention. Why hadn't she taken the bus back this time? Yet, she'd become so accustomed to walking, it hadn't crossed her mind to do otherwise. Perhaps it was time to change her routine, especially if she were being watched.

The familiar red brick of the residence was ahead, and she welcomed the sight. As she entered the door, she blew out a breath. Finally, she was in a safe place. Tomorrow, she'd be back in her routine, back to her normal life where dangerous people were kept behind locked doors.

The residence living room was full of nurses huddled in groups. Newspapers were strewn about as the women pointed and chatted. Lexie spotted Penny and strolled over to the couch where she and several other girls clustered together over a copy of the *New York Times*.

Penny looked up as she approached. "Hey, Lexie. Have you heard about the spies?"

If Penny only knew. Lexie feigned ignorance. "Spies?"

"Yes, spies! Come see!" Penny patted a spot on the couch beside her.

Lexie sat next to her roommate who held a newspaper at arm's length in front of her, pointing to the headlines. "See? Right here! I mean, they landed on Long Island, Lexie!"

Lexie pretended to be surprised. "Oh my goodness! I can't believe it!"

"Lexie, can you believe they were so close? I mean, what if you had run into them when you were out on the island?"

Lexie shook her head. "Thank God, I didn't." But she did.

"Here's their pictures." One of the girls folded the paper back to the page where the story continued.

Penny peered closely at the photos. "Say, Lexie. That guy looks like the guy we saw at the diner. Remember the nervous guy that was with the good-looking one?" She pointed to the spy.

Lexie glanced at the picture and shook her head. "I don't think so, Penny."

Penny held the paper closer to her face. "You sure? I don't know…"

"Penny, if that guy was a spy, where's the other one, the guy that said his name was, um, Cal? I don't see his picture."

"I guess you're right. Well, that's a relief." She put the paper down, then looked at Lexie with wide eyes. "Wouldn't that be something if we actually talked to spies?"

"That would be something all right. Good thing we didn't." Lexie hoped she sounded convincing. The paper showed seven spies in the pictures. But there were at least one or even two more. Did anyone else know about them? Should Lexie report what she knew to the authorities? *Lord, please show me what to do.*

When Lexie arrived on her usual floor at the psychiatric hospital the following day, Nurse Addams greeted her stiffly. "Good morning, Nurse Smithfield. I hope you enjoyed your weekend."

Lexie flinched at the nurse's condescending attitude. What had she done to warrant this tone?

"Is something wrong, Nurse Addams?"

The nurse's lips were drawn in a tight line. "Seems like your favorite patient has had a setback."

"My favorite patient?" Who? Then it struck her. "John Doe—I mean Mike Walker?"

"The one and the same." Nurse Addams gave a swift nod of her head.

Lexie's heart sank. "What happened? He didn't go back into catatonia, did he?"

"Oh no, quite the opposite in fact." She slapped her hand down on the desk. "He had another violent outburst, and we had to strap him down."

"Do you know why, what might have set him off?" Lexie figured there had to be an explanation for his anger. Now that he had his voice back, couldn't he communicate his needs?

"Dr. Kappas was in the ward. I had to leave to get something for the doctor, and when I got back, Mr. Walker had the doctor in a headlock, and I had to call the attendants for help."

Lexie shook her head in disbelief, disappointed to hear Mike was back in restraints. He had told Lexie he didn't like

Dr. Kappas, accusing the doctor of making a pass at Lexie. But what had triggered the recent episode?

"I'm really sorry to hear that," she said. "How long will he be in restraints?"

"Probably until his treatment," the nurse said. "He's scheduled for electric shock therapy tomorrow."

Her senses jolted, Lexie grasped for composure. The news affected her deeply, too much so, she realized. He was just a patient, and she was not an expert in psychiatric treatment, but she'd become personally involved in his progress. To hear he was slated for shock therapy was like hearing she'd failed a test, but more than that, somehow failed Mike.

She was speechless, afraid to voice her feelings. The nurse continued, "Since you're working tomorrow, you can assist in the treatment."

Lexie sagged like a boxer hanging onto the ropes of the ring after multiple blows. How could she possibly be part of Mike's torture? He would think she'd betrayed him. Did he know what they were planning to do? Had anyone told him yet?

She recovered her composure. "Who's administering the treatment?"

"Dr. Kappas says he wants to do it. He even suggested a lobotomy if the shock therapy didn't work."

Lexie swallowed the lump in her throat. Could things be any worse for Mike? Surely, he wasn't a candidate for a lobotomy!

"Well, here you are—your medication schedule for today." Nurse Addams handed her a clipboard. "Go ahead and get the doses ready."

Taking the chart, Lexie nodded, then looked it over as she

walked to the medicine cabinet, trying to keep her emotions in check when what she really wanted to do was check on Mike first. After assembling the necessary medications on a tray, she got the ward key from the head nurse and entered the ward.

The patients were unusually quiet and barely gave her a glance. Why was she unwelcome now?

She made her way around the room, handing out the medications, trying to keep her eyes away from Mike until she was finished. Even the men playing cards pretended not to notice her when she approached them.

"Good morning, gentlemen. How's the game?"

The men kept their eyes on the cards in their hands. Lexie was at a loss. She thought the men liked her.

Then Ronald wiggled his finger to call her attention. She bent over beside him and put her head close to his. "Dorothy, I need to tell you something." He spoke in a low voice.

"Yes, Ronald? What is it?" she whispered back.

"Be careful. You might end up like Mike. Don't make the doctor mad."

"Okay, I won't. But what did Mike do to make the doctor mad?"

The men glanced at each other and shrugged.

There was only one way she was going to find out—ask Mike herself. He had been prescribed a sedative, and she planned to give him his medicine last so she could talk to him. She braced herself to see him, afraid of how she'd find him.

He lay strapped down in bed, eyes closed. She touched him on the arm. "Mike?"

His eyes flew open, and he turned toward her. "See what

happens when you leave?" His voice was low and slightly slurred, no doubt the effect of the sedatives he'd been given.

Her heart gripped with regret. Was it her fault?

"What happened?" She plumped his pillow, then went to the end of his bed and cranked the head of the bed up.

"Your doctor friend. We had a little disagreement."

Lexie crossed her arms. "Disagreement about what?"

"Politics."

"Politics?" Was the doctor a Nazi sympathizer? But she was afraid to delve into the subject any more in case it would upset Mike again.

"Uh-huh. He gives me a headache."

"Have you been having lots of headaches?" She pushed his hair off his face.

"Not too bad." He gave her a twisted smile. "Just when that doctor is around."

"It seems that you two have a mutual dislike for each other."

He smiled broader. "You could say that. Can you keep him away from me now that you're back?"

She froze, remembering the treatment Mike was scheduled for the next day. He didn't miss her reaction.

"What's wrong? What do you know? Tell me, please." Her hand was near his, and he gripped it. "Please."

"The doctor plans to give you electric shock therapy."

Mike's eyes widened, and he wrestled with his straps trying to get up. "When?"

Lexie reached out to calm him, laying her hands on his chest. "Mike, calm down."

"How can I calm down?" His voice raised, and the other patients turned around to look.

"Shhh. Don't upset the other patients, please."

Filled with anger and fear, his eyes sought hers, and he lowered his voice. "Look, Nurse Smithfield, you know I'm not crazy." He cut his eyes at the other patients. "I'm not like them. I was hurt because I'm a soldier. Shouldn't a soldier be treated better than that?"

His words pierced her and echoed her sentiments. But what could she do?

"But Mike, what if the treatment helps you like it's supposed to? What if it makes your headaches go away? It has helped others."

"Don't I get a choice? I don't want to have it. Period, but no one has asked me what I want. Can't you do something to help me?"

"I'll try. I promise. I'll talk to the doctor tomorrow and explain to him that you don't need the treatment. But you must promise me you'll stay calm. I'll pray for you, too, if that's all right with you. Do we have a deal?"

He was silent a few moments, then said, "Deal."

"Good. Now, let's take your medicine." She picked up the syringe.

Mike eyed it and looked up at her. "What's it for?"

"It helps to calm you. So you won't get headaches," she said. Or get agitated, she didn't say.

He shook his head. "I don't want it."

She withdrew the medicine and tilted her head. "No? Why not?"

"It upsets my stomach." He tried to move his hand to his stomach but couldn't with the restraints on. "What am I supposed to do with these on if I get sick?"

Lexie considered his question, but no answer was good.

He glanced down at the straps across his body. "And I guess you're not allowed to take these off yet, right?"

"No, I can't. Not now." The head nurse told her the incident had happened less than twenty-four hours before.

"That's what I thought. So can we skip the medicine tonight? Please?"

It wasn't the first time a patient had refused medication, but Mike's refusal made sense. And it was one of the few things she could do for him. Even though she promised to talk to the doctor about the treatment, she doubted he'd change his mind. Another doctor might be swayed, but Dr. Kappas had made it clear he did not like to be challenged. In this situation, her family's former connections wouldn't make any difference.

"All right. You don't have to take it. But I'll have to make a note in your chart that you refused it."

Mike gave her a grateful smile. "You won't get in any trouble, will you?" The look of compassion on his face warmed her heart. Despite his predicament, he still cared about her. "You could tell them I was asleep, and you couldn't wake me up."

Lexie smiled at him. "That's a good story, but it isn't true, is it? I'd rather get in trouble for telling the truth than a lie."

"You're a good person, Nurse Smithfield. By the way, what's your first name anyway?"

She glanced around the room and lowered her voice. "Lexie, but you must call me Nurse Smithfield, or I'll get in trouble."

He grinned and whispered. "All right, Nurse Lexie Smithfield. I hope someday I'll be lucky enough to have a girl as nice as you."

She blushed and said, "Thank you."

But as she left the ward, she wondered if he already had a nice girl somewhere that he hadn't remembered yet. If he could regain more of his memory, maybe he could be released from the hospital. As long as he had no more outbursts.

At the end of her shift, she told all the patients good night and reassured Mike that she'd speak to the doctor first thing in the morning. He'd appeared happier when she left, and she prayed he'd be that way the next time she saw him.

Chapter Twenty-Seven

*R*ussell admired the verdant scenery of rolling pastureland as the army truck bumped along the Irish country road. Flocks of sheep grazed in fields on either side of them, a sharp contrast to the barren military base they'd just left.

Gloria sat between him and the driver, thanks to Artie's request. It took four trucks to haul the band and their equipment to each base. Artie was in the lead truck with some of the other band members. Gloria had an obvious hangover, so the open window helped to clear her head. Russell had offered to let her ride next to the window in case the road was too rough for her, but she'd refused, preferring to "have a man on each side" of her.

Her condition didn't seem to bother the young serviceman who drove them, as he appeared smitten with her charm. Russell wanted to talk with her, but not in front of anyone else. He wasn't sure what he would say yet but prayed God would give him the right words, and he could say something to help her. What he really wanted to know was why. Why did she act the way she did? Why did she throw herself at men? Why did she drink so much? He wanted to help, but he didn't want her to get the wrong idea about his interest.

Unlike her normally effusive self, Gloria hadn't spoken much since they'd left. It was apparent that she wasn't feeling well. If spoken to, she pasted on a fake smile and made a meager attempt to be congenial. Conversation in the loud truck required yelling, which was a tiresome way to communicate. He didn't want to stare at her, but he detected something else in her demeanor that might not be related to the hangover. Was it depression?

He leaned close to her ear to be heard over the rumble of the truck engine. "Are you feeling better?"

She faced him with a half-smile and questioning eyes. "Yeah, sure. Thanks for making me eat that toast. I think it helped."

"That's good. I'm sure you needed something in your stomach."

"Thanks for asking." She nudged him with her elbow. "You're a nice guy."

Russell shrugged. "Think you'll feel like practicing with us this afternoon?"

She turned back to face the road, appearing peeved by his lack of response to her compliment. "Of course," she answered. "Why wouldn't I be?"

The rest of the conversation would have to wait until they reached their destination. Hopefully, she'd stay sober the rest of the day, especially since she had become his responsibility. What would Lexie think?

When they arrived at the next base, the band dropped off their personal belongings in their barracks, then were treated to some sandwiches in the mess hall. Gloria was with them and was almost back to her old self, flirting and joking with the guys.

"Practice in one hour. We have two shows to do today, so we need to get ready," Artie announced, clapping his hands. "Would you please join us for practice, Gloria?" Artie's invitation was quite charming, if you asked Russell.

"I wouldn't miss it for the world, darling!" Gloria purred, batting her eyelashes.

Artie glanced at Russell, and he got the hint.

"I'll come get you in forty-five minutes," Russell said to the singer.

Gloria eyed him up and down, a sly smile on her face. "You will, huh? You'll do that for me? Then I should do something special for you."

Russell coughed, while some of the other guys chuckled. *Lord, help me. Please.*

"Just be ready. That'll be enough," he said.

Russell knocked several times before Gloria opened the door. "Are you ready?"

"Am I ready for what, darling?" Gloria wore a white chiffon dress with a plunging neckline and short skirt that billowed when she moved, sure to be a hit with the audience.

Russell's face heated, but he refused to be derailed from his mission. "Come on, Gloria. We don't want to keep the band waiting."

"Just a sec, darling, I need to get my handbag."

"I'll wait right here." Russell waited with his hands in his pockets, rocking on his heels until she came out. He eyed her for signs of drinking, but she seemed okay. She was chewing a piece of gum, which didn't look very attractive, but at least she was sober.

Practice went well, and Artie kept it short so they wouldn't be too tired to perform twice. Since there were U.S. soldiers at several bases in Northern Ireland, some would be trucked in from other locations instead of the band going to all the bases. Russell was amazed at the number of American servicemen in the country—over 40,000, from what he'd heard. They were obviously planning a big campaign somewhere, but where?

The band took an hour break before the afternoon show. Most of the guys just sat around or smoked cigarettes while they killed time. It was a long walk back to their barracks, so Russell stayed and hung out with the guys, much as he wanted to be doing something more productive. Gloria disappeared to find a restroom during the break, saying she had to freshen her makeup. Russell couldn't imagine her needing any more than she already had. That was another thing he liked about Lexie. Besides lipstick, she didn't wear any makeup and looked beautiful without it.

By showtime, the building was filled with excited soldiers, just like the previous night. Russell sat at the piano bench waiting for Artie's signal to begin.

Artie glanced over at Russell. "Where is she?"

An alarm shot through Russell. He hadn't seen Gloria for a while. He stood up and was about to go look for her when she appeared by the stage, a welcome sight to the band as well as the servicemen, who voiced their approval.

Artie smiled. "Are we ready? One, two, three!"

The set went on without a hitch, and Gloria seemed to be

enjoying herself, looking much happier than she had that morning. When they took a break, she excused herself and grabbed her handbag to go to the restroom and freshen up again. When the break was over, she hadn't returned yet, so Russell went to the restroom and knocked on the door.

"Gloria! You in there?"

"Just a minute!"

When she opened the door, Russell caught a whiff of whiskey. He extended his hand for her to walk in front of him, and he watched her to see if she was tipsy. She wobbled slightly on her heels, but then, who wouldn't, wearing those spikes? Maybe he imagined the smell of liquor.

She made it through the second set but seemed less steady on her feet. Was he seeing things, or was she tipsy? But how? There wasn't any liquor anywhere near them. If she had been drinking, where did she get it, and when?

After they finished, the soldiers gave them a rousing ovation, whistling loudly when Gloria bowed and curtsied. One thing for certain, the audience appreciated the show, and Russell was thankful they did. He waved at the men as they were dismissed, happy that he was able to give them some entertainment from home.

After they left, Artie said, "Let's go eat and take a breather before the next group comes. We have two hours."

He motioned to Russell. "Is she okay?" He nodded toward Gloria who was leaning over to sign autographs for a few of the men.

"I think so. Does she seem okay to you?"

"I'm not sure. Has she been drinking?"

"Not that I know of. I don't know where she would've gotten the liquor."

"Well, whatever her source is, make sure it stops before the next show."

"Will do." Was Russell making a promise he couldn't keep? He was pretty sure she'd had something to drink already, and he hadn't been able to prevent it.

Russell walked over to her and waited until she finished putting her signature on anything the soldiers handed her—hats, letters, you name it. She stood and winked at him.

"Would you like me to sign something of yours, darling?"

He took her by the arm. "Not today. Come on, let's go get some food."

She tried to pull away from him. "I'm not very hungry."

"Well, humor me. I need the company." He wasn't about to let her out of his sight before the next show.

"*Now* you want company! I've been offering to keep you company, but you've been refusing me." She pouted her red lips like a child.

"Let's go eat." Russell tightened his grip on her arm, trying not to hurt her as he pulled her along.

"Russell. I didn't know you cared," she teased, tossing her long hair over her shoulder.

The mess hall was the last building in a row of identical long barracks, and the rest of the guys in the band were walking to it, but Russell wasn't sure Gloria could walk that far in the shoes she was wearing. A young serviceman in a jeep pulled up alongside them. "Need a ride?"

"Can you take us to the mess hall?" Russell pointed down the road.

"Sure thing. Hop in."

"Aren't you the gentleman?" Gloria flashed her biggest smile at the young man.

Russell helped her into the front seat, then he climbed into the rear.

"Sure did enjoy your show," said the soldier. "Can't wait to let the folks back home know I gave a ride to Gloria Bentley!"

Gloria leaned over and gave the soldier a kiss on the cheek. "Now you can tell them you've been kissed by Gloria Bentley!"

Russell shook his head. The woman reveled in stardom. Then why didn't she seem happy?

When they reached the mess hall, the driver hopped out and came around to help Gloria. Russell climbed out beside her.

As he headed inside, giving Gloria a little push on her lower back, she stopped. "You go on inside. I'm going to look for a restroom," she said.

"Again? You feeling all right?" Russell studied her facial features and her body language. Maybe she was still feeling the hangover.

"Sure, darling. Don't worry about me. You run along, and I'll be in as soon as I find the ladies room."

Ladies room? A basic restroom would be more like it. He didn't mean to be nosy, but she sure acted like she was anxious to get rid of him.

"I'll go with you and wait outside for you."

Gloria put her hands on her hips. "Why are you babysitting me? I'm a big girl and can take care of myself."

Problem was, Russell didn't believe she could. "Come on," he said. "I'll go with you to find out where it is."

"So much chivalry." Gloria extended her arm toward the building. "Please, lead the way."

Once inside, Russell and Gloria joined the rest of the band at one of the long tables. The quartermaster was passing out meals, and Russell asked him where the restroom was. The man pointed toward the end of the building, and Gloria excused herself. Russell sat down and started talking with the other band members.

"Has anyone heard where these soldiers are going when they leave here?" Louis nodded toward the window where soldiers were lining up in formation.

Nick glanced over his shoulder, then lowered his voice. "I heard somebody say 'North Africa.'"

"Yeah, I heard that too," said Sal. "Boy, that's going to be a lot different than it is here."

"No kidding. From the pasture to the desert!"

"Rommel territory," said Harry. "That Nazi's been taking over since last year."

"Don't they call him 'the Desert Fox'?" asked Sal.

"Yeah, they do," said Louis. "But we've got Eisenhower. I put my money on him."

"You better. These guys need to win so they can go back home."

When they'd finished eating, most of the guys lit up for an after-dinner smoke. Russell went outside with some of the guys to watch planes taking off and landing at the small airstrip.

"Wonder what these people think about our military plopping themselves down in the middle of their country?"

"They should be happy to see them. The British need our help."

"Yeah, but look at this place. Don't you think it's strange to see airplanes landing in the middle of a sheep pasture?”

The drone of a plane coming in over their heads made them duck. “And the noise. I’m sure that takes some getting used to.”

“Maybe they’ll get earmuffs for the sheep,” Louis said, elbowing Nick.

“I’m going for a walk,” said Russell. “I want to see the countryside while I’m here.”

“I’ll go with you,” said Nick. He glanced around. “Where’s Gloria? Maybe she wants to go with us.”

Gloria. Russell had forgotten he was supposed to be keeping an eye on her. Drat. He better find her. He went back into the building to look for her. Finding the restroom, he knocked on the door. “Gloria? You in there?”

He listened for a response but didn’t hear anything, so he walked back to the kitchen area and asked the men working in there if they’d seen her leave. They all shook their heads and said they didn’t see her come out.

A warning signal went off in Russell’s head. Where did she go? What was she up to? Surely, she couldn’t be drinking. Where would she get the liquor?

He went back to the restroom and knocked again, but still no response from the other side. Privacy or no privacy, he had to find out if she was in there. He shifted his weight against the door and pushed hard. The latch on the other side gave way, and the door fell open. Russell’s eyes widened at the sight of Gloria sitting on the floor, leaning against the wall with her dark hair half covering her face. Her eyes opened when he walked in. “Oh, hello, darling,” she said with slurred speech. A glance at the flask resting in her hand beside her open handbag confirmed his worst suspicions.

She was drunk again.

Russell went to her and took the flask, tossing it in the trash can, then he put his arms under her armpits and lifted her from the floor. "Come on. We're getting you outside."

"Sure, darling, whatever you say."

He propped her up against the sink long enough to grab her shoes and put them in her handbag, picked it up, and managed to catch Gloria before she fell over. Turning the tap on, he splashed some water on her face.

"Hey! What are you doing?" Gloria complained, turning her head away. Russell retrieved his handkerchief and handed it to her so she could wipe her face.

"Let's go," Russell said, as he took her by the waist and helped her to walk out the door.

"Where are we going?"

"For a walk." Somehow he'd get her sober by showtime, even if it meant ruining her stockings.

More than a few people stared at them as they made their way down the road, her leaning against him for support.

"Can't we just sit down?" Gloria's weight sagged.

"Not yet. Just a few more steps."

They walked out the gate, where the guard's eyebrows were knitted in a frown.

Russell tipped his hat at the young soldier. "Just going for a walk," he said, and the soldier nodded.

Outside the base, Russell turned down the country lane bordered by the base fence on one side and a low stone wall on the other. A villager rode past on his bicycle, casting a subtle scowl before giving them a slight nod, characteristic of the locals who weren't happy with Americans, "Yanks," invading their countryside.

"Ouch!" Gloria jumped and grabbed her foot. The pain apparently awakened her senses. She lifted her head up and looked around them. "Where are we?"

"Northern Ireland." Where they'd been for a few days already.

"It's pretty."

"Yes, it's beautiful countryside." Russell pressed ahead, and Gloria walked alongside unassisted.

"Look!" she said, pointing to a pasture. "There's sheep!"

He had to smile at her childlike wonder, as if she were seeing the world for the first time.

The dirt road rose ahead, but the exercise felt good to him. He'd been sitting way too long. As they topped the hill, his breath caught at the scenery. Just beyond the road, the green pastures led to rugged cliffs that towered over the sea. The sound of waves crashing into the rocks below accompanied the gust of sea breeze that blew against them. Russell stopped and inhaled deeply, letting the peace and serenity of the setting fill his senses.

"Thank you, Lord, for this marvelous beauty," he said.

Gloria looked at him, lifting an eyebrow. "I should have known," she said.

"Known what?" He eyed her with curiosity.

"About you. I knew you were a good guy, but I didn't realize you were religious."

Russell put his hands in his pockets and gazed out at the panorama. "I don't consider myself religious. But I believe in God and try to live my life the way He wants me to."

She cocked her head at him. "Yeah? How do you know what He wants you to do?"

"Well, I read the Bible, and I pray, and I try not to do things I know are wrong." He regarded her. "What about you?"

"Me? Sure, I believe in God. Doesn't everybody?" She looked away, but not before he noted the sadness that cast a shadow over her face. "I don't think about doing what God wants me to do, though. I'm too busy trying to do what everybody else wants me to do."

"Everybody? Like who?"

"You know. Hollywood. Show business. I gotta be beautiful and sexy so people will like me."

"Why does it matter so much if people like you?" "What, are you crazy? Don't you care if people like you?"

"Of course, I care. But what people think isn't more important to me than what God thinks. I don't have to try to make people like me. I don't need someone else's approval. I'd rather please God than a million other people."

"So why are *you* in show business? Aren't you out here trying to get these people to like you, like your music?"

Russell shook his head. "No, that's not it at all. I'm not here to get attention. I'm here to do something nice for these guys, make them feel good while they're away from home, aren't you?"

"Sure, but … you know it's different with me. I have a reputation to live up to."

He fixed his gaze on her eyes. "Is it so hard to live up to your reputation that you have to drink?"

Tears filled her eyes and ran down her cheeks. "You don't understand how hard it is."

Russell grabbed her by the shoulders. "Gloria, quit trying to please others. God loves you, and that's enough. You're enough. You have a beautiful voice. Why don't you just let your beauty shine through your music? Be the person God made you to be and not somebody else. Trust me, you'll be happier, and you won't need anything else."

"You make it sound easy."

"It is, Gloria. You're making it hard." He took her hands. "Do you mind if I pray for you?"

She shrugged. "Can't hurt, I guess."

Russell lifted his face toward the sky. "Father, thank you for making Gloria the way you did. Please show her the beauty you created in her and let her know how much you love her."

When he finished, she wiped the tears from her face. "Thank you," she said. "But I don't know why God would love someone like me. I'm not good like you are."

"Gloria, I'm not good. In fact, I'm not any better than you are. But God loves me anyway, and He loves you too. Just because He's a loving Father, not because of anything we've done."

She focused on the ground. "I never knew my father. He was killed in the last war when I was two years old."

Russell's heart squeezed, and his attitude toward Gloria changed as understanding revealed itself to him.

"I'm sorry. So that's why you wanted to perform with the USO?"

She glanced at him with surprise. "Maybe so. You know, I never thought of it that way." She gazed out across the vista. "I guess I wanted to connect with my father somehow, through the soldiers."

"And you do, Gloria. Your singing reaches them and reminds them of home."

A broad smile took over Gloria's face. "I do? Yes, I do!"

The joy that transformed her lifted Russell's spirits as well. "Ready to go back now?"

"Yes." Then she looked down at her dress and dirty stockings where her toes peeked out the ends. "I think I need to change clothes before tonight's performance."

"I think so too."

"You gonna give me my handbag back? I don't think it goes with your outfit."

Russell glanced down at the purse he'd tucked under his arm. He laughed and handed it to her. "You might be missing something."

She squinted with thought, then widened her eyes with understanding. "That's okay. I won't need it."

Russell breathed a prayer of thanks as they walked back to the base. He was thankful he'd had the conversation with Gloria. Not only did it seem to help her, but it'd also given him a better understanding of himself. Maybe that's why he was on this trip. He enjoyed helping others and giving them encouragement, and that realization gave him an idea about his own future.

Chapter Twenty-Eight

"*T*his is the operator. Will you accept a call from Karl Mueller?"

"Karl? Karl Mueller?" His sister's familiar voice was sweet music to his heart. "Of course, I'll accept!" A muffled cry said, "Mother! Come here! It's Karl!"

"Sir, your call is connected."

"Hello, Karl? Hello? Karl, is that really you?"

"Hello, Gretchen. Yes, it's me, Karl. How are you?"

"We're good, Karl. But where are you? Are you in Canada?"

"No, I'm in the States. But tell me, how is Mother?"

"She's doing okay, Karl. But she misses you. We both do."

"I miss you too. Her health is good?"

"As well as can be expected. But she still misses Poppa, you know. And with you gone too, well, she says her men left her."

Karl swallowed hard, his throat constricted in anguish. "Good thing you are a nurse, yes? You can take good care of her."

"I try, but I cannot heal her heart." She paused. "But how are you in the States? When did you come back from Germany?"

"I, uh, I came here for a job."

"But how? I mean … wait, Karl. Mother wants to speak to you."

Her voice was weaker, more feeble than before. "Karl? Is this my son Karl?"

He bit back the tears. "Yes, Mother. It is me, Karl. Your son."

"Karl, I have been so worried about you. I pray for you every day."

He couldn't talk. Outside the phone booth, another man waited. A tremor of fear raced down his back.

"Karl? Are you there? Will you come here? Will you come see your mother?"

The operator interrupted. "Your three minutes is up. If you wish to continue the call, you'll have to deposit more money into the phone."

"Mother, I love you."

Click. The call ended. Karl wiped his eyes with the back of his hand, his heart racing.

Thank you, God, for taking care of them and letting me hear their voices once more.

He pushed back the hinged door of the booth and stepped out.

Lexie hurried through breakfast, eager to reach the psych ward before the doctor arrived. She rushed onto the floor, breathless when she approached the nurses' station. Nurse Addams wasn't in sight, though, so Lexie tapped her fingers on the counter, waiting until the head nurse arrived. Where could she be?

The door to the ward opened, and Nurse Addams walked out with Dr. Kappas. Seeing Lexie, she scowled and strode toward her. Dr. Kappas's eyes reflected recognition, but his demeanor was unlike his previous sociable personality. A tremor of fear rattled Lexie. Something was wrong. She readied herself for bad news, suspecting Mike was the subject. Was she too late? Had they administered the shock treatment already?

"Nurse Smithfield, we need to talk with you," Nurse Addams said.

"Yes? What is it?" She steeled herself.

With hands on her hips, the nurse asked, "Did you administer the sedative to Mr. Walker last night?" Dr. Kappas watched with arms crossed over his chest.

Mike's request not to take the drug flashed through her mind. "No, I didn't. He was still groggy from the previous dose and said it upset his stomach."

The nurse's nostrils flared. She glanced at the doctor, then back to Lexie. "So you disobeyed the doctor's orders?"

"I … the patient was in restraints. He said it would be difficult if he got sick and couldn't sit up." Lexie looked back and forth between the two. "Why? What happened? Did he have another episode? Did something go wrong with the shock treatment?"

Dr. Kappas dropped his arms and clenched his fists, glaring at her. "There was no shock treatment."

Lexie fought between relief and concern. "Because he

didn't have the sedative?"

"Because the patient was gone." Nurse Addams spoke through gritted teeth.

"Gone? Where?"

"We don't know, Nurse Smithfield. We are looking for him," Nurse Addams said.

"But how? When?"

Nurse Addams crossed her arms. "Sometime during the night when the janitor went in to mop the floor. Mr. Walker and some other patients overtook him. Mr. Walker exchanged clothes with him, strapped the poor man to the bed, and left the hospital."

Lexie's eyes widened. "He did? But how did he get his restraints off?"

The doctor spoke up. "Apparently, he was able to enlist the help of some of the other patients, but we don't know who because they're not talking."

Lexie shook her head in amazement. Where had Mike gone? Was he stable enough to be on his own?

"And you, young lady, may be in trouble for allowing this to happen." Nurse Addams frowned at Lexie.

"But how did I allow this to happen? I didn't undo his restraints."

"No, but if he'd had the medication, he wouldn't have been able to

coordinate such an act," said Dr. Kappas.

"And others might be in danger if he has one of his episodes now that he is loose, especially since he didn't have the treatment he was supposed to get," the head nurse added.

"I'm sorry if I had anything to do with his escape, but I thought I was doing what was best for the patient." *Escape* was exactly what Mike had done, and Lexie wasn't convinced it was wrong, in light of his circumstances.

"We'll see how this affects your training," Nurse Addams warned. She faced the doctor and said, "Doctor, I apologize for this whole unfortunate episode."

He nodded, then cast an arrogant glance at Lexie before he walked off.

Lexie faced her superior. "What do you want me to do?"

The nurse walked around to the other side of the nurses' station and sat down. Steepling her fingers, she considered Lexie's question. "Right now, I want you to perform your regular duties. See if you can find out anything else from the patients." She handed Lexie Mike Walker's chart. "I see that you noted you did not give him his medicine."

"Yes, of course."

"Your honesty may save you, then. It shows you weren't trying to hide anything."

"Why would I hide anything?"

Nurse Addams allowed a slight smile on her lips. "Exactly." She reached for the chart, and Lexie handed it back. "Now go see about your patients."

"Yes, ma'am." *Her* patients? Did that mean she would be allowed to stay? All she was sure of was that one of *her* patients was missing, and she didn't know where he was, much less what kind of condition he was in.

When she walked into the wardroom, the men acted sheepish. She placed her hands on her hips and scanned the room. "Good morning, gentlemen. I've lost Mike Walker, and I don't know how to find him. Are any of you hiding him?"

Several people shook their heads. Lexie started going

from patient to patient as was her normal routine. When she got to Bob, he peered at her over his handful of cards.

"He left," Bob whispered.

"Aha. How did he do that, Bob?"

"He changed places."

"I see. Do you know who unstrapped his restraints?"

Bob shook his head. "No. They were hard to get off."

"So you helped each other?"

He nodded. "Yes, we all helped."

"And did Mike tell you where he was going?"

"He said he had to go somewhere very important. He needed our help to go."

"I'm sure he was very thankful that you men helped him." Bob smiled.

"He said we were his fellow soldiers."

Lexie bit back a smile. "And that made you feel good."

Bob nodded with vigor. "Yes, I'm a soldier." He straightened his back and sat taller.

"So, Bob, did he tell you anything else about where he was going or if there was anyone he was going to see?"

Bob looked deep in thought. "He said somebody missed him, and he wanted to see them."

Lexie's interest piqued. Did Mike regain his memory? "Bob, this is important. Did he say a name?"

Bob shrugged. "I don't remember."

"Do you think anyone else in here remembers?"

Bob looked around the room. "Maybe Frank remembers."

No one else in the room was interested in talking, much less answering any questions. No doubt Nurse Addams had already tried to get information from them. Lexie finished making her rounds, then headed toward the door. As she reached for it, Bob called out.

"His uncle. He was going to see his uncle Sam."

Lexie looked over her shoulder at Bob who was nodding and smiling as he studied his cards. Uncle Sam? Did that mean he was going back to the Navy or was it just a coincidence that his uncle's name was Sam? Either way, it sounded like Mike had regained his memory or at least some of it.

She went through the rest of the day trying to find out more about Mike's departure, but nothing else was revealed. Her emotions hovered between joy that Mike was healthy enough to devise such a scheme, fear that he wasn't well, and worry that he would get into trouble. If only she could talk to him and find out his intentions, but he had probably left the area to avoid being caught.

That afternoon, two uniformed Army officers arrived on the floor. They informed the nurses that Mike Walker was an Army Air Corps pilot who had gone missing when his plane crashed near an island in the Philippines. His parents and younger siblings lived in Michigan, but no wife or children were mentioned. The officers had been sent to the hospital to find out about his disappearance. Lexie had little to tell them since she didn't really know where Mike had gone. Thankfully, Nurse Addams didn't implicate Lexie in his escape either.

"What will happen if you find him?" Lexie ventured.

"He's considered absent without leave, so he'll be arrested," the older officer said.

Lexie's heart restricted. "But what if he returns to the Navy on his own?"

The two men glanced at each other before the same officer

answered. "That depends. There will probably be a hearing to determine what course of action will be followed."

"And if he wants to return to active duty?"

"Then things will go better for him, that is, of course, if he's deemed medically well enough." He touched the brim of his cap. "Thank you, ma'am."

"Sir, would you please let us know if you find him?" Lexie had to know what happened to Mike.

"Yes, we'll do that." The two men nodded, then turned and strode to the elevator.

After the elevator door closed, Nurse Addams turned to Lexie. "Do you think he might return to the Navy?"

Lexie shrugged. "I don't know. In a way, I hope so, so he won't get in trouble."

"Out of the frying pan into the fire," said Nurse Addams.

"What do you mean?"

"Oh, it just sounds like Mike Walker's life has been complicated lately."

"Maybe if he remembers his family, he'll go see them."

"Perhaps, and I'm sure the Navy is expecting that too."

Which uncle was Mike going to see?

Lexie's heart was heavy as she walked back to the residence. She wasn't ready to face Penny yet, knowing she'd probably heard about Mike Walker's escape and would have to go over it again. When she discovered her roommate hadn't returned yet, she breathed a sigh of relief, kicked off her shoes, and sank down on the bed. An overwhelming feeling of abandonment surrounded her. First Russell, then Cal, then Mike. They all left her. What was wrong with her? A puddle of tears pooled in her eyes before overflowing down her cheeks.

Of course, they were all different. Russell was coming back, wasn't he? And he didn't leave because of her, or did he? Cal was another story altogether. He left so he wouldn't get caught, but he had betrayed her, and that only added to her pain. And Mike—she wanted to help him get better so badly, but now she'd never find out how he was. He'd simply disappeared like Cal, but not like Cal.

Penny walked into the room and, seeing Lexie upset, rushed over and sat down beside her. "Lex! What's wrong, honey?"

Lexie turned onto her side facing Penny and sobbed. "Penny, I'm such a failure!"

"You? A failure? That's impossible! You're the top of the class. Why would you say that?" Penny grabbed a handkerchief out of her purse and handed it to Lexie.

Taking the handkerchief, Lexie wiped her face and nose and stopped crying. She took a deep, trembling breath. "I guess you heard about the patient that escaped from the psych ward."

"Yeah, it's all over the hospital. Pretty clever, if you ask me, but I hope he's not dangerous."

"He's not, at least I don't think he is."

Penny's eyes rounded. "You knew him, Lexie? Oh, that's right. You work that floor a lot."

"Yes, I knew him, or I thought I did. His name is Mike Walker. He's the one they brought in that was catatonic several weeks ago. Remember?"

"Oh, yeah. Guess he's not catatonic now. Wait. Do you think he was faking?"

Lexie sat up, unpinned her nurse's cap, and tossed it over on the dressing table. "Oh no. He really was catatonic. I'm positive about that. He had come out of it and was getting his memory back."

"So why do you think he left like he did?"

"He knew they were going to do electric shock therapy on him, and he didn't want them to do it."

"He told you that?"

Lexie nodded. "Yes, well, he didn't tell me he was going to escape, though. But he did ask me to see if I could keep them from administering it to him."

"Oh. Do they know that at the hospital?"

"No." Lexie shook her head. "I didn't tell them why he left. They'd think I had something to do with it. As it is, I worry that this whole incident might affect my graduation."

"Lexie, I don't think you could be held responsible for him escaping. Sounds like he was pretty smart. You're not a failure!"

"But I feel like one. It's just that things haven't worked out like I expected." Lexie couldn't share her feelings about Cal's deceit. Best leave that story alone. She'd tell Russell, but when? Tears threatened again, and she sniffed, hoping to stem the flow. "And I miss Russell. Guess I didn't know how much." A tear dropped onto her lap.

"I know you do. You've just had a lot on you lately." Penny stood and began taking off her uniform. She stopped and turned to Lexie. "Say, you know this weekend is the Fourth of July. Why don't you come home with me and spend it with my family?"

Lexie got up to change clothes as well. "Thanks, Penny. But I'm going back to East Hampton. I told the Maurice sisters I was coming."

"No offense, but won't you get bored there? I mean, no

Russell, no fireworks, just the two old ladies?"

How could Lexie explain to Penny that the sisters' cottage was her retreat, her "safe" place? "It won't be so boring. We'll go to the club and watch the tennis tournament they're having. The Fourth is going to be pretty quiet this year anyway. You know, most of the factories will be open, and a lot of people are working as usual. Apparently, that's supposed to show our support for the soldiers fighting for our independence."

"Well, we always have a gang at our house, so it's never quiet. We'll have a cookout and lots of fun. Are you sure you don't want to go?"

"No, but thanks anyway."

"Say, I know what we need! Let's go down to the diner and get a milkshake. We haven't done that for a while. What do you say?"

The diner? The place where she'd been friends with a Nazi spy? She shuddered. She'd never intended to go there again.

"I don't think so, Penny. I don't really feel up to it."

"Why not? You deserve a treat after all this. Come on!"

How could she explain to Penny? But maybe she was being silly. Cal was gone now, and so were the others. Surely she would be safe going there with Penny to get a milkshake.

"Okay. Why not?" They put on their street clothes and headed down to the familiar place. Lexie kept looking over her shoulder on the way.

"What are you looking for?" Penny asked. "You expect to see that guy Mike from the hospital? I kind of doubt he'd be easy to spot since he doesn't want to be found."

"Mike? No, I don't expect to see him."

Lexie focused ahead. Who *was* she looking for? If not

Mike, then Cal? But she really didn't expect to see him either. So why did she still think she was being followed?

The diner hadn't changed, but it had lost its usual comfort. Without Russell and Cal, the place was full of strangers. The only familiar faces were the waitress' and the owner's. When the waitress took their shake order, Lexie feared the woman would mention her previous dining companion, Cal. But the waitress only nodded at them and left in a hurry to pick up orders the cook called out from the grill.

She returned with the shakes and put the cold refreshments in front of them. The cold chocolate drink slid down Lexie's throat as she stared out the glass window watching people walk by while Penny jabbered on about something. A group of guys dressed in army uniforms passed the diner. Where would they be sent? Would they go where Russell was? Would his band play for them? She sighed, letting her shoulders sag.

"Lexie? Lexie, did you hear me?" Penny grabbed Lexie's wrist across the table.

Lexie started, glancing down at Penny's hand on her. "Hmm? I'm sorry, Penny. What did you say?"

"I asked you if you had gotten a letter from Russell yet."

Lexie shook her head. "No."

"Did you check today's mail?"

"No. I didn't think about it. I went straight to the room."

"Maybe you'll get one today." Penny glanced out the window. "Say, isn't that the German baker? Wonder how he feels about those Nazi spies?"

Lexie almost choked on her shake. "Where?"

"Over there," Penny pointed. Lexie jerked her head to look, but a bus blocked her view. When the bus passed, there was no sign of the baker.

"I don't see him, Penny. Are you sure that's who it was?"

Penny scanned the street outside and shrugged. "I could've sworn it was him. Maybe he got on that bus."

Lexie shuddered at the thought of the man. Why was he still around if he were a spy? The last time Lexie had seen him, he was arguing with Cal. What was their connection?

"He's always got that nasty cigar in his mouth," said Penny. "I hope the ashes don't fall on the food in the bakery."

Lexie hadn't finished her drink, but it had lost its flavor. Coming here had been a mistake. She wanted to get away from the place, never come back, and never see that obnoxious baker again. "Penny, I'm ready to go. Are you?"

Penny drained her shake. "Sure." The girls slid out of the booth, paid the cashier, and went out the door. Lexie quickened her pace down the sidewalk.

"Lexie, what's the rush?"

Lexie slowed. "Sorry, guess I'm just used to being in a hurry."

"Well, you're not at work now, so relax."

How could she relax, though, with the smell of cigar smoke lingering in the air?

Chapter Twenty-Nine

My Dear Lexie,

How are you? Has the hospital been keeping you busy? I can picture you now as you take care of your patients and know how blessed they are to have you as their nurse. Your attention and desire to provide excellent care are characteristics I admire so much. Things are going well over here. The guys on the bases are really happy to see us, and it's gratifying to know we've cheered them up and given them a taste of home. We've filled up Northern Ireland with our troops, and some of the locals aren't very happy about it. You can tell by the looks we get when we pass by them on the road. They're pretty close-knit over here and keep to themselves. A couple of the guys have gotten into barroom fistfights, one of the unpleasant side effects of getting drunk, especially among unfriendly villagers. Of course, the soldiers were reprimanded, and the bar was made off-limits for a while.

I wish you could see this countryside. It's so beautiful, lush and green, with houses and stone fences that make you think you've stepped back into another time. You don't see many cars, as most folks walk or ride bicycles. The only complaint you hear from the Americans is the weather. It's cold and damp much of the time, even though it's summer.

The guys in the band are nice and fun to be around. They call me "the chaplain," I guess because I don't smoke or drink or use profanity. Plus, when I get a chance between sets, I play hymns like I used to. I did meet a chaplain here that I've enjoyed getting to know. He'll ship out with all the other soldiers when they leave.

We don't know when or where they're going, but rumors have been flying around about North Africa.

I suppose you're going to spend the Fourth of July with the Maurice sisters like we had planned. Sorry I won't be there to spend it with you.

I really miss you, Lexie, and think about you all the time. I miss your bright smile that lights up your face and every room you walk into. I'm so thankful you are part of my life, even though not as large a part as I'd like. I sure do wish we could talk on the phone because I miss hearing your voice. Every day, I pray for you and your safety, and I thank God that someday I can call you my wife.

All my love, Russell

Lexie stared at the letter in her hand, her only connection to her fiancé. He hadn't forgotten her. A tear trickled down her cheek. She wiped it off and smiled. Russell really did love her. Why did she doubt it? Deep inside, she knew their relationship was solid. Where did these ridiculous negative thoughts come from? Her mother. That was the way her mother thought—worried about everything until the fears consumed her. But her daughter wasn't like that. She wasn't going to live her life afraid of everything and everyone.

And yet, maybe there were some people she should fear.

Should she have feared Cal, who was a real threat to her country? Should she have feared Mike? The hospital thought his outbursts made him dangerous, so they'd sedated him and restrained him. But she didn't think he was. Was she wrong about him too? And why was she still looking over her shoulder? Was this a habit she'd acquired at Jekyll Island when there really was someone out to harm her? *Lord, please give me wisdom about what and who to fear and protect me from real danger.*

Lexie picked up the phone in the residence living room and dialed the Maurice sisters.

"Hello?"

"Peg? This is Lexie."

"Oh, hello, Lexie." The older woman chuckled. "Jane is out running errands if you're wondering why I answered the phone. Are you still coming this weekend?"

"Yes, if you'll still have me. That's why I'm calling."

"Of course, we'll still have you! Are you coming Friday night or Saturday morning?"

"I'd like to come Friday night if it's not too much trouble."

"None at all. Do you know what time your train will arrive?"

"I hope to catch the five o'clock train and get there by eight thirty, but if I miss the early train, I won't get there until nine. Why don't I just call you from the phone booth at the station when I get there? I'd hate for Homer to have to wait for me."

"That sounds fine. We'll just be looking for your call Friday. Be careful."

"I will." Why did people always say that? Of course, she'd

be careful.

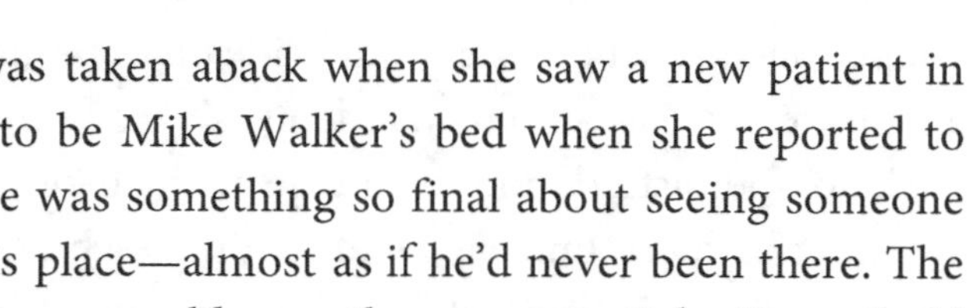

Lexie was taken aback when she saw a new patient in what used to be Mike Walker's bed when she reported to work. There was something so final about seeing someone else take his place—almost as if he'd never been there. The new patient was an older gentleman, a new John Doe, who'd been found wandering in Central Park, dirty and confused. Nurse Addams said they'd cleaned him up and were waiting for his family to file a "missing persons" report. Hopefully, he had a family who cared about him and would look for him. Meanwhile, he'd made friends with Bob, who was teaching him how to play cards.

All day long, Lexie expected to hear that Mike Walker had been found. She couldn't help but worry about him. Where was he? Who was taking care of him? Had he tried to contact his parents, that is, if he remembered them? But no news about his whereabouts arrived at the hospital, and she could only pray he was safe and healthy. She prayed for his memory to be restored as well and for his headaches to go away. If only she could talk to him again and see for herself what kind of condition he was in.

Lexie's shift had been changed to days, but Penny now had night duty, so they didn't see each other for the next couple of days, and her room was unusually quiet without her animated roommate. After work on Thursday, she changed clothes and tried to study, but she was restless. The photo of her and Russell standing beside their bicycles at Jekyll Island beckoned to past times of fun and freedom.

She was so naïve to think those times would last forever. Why did you have to lose something to truly appreciate it?

If he were here in the States now, they'd be going to Long Island together where they could ride bikes beside the ocean again. But he wasn't here. Suddenly, she couldn't wait to get back to the sisters' house and go for a bike ride. Russell wouldn't be there, but she could reminisce about their rides and imagine him being alongside her anyway. She couldn't wait for tomorrow, Friday, to get out of town. She pulled out her suitcase to start packing so she'd be ready to leave right after work.

A tap on her door made her turn around. Nancy stood just outside the threshold, looking lost.

"Hey Lexie," said Nancy, in her quiet, timid voice. "Hi, Nancy."

Nancy pointed to Lexie's open suitcase. "Are you going home today too?"

Lexie glanced down at her suitcase, then back at Nancy. "No, I'm not leaving today. I have to work tomorrow."

"Oh." The girl seemed depressed, and Lexie remembered her boyfriend had shipped out.

"Nancy, is there something wrong?"

The girl trembled, and a tear slid down her cheek. Lexie went over to her and took her arm. "Come in and sit down."

Nancy sat on the end of the twin bed, and Lexie sat down next to her. Lexie searched her face. "Do you want to talk about it?"

Nancy sniffed, and Lexie got the Kleenex box from the bedside table and handed it to her. Nancy took a tissue and wiped her nose. "I have to go back home today. My grandmother died." She choked back a sob.

Lexie patted her hand. "I'm sorry, Nancy." An image of her own grandmother came to mind, and she felt a twinge of sadness. "I remember when my own grandmother passed away."

The other girl nodded and dabbed her eyes. "My mother was really upset when she called to tell me."

Lexie searched for the right words to say to comfort Nancy. "I'm sure she'll be glad to have you there."

Nancy nodded again, then her lip trembled. "I wish James was still here."

"He's your boyfriend?"

"Yes. If he were here, he'd come get me and take me home. We lived in the same town upstate. But he left for the Army last week." Her shoulders shook with another sob.

Lexie's heart went out to the bereft girl who seemed so much younger than she. "So how are you getting home? Is someone else coming to get you?"

Nancy shook her head. "Nobody else can. Mother told me to take the train. I've never ridden the train by myself before."

Lexie pitied the poor girl. Apparently, she was unaccustomed to life in the city. "It's not that bad. I've ridden it lots of times by myself."

"I know. You seem to be much braver than I am. I don't even know how to buy a ticket or find the right train. Penn Station is so big it terrifies me."

Lexie could understand the girl's fears. She'd certainly had enough of her own. However, she did know her way around the train station. Maybe she could help.

"I have an idea. I'll go to Penn Station with you and help you get your ticket and find your train. Are you packed and ready to go?"

Nancy looked at Lexie with a glimmer of hope in her eyes. "You would do that for me? You'd go with me?"

"Sure. I don't have anything else to do before tomorrow. Let's get going so you can catch the next train." Lexie jumped up from the bed.

Nancy stood and said, "Okay. I'll get my suitcase."

When Nancy returned with her suitcase, the girls went downstairs together. They stepped outside just in time to catch a bus to the train station. Lexie breathed a sigh of relief as they boarded the bus since she'd been avoiding walking anywhere other than back and forth to the hospital. For once, she was taking everyone's suggestion to be careful seriously.

At the station, Lexie took Nancy to the ticket window where she bought a ticket. The teller told her where the train would be, but the girl looked lost, so Lexie walked downstairs and waited with her on the platform until the train arrived.

"Here you go," Lexie said, motioning to the train as it screeched to a halt in front of them.

Nancy gave Lexie a tight hug. "Thank you so much! You're the best!"

Once Nancy was on board, Lexie waved goodbye to her and watched the train disappear down the track. Lexie slowly climbed the stairs back up to the main lobby, her thoughts on Nancy and her situation. Dusk had descended on the city when she stepped outside and walked toward the bus stop. She glanced up in time to see her bus leaving the curb. Panic tightened her chest. Why couldn't she have gotten there just a few minutes sooner?

Now she'd have to walk back. A sense of dread weighted her steps as she realized she'd have to go the distance alone.

Nancy had called her "brave." But if she only knew how much Lexie dealt with fear. Still, she had walked the distance before, and there was no reason she couldn't do it again. She started back the usual way, passing the Martinique and thinking of Russell. But as she neared the diner, she deviated from her usual path and crossed to the other side of the street to distance herself from the place.

The sidewalks were almost empty since most people had gone home from work. Except for the occasional car that passed, the city was quiet enough to hear her shoes clicking on the pavement. She couldn't help but constantly scan the area around her. When she was a child, Russell and her brother had called her "scaredy cat," and she had gone out of her way to prove them wrong. Maybe they had been right, though.

As she glanced over at the diner across the street, she noticed Mack had turned the lights on inside already because restaurants weren't allowed to display their outside neon lights during the dimout. What irony that the enemy they were hiding from had eaten in this very place. Nothing appeared out of the ordinary, but when a prickly tingle ran down her spine, she knew she was being watched. Her eyes and ears were on full alert to detect movement. Did she hear footsteps behind her? A quick glance over her shoulder revealed no one. Still, she couldn't shake the way her skin crawled. She quickened her step as the dim streetlights came on.

She felt an urge to hum "Amazing Grace." But why now, out in public? Not that anyone was around to hear her. The urge persisted, and she remembered Mike asking her to sing the words. So she began singing the hymn, feeling just a little peculiar as she started out in a very low voice, but gaining volume as the words resonated with meaning for her.

Only a few blocks remained as she passed an alley between two buildings. Her song was cut short when a hand came from behind and covered her mouth. Alarm raced through her body as she was dragged into the alleyway. Who? She couldn't see her attacker in the dark as she struggled to get free, but the man pushed her against the brick wall, and with cigar breath, he said, "You are the reason the plan failed. You will pay." Cold metal touched her neck, and she knew she was going to die. She closed her eyes, waiting for her death, but then there were more voices, one in German and one in English. Her attacker released her as he himself was attacked. Someone yelled, "Run, Lexie!"

She didn't look back and ran as fast as she could toward the residence. Just as she reached the building, she heard a gunshot. She paused a second, then raced into the nurses' quarters, out of breath and trembling. Thankfully, no one else was in the living room, and she dropped onto a chair, her heart racing as she tried to recover.

Who had come to her rescue? Someone who spoke German? Cal? But there were at least two more voices. And one of them knew her. Was that Mike's voice that told her to run? Who had been shot? She hoped it wasn't Mike. But what if her attacker was still loose?

So many questions, but no answers. All she knew for sure was that she'd been protected, somehow, by somebody. Which meant she really had been watched. Thank God, she made it back to the residence. And thank God, He had been watching over her.

The next morning, Lexie tried to dress quietly without waking Penny since she'd worked late. But Penny woke anyway, yawned, and stretched. "Hey, Lex."

"Hi, Penny. Sorry I woke you up."

"Don't be. I need to get up anyway. I'm going in early today so I can get out of here and head home for the weekend." She sat up on the edge of the bed.

"I had the same idea. It's been a long week."

They dressed and went downstairs where the other nurses were gathered.

"Did you hear what happened last night?" one of the girls said.

"A guy was killed not too far from here." Another spoke up.

Lexie's heart fell. Penny jumped into the conversation. "Who was killed? Where?"

Lexie strained to hear the answer.

"I heard it was the German baker. He was shot."

"Oh, my!" Penny covered her mouth. "Somebody hates Germans that much?"

Lexie's mind raced. Her attacker was dead, but who shot him? Did that mean she was safe now? She couldn't wait for the day to end so she could be on her way to East Hampton.

After her shift was over, she changed clothes as fast as possible, told Penny bye, and hurried to Penn Station. The grand lobby was full of people leaving town for the weekend. As she crossed the room, a man bumped into her. Her breath caught when she glanced at his face. Although the hair was black, the face was familiar.

"Cal?" She froze. What should she do? Yell for help?

Then he smiled. "Happy to see you again."

She had so many questions but found it hard to speak. "You're still here."

Cal nodded. "I leave today." He glanced around, then looked back at her, his gaze penetrating. "I want to thank you for your friendship. You helped me make some important decisions."

"But…"

He touched his finger to his lips. "Because of you, there won't be any fireworks."

"Me? No, there's no fireworks because of the blackout."

He winked and smiled, tipping his hat. "I pray you and your future husband will live happily ever after."

Before she could answer, he turned and walked away quickly, disappearing into the crowd toward the exit for the northbound train. Stunned by the encounter, she tried to understand what he meant by "no fireworks" as she continued toward the Long Island train.

Then she heard her name. "Lexie!" A male voice called out from across the room, the same voice she'd heard the night before. She spun to look, and her mouth dropped open when she saw Mike Walker, his hat barely hiding a black eye. He grinned and gave her a thumbs-up, then turned and vanished beyond the sign that read "Westbound Trains."

Chapter Thirty

Lexie stretched out on the chaise lounge on the cottage patio, gazing up at the stars in the nighttime sky. Her muscles were tired but in a good way.

"We sure are glad you were here today, Lexie." Peg sat on the chair to Lexie's right.

"Yes, we are. And Mr. Coleman is too. He wouldn't have had a partner in the tennis tournament if you hadn't been here since his partner twisted her ankle yesterday," Marian added.

"Wasn't he the lucky duck? Not only did he get a partner, he got the best partner!"

"Oh, you two. I'm not the best," Lexie said.

"I'd say second place is pretty close to the best," said Marian.

"Well at least we gave the number one team a run for their money,"

said Lexie.

"Yes, you did. We're so proud of you!" said Peg.

"Thank you. It did feel good, I must say." Lexie sat up. "It's been a while since I played, and I'm glad to know I haven't forgotten how."

"Ha! I don't think that would happen," said Marian.

"Well, we didn't have any fireworks tonight, but we had a good Fourth anyway."

The phone rang in the house, and the women glanced at each other. "Who could be calling us this time of night on the Fourth of July?"

"Lexie, would you mind getting it? There's no one inside to answer."

"Of course." Lexie jumped from the chair and ran into the house, picking up the phone in the hallway.

The phone crackled, and an operator's voice came on. "Call for Lexie Smithfield. Will you accept?"

"Yes. This is Lexie Smithfield."

"Go ahead, sir, with your call."

"Hello? Lexie?" The reception was weak, but she knew his voice. "Russell?"

"Yes, Lexie. It's me, Russell. Happy Fourth of July!" Lexie wiggled with delight.

"Russell! It's so good to hear your voice!"

"Yours, too, Lexie. I finally finagled a call through to the States, but I can't talk long. Have you had a good Fourth?"

"Yes, Russell, I did. I had to sub for a hurt player in the club's tennis tournament today."

"Good for you. I hope you won."

"Second place."

"That's great. Say, Lexie, is everything going all right? I mean, anything strange happen?"

She couldn't possibly tell him about last night during the call. "Why?"

"Well, last night around midnight our time, I had this

impression that I should pray for you, that you were in danger. So I got down on my knees and prayed. Did something happen?"

Lexie calculated the time difference of five hours between New York and Ireland. Midnight for Russell was the same time she was attacked.

"I'll tell you all about it when you come back. But thank you for your prayers. They helped. And you don't have to worry. Everything's fine now."

"That's good, Lexie. I miss you, and I can't wait to see you again."

"I miss you, too, Russell. Do you know when you'll be back?" "Two more weeks here, then we'll take a ship back. I should be home before the end of July, and we can discuss our future." Her future was still secure. "I love you, Russell."

"I love you, too, Lexie. And give Peg and Marian a hug for me."

"I will. Thank you for calling."

"Believe me, it was my pleasure. See you soon. Good night."

"Good night, Russell."

Lexie put down the receiver, walked back through the house, and stepped outside. As she did, a shooting star raced across the sky.

God had provided the fireworks, just like He'd provided for everything else.

Epilogue

December 1942

"There!" Peg finished pinning the headpiece of Lexie's shoulder-length veil onto her hair and stepped back, studying her handiwork.

"You're perfect!" Marian clasped her hands as she stood beside her sister and pointed to the mirror. "Look!"

Lexie whirled around to the Cheval mirror and marveled at her reflection. Was that really her in that long white satin wedding dress?

"I can't believe I'm really getting married today." She couldn't keep from smiling as she spun around again, her skirt flaring. "I feel like Cinderella."

"And your Prince Charming is waiting downstairs," Peg said. "Russell will be dazzled when he sees you."

"I don't believe I've ever seen a more beautiful bride!" Marian gushed. "So you have something new—your dress, something borrowed, our mother's pearl earrings, something old—your grandmother's lace handkerchief, and something blue—that lovely sapphire cross pin from your friend in Canada. What a nice touch to your headpiece.

Looks like you have everything you need," said Peg.

"She does, Peg. She's got her nursing diploma, and she's marrying a handsome chaplain's associate."

"Lexie, who was that telegram from this morning? Your face lit up like a candle when you read it."

"Oh, just a former patient congratulating me on our wedding."

The telegram had read, *Congratulations and may God bless your wedding and marriage. Thank you for your help. Yours truly, Captain Michael Walker, United States Army Air Corps.*

"Well, how nice! I love happy endings!" Marian's smile spread across her rosy cheeks.

Lexie glanced out the window at the snowflakes that drifted down and painted the landscape with story-tale charm. In this pure, white world, there were no shadows, only happy endings.

Acknowledgements

$\mathcal{A}$ historical book requires a lot of research, even when that book is a novel. As the author, I'm obligated to be as historically accurate as possible, even though my characters and parts of the story are fictitious. Without the help of others, I'd never have found the information I needed to write this book set in New York in 1942.

Consequently, there are many people to thank. On my trip to East Hampton on Long Island, I had the joy of finding the charming East Hampton Library where Gina Piastuck provided invaluable help for my research of the East Hampton and Amagansett area, including the online archives of the *East Hampton Star* newspaper. In addition, I want to thank Henry Osmers, the historian at Montauk Point Lighthouse, who opened my eyes to the area during the war and also referred me to Gina.

Trying to get information about Bellevue Psychiatric Hospital and the nurses' training for the year 1942 was a challenge. Much has changed since then, and the hospital where Lexie trained is no longer in use. Huge thanks to

Allison Piazza, reference librarian for the New York Academy of Medicine for her help and the awesome floor plan she provided for the Bellevue Psychiatric Hospital during Lexie's time. The Martinique Hotel is still operating now as the Radisson Martinique, and although there have been renovations since 1942, Tara Williams, Director of Revenue for the hotel, knows a lot about its history. Tara also helped me understand the hotel's location in proximity to other Manhattan landmarks. A big shout out goes to Steve Fielding at the Northwest Florida State College Library for his relentless research about the history of nursing and Bellevue. Steve provided me with wonderful access to files of the *New York Times* where I could read current events in Lexie's life.

In addition, the New York Public Library research department and the New York University Library research departments and the New York Transit Museum provided information for my book.

I also want to thank my nurse friends—Dr. Beth Norton, professor of nursing at Northwest Florida State College, Beth Tritschler, "retired" nurse, who advised me on treatment and medication for psychiatric patients in 1942, and Word Weaver nurse Susan Neal. Speaking of Word Weavers, thank you to Chris Manion for her chapter critique.

And last, but certainly not least, I am so thankful my husband Chuck worked my research into our family vacation so that I was able to visit the Long Island area of the story. What a treat to see the newly restored coast guard station near the beach where the Nazi saboteurs landed!

Discussion Questions

1. Lexie accidentally befriended a spy. Do you think she should have gone to the authorities when she found out? If she had, what do you think would have happened to her? What do you think Russell would have suggested if he'd known about the spies?

2. Lexie struggles with when to believe a fear is valid and when it is a phobia because of her mother's mental health problems. Do you ever have fears? Phobias? How do you handle them?

3. Do you think Russell did the right thing by going overseas with the USO? Why do you think he went? Have you ever known someone with a handicap that kept them from serving in the military? Did they want to?

4. Karl (Cal) thought he owed his allegiance to his ancestral country of Germany. But he grew up in the United States. What did he ultimately decide his allegiance was to?

5.   Through their conversation, Lexie influenced Karl to evaluate his beliefs and change his mind about his mission. Have you ever had that effect on someone? How?

6.   Nurse Nancy was young and afraid. She needed a strong person to help her, and Lexie became that person. Have you ever become stronger when someone else needed you?

7.   Dr. Dimitri Kappas is a womanizer. Have you ever known anyone like him? Why are some women deceived by his type?

8.   Dr. Kappas and Mike didn't like each other. Why do you think that is so?

9.   Many people in the 1940's were institutionalized because their families didn't want to be bothered by them. Do you believe that still happens today?

10.   Lexie was upset because Karl was not who she thought he was. She felt deceived and betrayed. Have you ever misjudged someone and felt like a fool when you learned the truth about them? Do you think Karl was a nice person or not?

11.   Were you aware of the real Nazi spies that landed on U.S. shores? How does it make you feel to know how easily they landed on our shores undetected? Called Operation Pastorius, you might want to research it further.

12.   Mack's Diner was a popular place. Have you ever gone to a diner? What did it look like? What did they serve? Was it open 24/7?

Find out more about Lexie and the shadow that darkens her family's lives in Book 1 of Suspicious Shores,

The Gilded Curse

Silver Scroll Merit Award for Fiction

A simple task becomes a dangerous venture when Lexie Smithfield returns to the island paradise of her childhood . . .

Now that the Depression has ruined her finances, all Lexie wants to do is return to Jekyll Island and dispose of her family's grand old cottage at the Millionaires' Club resort. As the only living heir, the place that had once been a gilded getaway is now a place of painful memories and, according to her deceased mother, curses.

Lexie doesn't believe in curses—or blessings, for that matter. But when she arrives on the island in January of 1942 she finds an unknown intruder in the family cottage. With German subs threatening U.S. ships along the coastline, Lexie realizes she is being stalked by a stranger. What does *she* have that anyone would want?

Russell Parker, a childhood friend, has become the superintendent of the Jekyll Island Inn and keeper of the club members' secrets: including the secrets of Lexie's own family. As Lexie and Russell seek to solve the mysterious happenings surrounding the cottage—and identify the phantom stranger—an unexpected romance blossoms.

But can they act in time? Or will Lexie succumb to the island's deadly curse?

Follow Lexie and Russell's adventures in
Book 3 of Suspicious Shores,

The Seaside Curse

When your country is at war overseas, shouldn't you feel safe at home?

Lexie and Russell Thompson have settled down in a new seaside community near the Portsmouth Naval Shipyard where Russell is the interim chaplain. Adjusting to her role as a stay-at-home new mother, Lexie seeks to fit in to the comfortable neighborhood. It's been two years since she befriended a Nazi spy, and the ring he was in has been arrested and prosecuted. Now that Lexie and her husband Russell have left busy Manhattan, Lexie is thankful for the quiet, peaceful atmosphere of her new home and neighborhood.

The year is 1945, and patriotism is running high with most of the population working to aid the country in its war effort. The shipyard builds submarines and currently employs 25,000 people, civilians and military. Most people in the surrounding towns work at the shipyard, including Lexie and Russell's neighbors. Lexie is happy to find a new friend who helps watch her toddler son Robby when she returns to work. But are her neighbors as nice as they appear to be, or are they hiding a dangerous secret?

www.ingramcontent.com/pod-product-compliance
Lightning Source LLC
Chambersburg PA
CBHW072045190726
48294CB00005B/1410